hc

The Dreamer's Legacy © Celu Amberst[...]

Published by Kegedonce Press
11 Park Road, Cape Croker Reserve
R. R. 5, Wiarton, Ontario, N0H 2T0
www.kegedonce.com
Administration Office/Book Orders
RR7 Owen Sound, ON N4K 6V5

Copyeditor: Suzanne Stephenson
Cover Art: Jason Odjick
Cover Design: Red Willow Designs
Layout Design: Eric Abram

Library and Archives Canada Cataloguing in Publication

Amberstone, Celu, 1947-
    The dreamer's legacy / Celu Amberstone.

ISBN 978-0-9784998-9-1

    I. Title.

PS8551.M35D74 2011   C813'.54   C2011-902898-0

Sales and Distribution - http://www.lpg.ca/LitDistco:
            For Customer Service/Orders
            Tel 1-800-591-6250 Fax 1-800-591-6251
            100 Armstrong Ave. Georgetown, ON L7G 5S4
            Email orders@litdistco.ca

Kegedonce Press gratefully acknowledges the generous support of:

ONTARIO ARTS COUNCIL
CONSEIL DES ARTS DE L'ONTARIO

*We acknowledge the support of the Canada Council for the Arts which last
year invested $20.1 million in writing and publishing throughout Canada.*

Canada Council   Conseil des Arts
for the Arts   du Canada

Kegedonce Press · Kegedonce Press · Kegedonce Press

THE DREAMER'S LEGACY

Celu Amberstone

Dedication

This book is dedicated to all the refugees and displaced indigenous peoples around the world. It is also dedicated to my children and grandchildren. Because I am not a woman of material wealth, my writing is my legacy to both them, and all the children who are our cherished future. Also in dedication, I offer my eternal gratitude for the traditional teachings of my grandparents, aunties, and the other Elders I've met over the years who have taken the time to teach me. The wisdom and strength of my Elders has always been, and will continue to be, an inspiration in my life.

Acknowledgements

I would like to thank for their support my four sons, my father, my brother and sister, and my friends Brenda, Katie and Paddy, Mia, Nina, and many others for being there when I needed them. Clélie and Paula, your friendship and help with proofreading and other editing was greatly appreciated. Daniel, your edits and suggestions were beyond price.

I would also like to thank the folks at Kegedonce Press for their dedication, hard work, vision, and fearless determination to encourage Aboriginal writers of all types.

Part One

* * *

The explorers from the empire who came north named all the tribes they found in the arctic Zacatik. And somewhere along the way they shortened it to "Zaunk" when they wanted to ridicule us and make us feel small. I'm not sure what either word meant to them, but we called ourselves the Qwani'Ya Sa'adi. Loosely translated, it means "Fish People" in today's common tongue. We caught whitefish mostly. Summer and winter, smoked or baked— even sometimes raw—we ate a lot of fish. Our traditional home was on the southern shores of the Big Ice Lake, not far from where it flows into the Socanna River.

Like the land that has tasted our blood and shared our memories, we can endure almost anything. A quiet people and shy around strangers, we stand back and observe before we speak. Some outsiders mistake our reticence for stupidity, but they are the foolish ones. In currents of jade green, indigo, and black, our thoughts run deep. In our dreams we swim the Big Ice Lake's hidden currents with Dalo the Loon, Qwa'osi the Otter and Co'yeh the Lake Seal, to bring back the magic found in the caves of the Great Aseutl Kunai.

Our healers and wise ones found their power in natural things such as winds, rocks, ice, and the whistling fires of the Spirit-Lights. The land doesn't belong to us; we belong to the land. It holds our Qwakaiva, our ancestor's bones, and our tribal memories. My daughter Qwachula's mentor with the long Chamuqwani nose and kind eyes gave me a quizzical look when I first said this to him, then he thought about it some more and nodded his head in agreement.

I promised my daughter to recount the story of my youth, but the world has changed so much. Why should these children who have grown up in such a different way believe me? They will think my memories lie, or worse yet, that they are the demented ramblings of a senile old man.

But I suppose I must tell them. What does it matter that most will think these memories just the fancies of my imagination? The ones with Qwakaiva, the ones in whom the Blood runs true, they will be empowered and keep the ceremonies alive that bind the world together. The past may be gone forever, but we must remain a tribal people in the world bequeathed us or we will not survive our present to gain a future for our children.

Chapter One

"You're not welcome here. Go!"I froze with one foot upon the trading post steps. Mother had sent me for more tea, but I'd no wish to enter if the trader was angry. Jombonni had repeatedly warned his son Kutima and me not to raid the candy barrel, but did we listen?

No.

I peered through the open door into the store's dim interior. Maybe I should find a cousin to get the tea ... dog fart! Only a coward would run and hide, I told myself. If he knows about the candy, I should go in and confess.

But Jombonni wasn't talking to me; the trader hadn't even seen me. He faced two broad-shouldered men wearing wide brimmed hats and dirty canvas trews. I breathed a sigh of relief and stepped onto the porch.

The strangers had their backs to me, intent on the thin, pale-skinned man in the white apron behind the counter shaking his fist at them. Miners. I hated them. I wished there were no yellow rocks in our streams. I wished they would go away and leave us alone.

Unfortunately, the only trading post in the northern mountains was at our end of the Big Ice Lake.

"What's a matter, Trader -Man? We got dust enough to pay your price," one of the surly pair growled.

"I don't care. No more liquor. You and your brother are nothing but trouble. Now get out."

Oh, Qwa'osi, it was the Jomash brothers!

Where were Uncle Tli and his friends? If they saw these particular men, there was going to be a fight, like last time.

"The Mud-Grubber deserved the licking we gave him," the other brother protested. "The crazy Zaunk started it."

Jombonni slammed his hand down upon the counter top. "I said get out, and I meant it. I'm not selling you anything."

The second man to speak put a hand on the long-bladed knife holstered at his hip. "You Zaunk-loving bastard, I'm gonna...."

Jombonni's pale face turned a bright pink. One of his hands dropped beneath the counter as if reaching for something. "Do what? Kill me, too?"

"I don't know what you're talking about."

A man from downriver had made the mistake of arguing with these same brothers at the post, and later when the fisherman went missing, even Jombonni, who tried not to take sides, thought the disappearance suspicious.

Jombonni's flushed face turned a deeper shade of crimson, and his mouth hardened into a determined line. "Get. Now!"

A boy's frightened face materialized from behind a barrel, then it disappeared back into the storeroom. A moment later two of the post's burly workmen appeared in the warehouse doorway, walking in to flank their boss. The other miner saw them and placed a hand on his brother's arm.

I hastily scanned the surrounding buildings and dock area. No one seemed to be loitering nearby, but Uncle Tli and his friends had threatened revenge on the brothers when next they saw them. Raising my hand to shade my eyes, I searched farther along the shore....

The sun had risen above the eastern peaks, fanning out in a ribbon of silver across the green water. Several fishermen were over by the beached canoes. But their faces were lost in shadow, and I couldn't recognize them.

Oh, Uncle, please stay away.

Then without warning the light reflecting off the water intensified. The knot in my gut tightened. I stifled a cry and closed my eyes.

Too late.

As hard-edged and piercing as glass, the brightness was trapped inside my head. There was no escaping the Spirit-Sending devouring me. Suddenly powerless and terrified, I clung to the doorframe, determined not to draw the attention of the foreigners inside the post.

Ensnared within a whirling storm of disjointed images, I saw scavenging dogs, Wannigua demons, and dead men and women lying in the snow. A village was in flames, people screaming. What village? I wanted to see, but the mists thickened.

"Let's go. The Zaunk-lover will sing a different song when the steamboat gets here," one of the miners said, his voice echoing through the tumult of the foretelling.

"Things are gonna change around here. Just wait and see, Trader-Man, when the steamboat comes."

When the steamboat comes—comes.... The miner's words reverberated in my head. I trembled. The paddlewheeler was coming, true enough. But unlike other visits, this year its bounty of trade goods was an illusion. Hidden among its many boxes and barrels was an unspeakable evil. Change was coming, certain and terrible.

"No. It's not true," I begged in the mind-speech of Spirits.

Smothered by smoke and blackness, I heard a mechanical roaring and the thunder of fast water over boulders in a narrow channel. My body convulsed. I choked on the stench of hot iron and fish slime. Suddenly I was drowning in foaming water, dark currents sucking me down into the abyss. Panicked, I struggled to get away. Discordant laughter mocked my efforts.

"Qwa'osi, Otter Warrior and Guardian, save me!"

Determined to swim out of the chaos, I focused my Qwakaiva, as Grandfather had taught me. And with the Spirit's aid I banished the sounds and images of the foretelling. Still dizzy and weak, my Spirit returned to my body. I shivered, the summer sun's heat unable to stop my trembling.

The world before my eyes revealed a new jagged clarity. The glowing Spirit-Fires around living things had a bluish-grey tinge that warned of some unspeakable sorrow. I was vaguely aware that the men inside the store had stopped talking. The enraged brothers were heading for the doorway, where I stood shivering and gulping for air. I needed to get away, before the torrent of red anger and black fear engulfed me, but at that moment my body felt too sluggish to move.

As the taller of the two yellow-haired brothers came out onto the porch, he backhanded me with a blow that sent me sprawling. "Out of the way, brat." Without looking back, the miners stomped off the porch heading toward the dock.

I'd always given the miners the healthy respect I might a vicious sled dog, staying out of their way when I noticed them lounging round the post. But at that moment I wished I already had the knife Uncle Tli had promised me next time the steamboat arrived.

If I had my gifting knife, I'd show them...

I picked myself up off the porch's weathered floorboards and wiped my mouth, leaving a trail of scarlet down my forearm.

My face throbbed. Stumbling away from the post, I headed down the beach in the opposite direction of the miners. Once out of sight, I crouched and splashed cold water over my aching face.

"Tas? Are you all right? Kutima told me to come find you."

Still dripping, I turned. My brother-cousin Samiqwas stood on the shingle. When he saw my face, his brown eyes widened. "What happened?"

I waded out of the water and started walking down the beach, not wanting to talk to anyone, not even my best friend. "It's nothing."

Samiqwas fell into step beside me, frowning. "Did Matoqwa do that? If he did, I'll...."

"No. I haven't even seen Matoqwa today. Just forget it. I don't want to talk about it." Samiquas snorted, calling me a bad name in the traders' language. I balled my fists and rounded on him. "Take that back, Dog Fart."

Impatient for an answer, he hopped out of reach of my swing. "Some angry miners were getting into their canoe a while ago. Did they try to steal you? Did they want to make you their slave?"

Samiqwas had reason to be worried; it had happened before. "No."

Samiqwas was a square-built boy with his mother's round face, and his father's large hands and feet. He was proud of the length of his twig and how far he could piss. Being a year older, over the past winter he had shot up in height, making the difference in our ages more apparent.

Glancing towards the trading post, I swatted at a mosquito and watched the glowing disk of the sun illuminate the blue ice of the glacier across the lake. The dark silhouette of the brothers' canoe made its way up the eastern shore. Still furious and hurting, I focused my anger on the disappearing canoe.

"Kunai, I seek vengeance. Open your enormous jaws and swallow them, boat and all."

In the shadowy depths of the lake a being of immense power stirred, roused from its dreams by my summons. Cold yellow-green eyes opened and contemplated me. Appalled, I shrank from that enigmatic gaze.

I must have cried out, for suddenly strong hands grasped my shoulders, breaking the contact, plunging my Spirit back into my physical self. I took a ragged breath and opened my eyes. Samiqwas was holding me.

"Tas? What's wrong?"

My tongue frozen to the roof of my mouth, I shook my head, unable to speak. Everywhere I turned, evil omens assailed me. I pushed myself away from him. His touch burned like stinging nettles brushing against my skin.

When I remained silent and started walking, he spun me around to face him.

"Tas, answer me. What's wrong?"

Before I could guard my tongue, I blurted, "The steamboat hasn't cracked on the rocks like the traders fear. It's coming ... soon."

He beamed. "Haya! That's wonderful news."

Taking a petty delight in shattering his excitement, I growled, "No, it isn't! I wish the steamboat would go away—drown." Before the shadow onboard it covers us all.

In those early days as the ice cleared, the old paddlewheeler chugged north each year up the Socanna River from Fort Protection to our home on the Big Ice Lake. The boat's arrival, and the trading that followed, was the most important event of our year. During the summer, children spent every spare moment on the lakeshore, hoping to be the first to sight the steamboat. There was a bag of hard candy waiting at the post as a prize for the lucky one who brought the news. But the steamboat was late that year. The snowmelt from the spring runoff had passed through the river's channel already, and still there was no sign of the boat.

Samiqwas stared at me as if moose antlers had just sprouted from my skull. Then, trying to be reasonable, he said, "Tas, everyone will suffer next winter without those tradegoods. Why would you say such a terrible thing? You aren't making any sense."

"I know," I grumbled. "Stop pestering me." I took several deep breaths as Grandfather had taught me, trying to dispel my emotions and bring back clarity....

"Well? Is the paddlewheeler coming or not?" Samiqwas pressed.

Fighting back nausea, I mentally kicked myself. Why hadn't I kept my big mouth shut? Kunai's sudden interest in me, a village in flames—how could I tell him what I'd seen? My brother-cousin's spirit was like a hunter's blade, bright silver and sharp edged; he wouldn't understand. Even I didn't understand.

"Yes. It's coming," I said, my voice taking on a longsuffering tone.

Walking a few paces closer to the water, he held his hand to his eyes and looked out across the lake. "I don't see anything."

"So? I said the boat was coming, didn't I? It'll be here by tomorrow, maybe later today, but...."

He made a rude noise, sparking my anger anew. Still glaring at his back, I hurled a stone into the water with more force than necessary.

Would that nasty miner have hit Samiqwas if he'd found him standing in the doorway of the store?

I hurled another stone. Probably.

Another stone. But maybe Samiqwas would have fought back. "Uncle Tli is going to buy me a bright steel knife of my own this year."

"So?"

Samiqwas picked up a flat stone and skipped it effortlessly over the water. The stone hopped three times before it sank. A smile curving his lips, he patted the knife resting in its worn leather sheath at his hip. "I already have a steel knife. Uncle Tli can buy me a fox trap if he wants to give me a present."

To have a knife made of iron, not one made of bone or chipped stone, meant that a boy was recognized by the hunters of our village as nearly a man-grown.

I had no such knife, and still slept in my mother's furs....

Samiqwas and I were brothers, as was the custom for maternal cousins among my people. I loved him, but his drawing my attention to his father's gift and his new status only fuelled my annoyance with him.

"Yes, you have a knife. But it's just an old one your father didn't want any more. Mine will be new."

Out of the corner of my eye I saw his mouth tighten, but I pretended not to notice. I picked up a rock and arched it out over the lake, trying to imitate his throw.

The rock sank, much to my disgust. It was so humiliating. Boys half my age could skip rocks better than I could. I dared not look around for fear he would be laughing at me. My aching cheek hurt all the more for the flush I was sure darkened it.

Too short for my own liking, my face oval not round, my hair wavy not straight, my eyes a deep violet rather than a warm brown, I hated all the differences that set me apart from my relatives.

Swallowing down the lump clogging my throat, I kept my eyes focused on the water. I tossed my next stone, with similar results. Then I threw another, deliberately casting wide, so that the rock hit his leg instead. He whirled round to face me with fist raised. I thought he was going to hit me, but whatever he saw in my face made him change his mind.

Stifling a grin, he stepped up beside me. "You're holding them wrong, look." He scooped up a handful of stones and patiently showed me the proper way to hold them.

His generosity in choosing to ignore my childishness shamed me all the more. I knew he was being kind, trying to make peace between us, so I did as he suggested. I let go of my anger and my fear for the future. I let my bad feelings sink into the lake with the stones.

When Samiqwas saw I understood how to skip them, he became bored. Looking around for something else to occupy his energy, he spied his father and his uncle down by their moored fishing canoe. Waving a farewell, he headed in their direction.

"Hey! Where are you going?"

He turned round to face me, still walking backward. "Why to tell them what you said, of course. Maybe they'll want to take the canoe out to look for the paddlewheeler. If they do, I'm going."

I flung my handful of stones into the water, not bothering to watch where they fell. "Wait for me," I shouted. "I'm the one who told you. The bag of candy is my prize."

He laughed. "Careful, Tas, or your belly will grow as big as old Grandma Bear's. Don't worry. I'll share the prize when we get back."

Chapter Two

I raced up the beach, panting like a dog. Samiqwas waved, stifling a grin as his father and his uncle paddled out into the lake. I kicked a twig off the dock in frustration. I was the one who had seen the steamboat first; it wasn't fair that Samiqwas would get the sweets.

I considered telling Jombonni, before they got back, then I decided against it. The southerners didn't believe in Spirit-Sendings. Jombonni had to see something with his eyes to believe it. He would only laugh at me if I told him my vision.

But Uncle Tli would believe me. Now that the miners were gone, and it was safe, maybe Uncle would even take me out on the lake to see the steamboat, too.

If I could find him....

His canoe lay upturned by the big fir, but no Uncle. Leaping off the dock I raced back to the village.

My elder-uncle Da'wabin had married into a village down the Socanna River. I rarely saw him, but Uncle Tli, Mother's younger brother, lived with his wife's family in our earthen-lodge settlement.

I arrived out of breath at Uncle Tli's home, barely able to gasp out a greeting. From inside a woman's soft voice told me to enter. Her face as round as the moon for which she was named, Shilshigua smiled when she saw me and held out a steaming basket. "I have some fresh seed cakes. Would you like one?"

I shook my head, still gulping for air. "No. Thank you." I glanced about the lodge's dim interior, hoping to see Uncle Tli, lounging on his bed platform, playing with his new daughter. "Where is Uncle?"

Putting the basket back on the hearth, Shilshigua resumed stirring a pot simmering in the hot coals. Fragrant smells of wild onions, meat, and seal fat filled the lodge, making my mouth water. "He went fishing with my brother Chugai early this morning."

That explained why Tli's canoe was still on the beach. Then suddenly I was angry. "Why am I always the one staying home with the women?" I cried. "Why isn't Uncle here to bring me out on the lake? Or my father?"

An unreadable look came over her face. Then, dropping her eyes, she turned away to stir her pot once more. "Why don't you ask your mother that question, my husband's nephew. I don't know the answer."

Of course she didn't know, and couldn't help me understand. Shamed by my rude outburst, I fled from the lodge.

I marched into my home, planting myself in front of Mother with my arms folded across my chest. Sunlight streamed down the open smoke hole, illuminating the lodge's interior with a golden hue. The embers of the cook fire sent up lazy tendrils of blue smoke to mingle with the sunlight.

My mother was a slim woman with luminous dark eyes and clear brown skin. Wearing the wistful expression she often had when she thought no one was watching, she sat on our sleeping platform, stitching a pair of winter boots to sell to the trader. Grandmother was also in the lodge, sitting on her own bed, her thick body bent over her sewing.

Taking in a deep breath, I asked, "Amima, why don't I have a father of my own? I want a father, like Samiqwas."

Without looking up, she laughed softly. "Like Samiqwas, eh?" Then she returned to her sewing.

"Amima?"

Was her only answer going to be silence and laughter? Did my feelings mean nothing to her? When I remained, glaring at her, silently demanding an answer, she sighed. "Always running here and there, chasing seeds and berries. Little Rock Squirrel, be patient. You may meet him someday."

"Someday? What kind of an answer is that?" I was furious with this unknown stranger who'd sired me and then left. Once again I forgot about respecting my elders, and demanded, "Why did he go away? Did you do something bad that made him leave us?"

Mother glanced up, frowning. Her eyes widened when she saw my bruised face and bloodied lip, but she made no comment.

Grandmother, who had been silently observing us, chose that moment to make a sound of disgust deep in her throat. "I warned you this day would come. Tell him."

Jabbing her needle into the soft moosehide with a savage intensity, Mother refused to glance in Grandmother's direction. "There's nothing to tell, and you know that as well as I."

"Do I? Tell him, Qwadalah."

When Mother refused to answer, Grandmother focused her grim stare on me. I shuddered; did I really want to know the truth about my father?

On this day of all days, maybe I'd been foolish to press for answers.

"There's more to the world than this tiny village, Grandson." Grandmother had such an expectant expression that it diverted my attention. "Perhaps your father, when your mother chooses to summon him again, will take you home with him and teach you. Would you like that, Little Rock Squirrel?"

"Take me away? Leave all my relatives?" I gaped. That was a sobering thought, and one I hadn't considered. "But why would I have to go away, Ami? Ko lives with us. Why can't my father?"

"Ko." She made a face, disgusted. "Any man in the village can show you how to hunt and fish, but your father's Qwakaiva is different. He could teach you wonders."

"Wonders? But I don't need a father to learn about my Qwakaiva. Grandfather's teaching me."

"Is he?"

I dropped my eyes and murmured, "He's trying. It's just...."

"I don't believe my ears!" Mother said. "Now you want him to come back to us? You sang a different song when you learned I was pregnant."

"Did I? I don't recall that."

"How convenient."

"Well, perhaps I did, but now that these foreigners are trying to steal our land, I have reconsidered my earlier rashness."

Mother snorted and jabbed her needle into the leather hard enough to prick her own finger. "Don't fill the child's head with such foolish notions. Tasimu can't do anything about the miners. Nor can he go with his father. It isn't possible."

"Of course he can go with him. You don't truly believe that do you, my girl? Surely the blood—"

Her voice nearly a shout, Mother took her bleeding finger from her mouth and cried, "Stop! I won't listen." Pushing her sewing off her lap with an impatient gesture, Mother walked to the wooden grub boxes by the wall and began rummaging around in the nearest one.

Grandmother remained unruffled. The fine steel needle she was using to sew a pair of mitts went into the wolverine skin, without a break in its rhythm.

"Surely you miss your handsome Star Swimmer under your furs?"

Mother let out a startled sob, tears pooling in her eyes before she turned away. "My son is all I need. Why do you torment me?"

I heard no more after that. Not finding what she was looking for in the box, Mother realized at the same moment how closely I was listening, and vented her frustration upon me.

"Tasimu, where is the tea I sent you to bring back from the post?"

Tea. With everything else that had happened that morning I'd completely forgotten about my errand to fetch more tea. I hung my head, staring at the smooth stones by the hearth. "I'm sorry. I forgot."

Mother slammed down the wooden lid on the box and straightened. "Well, go right now and get it." She made a shooing motion with her hands. "Go on, quickly now. Your grandmother will be thirsty soon."

The tea was only an excuse to get rid of me, but I did as she wanted. She wasn't going to tell me anything more about my father with Grandmother sitting there.

I was determined to ask Mother more questions, but by the time I returned both women had left our lodge. Aunt Tuulah was like my second mother. She'd nursed me along with Samiqwas when I was small, and my own mother had been not right in her mind for a time. She might tell me—if she knew, and I could find her. I put the packet of tea in the grub box and wandered outside, unsure where she'd gone.

Then three of my small girl-cousins saw me. They cried out, wanting me to come be their sled doggie and pull them on an old reed mat. That was the last thing I wanted to do, so I hid behind the woodpile until they gave up looking for me.

Fearing they might find me again if I stayed to search for Mother or Auntie, I left the settlement by the back route, taking the path to Hot Springs Creek.

As the village disappeared from view, a raven cawed. Suddenly dizzy, I cried out and slammed into a tree, tiny lights exploding behind my eyes. When my vision cleared everything had changed. Instead of the familiar trail through the summer forest, an old man knelt in the snow ahead of me, coughing up blood. I swayed as the smell of smoke seared my throat, and again the ghostly sounds of wailing people echoed inside my head.

I ran ... and kept running until the vision dissipated, and my breath came in ragged gasps. I needed help—someone who could protect me from the evil revealed in unwanted visions.

Uncle Tli was out on the lake, and I had no father, but my grandfather, our village's Qwakaihi, was a man used to unravelling mysteries, and I had a good idea where I might find him.

Chapter Three

When I stepped out of the willows, composed once more, Grandfather was sitting on a log by the creek. He was wearing the blue and red woollen shirt Aunt Tuulah had made for him, caribou-skin leggings, and high-topped, moose-hide boots with greased rawhide soles to make them waterproof. In spite of his age, his square body retained a hunter's strength. He had just finished his bath, his grey hair hanging down his back in long ropy strands.

Not wishing to disturb his contemplation until he was ready to acknowledge me, I sat down quietly on the other end of the log and gazed out over the lake, waiting for him to finish smoking his pipe.

Tucked among the folds of glacier-capped mountains, the Big Ice Lake was long, narrow, and very deep. Its water had turned indigo in the afternoon light. High up among the eastern peaks, grey clouds hovered.

In such a long, narrow valley a storm could blow out of nowhere, churning the water from a placid green to a milky froth in moments. Our fishermen were always alert to the slightest change in the weather. But in spite of all their precautions, someone was occasionally lost to the many shadowy creatures in the bottom of the lake.

Grandfather had always warned me about Co'yeh if I should be by the lakeshore alone in the evening. He was a Seal; he was an enemy. Lake Seals stole fish from our nets whenever they could. Women with no husbands were in danger from Co'yeh's Warriors who disguised themselves as men during the seals' mating season. And an unwary person could be lured to his death listening to the Seals' sad song out on the lake in the summer twilight.

In the long-ago time when the Otter Qwa'osi, Matoqwa the Bear, and the people living on the lakeshore made war against him for taking too many fish, Co'yeh, fearless warrior, deep swimmer, won a bone game with Kunai the Aseutl living at the bottom of the lake, thus forming his own alliance.

Had Co'yeh, rival of Qwa'osi and enemy of our village, lured that fisherman to his death and stolen his Spirit so that Kunai could kill and eat him? Or maybe it had just been the miners who had killed him as Uncle Tli claimed, then sank his canoe, leaving no trace of their crime. So many possibilities....

"The Aseutl is a capricious beast," Grandfather said, as if he'd been thinking of the killing, too. "Sometimes he will gift a seeker with power—if the seeker pleases him. At other times, when he's tired of fish, and hungers for the taste of red meat, Kunai will claim a human for his meal, feasting on both the unfortunate's flesh and Qwakaiva."

Recalling shadowy creatures swimming to me and imparting unwanted knowledge of things to come, I said, "Was it Co'yeh, or the Great Aseutl's touch I felt when I fell out of Ko's boat in my fourth summer?"

Grandfather sucked on his pipe, considering the question. "The first touch of the Unseen Ones is always frightening. When you are older, perhaps they will speak to you of that time. Then, you'll know who is your Spirit's Companion, the one from whom you receive your Qwakaiva."

"I hope my Spirit's Companion will be one of Qwa'osi's Otter Warriors. I want to heal people and protect them as you do, Grandfather."

He smiled. "Yes, that's my wish for you, too. Any being emerging from the depths of the lake to claim a human for its Spirit Companion would be more curse than blessing."

More curse than blessing.

A chill ran down my spine. "But what if I don't like the one who speaks to me? What if it's Co'yeh and he steals my Spirit, but leaves my body to walk among my relatives?"

Then, remembering the mysterious green eyes that I'd envisioned contemplating me earlier that day, I blurted, "Or what if it is Kunai?"

"Kunai—not Co'yeh, then?" Grandfather laughed, but his mirth seemed forced. "Do you believe the Master of Enigma himself favours you? What a strange notion."

His tone of voice was teasing, but this time his smile was brittle, more like a grimace than a friendly grin. Crooning softly, he stroked my tangled hair. "Now, now, Little Rock Squirrel, don't be afraid. I was only teasing you. Kunai rarely interests himself in the affairs of the People. And we have Qwa'osi, the Otter Warrior, to befriend us in the Spirit-Realm, remember? Qwa'osi is a sly one, you know; you wear his token. Co'yeh the Lake Seal and his allies can't hurt you."

He lifted the otter claw that always hung around my neck on its leather thong, showing it to me. "See, the Otter favours you. I've spoken to him on your behalf. You're safe as long as you wear his token."

Safe? Qwa'osi, why aren't you protecting me better?

"Ati, why is the Otter our protector and not his brother?" I blurted. "Co'yeh is the better fisherman. And he can swim the dark waters under the Earth like Kunai. Maybe he would be a more powerful Protector for us."

For me.

Taken aback by something in my tone of voice, he studied me for a long time before answering. "Yes, Co'yeh is a better fisherman. Seeking the mysteries of the twilight world where only Kunai can dwell, he swims into the black depths to gain prophesy, among other hidden knowledge. But Qwa'osi is both a fisher in the lake and a hunter upon the land. He can travel and protect us in both worlds and that's why we are blessed to have him as the Guardian of our village. Be at peace, Grandson."

Unlike other times when the shadowy beings swimming at the edge of my consciousness threatened, that day, his reassurances didn't comfort me. "I hate my Qwakaiva," I cried. "If Qwa'osi is so strong, tell Him to take it back. I don't want it."

The vehemence of my tone startled him. Then his expression smoothed, and he shook his head. "I can't do that."

"Why not? You're a man of Power."

"That ability is beyond my skill."

"And what of my father, can he do such a thing?"

"Your father?" I suspected he was studying me with his Spirit-Sight, but I didn't care.

"Who has been talking to you about your father?" His tone was gentle, but with my own Spirit-Sight, I could see red spikes of fire surrounding his head. He was angry, but with whom, me—or someone else?

"No one has been talking to me. That's the problem," I grumbled. "Samiqwas has a father. I want a father, too."

Seemingly relieved by my answer, he chuckled. "I'm sure you do, but I doubt if your father will be back anytime soon, and that's for the best, believe me." He patted my shoulder, but his heart wasn't in the gesture. "So you'll just have to make do with only me and your Uncle Tli."

"For the best?" I swallowed down the lump of sadness, suddenly choking me.

"I can see by your face that you don't agree with me, you think perhaps I'm being unnecessarily cruel, but I'm only hoping to spare you future pain when I say this. Trust me; it's for the best."

"Grandmother doesn't agree with you," I blurted angrily. "She wants my father to come here to make the miners go away."

"Oh, she does, does she?"

"Yes. Could he do that?"

"I doubt it, nor would he want to."

"She also wants him to teach me special things. But I hate my Qwakaiva! Please, Ati, take it away."

He put an arm around me and squeezed me close. "I'm sorry. I can't take away what the Unseen Ones have gifted. Qwakaiva is given to someone for a purpose. It is to be used for the good of the People, never selfishly. I doubt if even your father could change your life's pattern."

I sniffed and wiped my nose on my sleeve. "Then will you tell me about him? I'm not a baby now. I want to know."

Alas, Grandfather's answers weren't any more enlightening than those of my female relatives. He was as sly as the Otter whose power he borrowed for his conjuring, and it was only later I realized how he'd tricked me. As I pestered him with questions, he must have used his Gift to divert me. I suddenly became very interested in finding tree fungus we could later carve.

As he'd hoped, I forgot all about my father, but I also was distracted from warning Grandfather about the disaster I'd witnessed in my vision.

Chapter Four

When Grandfather and I returned from Hot Springs Creek, Mother told me to stay and help Grandmother while she took some fish soup to an ailing relative. I didn't mind at first; I was looking forward to spending more time with Grandfather. However, he left soon after he ate. Not wanting me to sit idle, Grandmother told me to chop more wood and stack it in the structure we had tacked on to the front of the lodge to keep out the drafts.

In the old days we lived in small family groups spread throughout our territory, but by the time I was born, most families were building warm earthen-lodges on the slope above the Big Ice Lake, to be close to the trading post. Many of the Chamuqwani called our homes dirty, because they were made of earth and poles. I didn't care what they said; our lodges were warmer in winter than their cabins by the bitterly cold lakeshore.

It seemed like I'd been stacking firewood against the wall forever when the paddlewheeler's high-pitched whistle blew down by the wharf. Dropping the kindling I'd just started to arrange in its basket, I poked my head outside.

Samiqwas waved as he raced past shouting the news. "The steamboat is almost here. Everyone come, quick!"

Several relatives pushed back hide door flaps to listen, then disappeared inside to get ready. From beyond the blanket that led into our living quarters, Grandmother grumbled, "What was that boy yelling about?"

Warm air and the smells of wood smoke and fried mushrooms brushed against my face as I pulled open the blanket. "Samiqwas says the steamboat is here."

Grandmother and my youngest sister-cousin Seicu were the only ones in our lodge at that moment. While Grandmother cleaned up after a recent meal, Seicu sat on her mother's bed, dressing her wooden-headed doll in its new fur garment. Grandmother was unimpressed by my news. She grunted and continued sweeping.

Did she really expect me to continue with the chores she'd assigned me now? I could hardly stand still, I was so excited. In the distance Samiqwas continued to shout as he ran up the hill to where some of the men were chopping down dead trees.

Behind Grandmother's broad back, Seicu stared at me wide-eyed. As if she had read my mind, she asked, "Want go see, Ami?"

Seicu was the family's youngest. Everyone but Grandmother spoiled her, because she'd been a sickly baby. Though she'd grown stronger in the last two years, the habit hadn't waned.

When Grandmother ignored her, Seicu's eyes grew moist with tears. The elder hated when Seicu cried to get her way. If Seicu tried that ploy now, we might be stuck here until Mother or Aunt Tuulah returned to rescue us, and that wouldn't happen any time soon.

Outside people were talking in excited voices as they hurried down the path. Hoping to ward off trouble, I said, "I'm done with the wood, Ami. If you don't need me, I'll take her to the dock, so she can see the steamboat."

Grandmother glanced at Seicu, and gave me a sour look. Then she relented. "All right, you both can go."

Doll in hand, Seicu hopped down from the bed platform and took my hand. I let the blanket fall, and we hurried outside to join the people heading for the dock.

To my surprise, along with the boat's usual cargo came a large number of soldiers and miners. Pale-skinned or dark, they leaned over the railing to gawk, as the steamboat pulled alongside the pier. Trailing behind the boat was a string of flatboats and rafts, burdened with additional newcomers and mounds of supplies.

All the men at the rail laughed and joked with one another in their loud foreign voices "Dirty Zaunks." Someone jeered.

"Ugly ain't they?" another said.

A miner with a broad-brimmed hat that hid much of his face laughed. "Ugly or pretty, who cares what a woman looks like under a blanket. It's dark most of the year this far north anyway."

Many of my Qwani'Ya Sa'adi relatives could understand the foreigners' language better than they could speak it. A few young men must have understood the newcomers, as I had. Spirit-Fires brimming with hostility, they whispered among themselves, glancing often at the strangers.

More miners, more trouble. I turned away and led Seicu deeper into the enthusiastic crowd.

The sun had slipped behind the mountains by the time the paddlewheeler was moored securely to the pier. The grey clouds hovering over the eastern peaks earlier were gone. No rain, and the long summer twilight would offer plenty of light for unloading.

The adults in my village were as excited as the children. Everyone hung around the dock and the store, getting in the way. They discussed what they hoped the trader had ordered for them, and what they would buy first with their credits.

Each year it was amazing to see how many canvas-wrapped bundles, wooden barrels, big trunks, and other supplies the Chamuqwani could fit on their steamboat. We examined anything left unattended, jumping out of the way of the cursing workmen, only to resume our explorations unrepentant when they returned to other duties. In the boxes and trunks there were mysteries to discover and dream of owning some day. I would hardly sleep that night knowing that tomorrow there would be so many wonders to stare at on the restocked store shelves.

Thinking about all those marvels reminded me of the candy prize that rightfully belonged to me. Lifting Seicu to my shoulders, I said, "Can you see your brother?"

She squirmed about, slapping her doll into my face. "No."

I spat fur out of my mouth and urged, "Keep looking. If you find him, he'll give us sweets."

She wiggled some more, slapped me with her doll a few times, then pointed. "Brother there. Has candy?"

"Yes." Grabbing her swinging feet, I stopped to peer through the press of bodies, wishing, not for the first time, that I was taller. "Where, Little One? I can't see him."

She tipped her head forward so she was looking at me upside down, her eyes bright with excitement.

"Where?"

She pointed more insistently towards the far end of the dock, away from the unloading. "There."

When I still hesitated, unable to see over the backs of two Chamuqwani carrying a heavy chest, she whacked me on the arm with her doll. "Oh, you too short, Little Rock Squirrel. I show."

Before I could take another step, Seicu grabbed one of my ears as if it were the lead on a dog sled harness, and twisted my head in the direction she wanted me to travel.

"Ouch! Stop that." I pried her fingers off my ear and rubbed it. "That hurt, and don't call me that baby-name."

Seicu giggled. "A'right, baby." Then she grabbed my hair instead, swinging her feet. "Ah'hup, doggie." I growled as she pulled on my braid, and that got her giggling even louder. I started moving before she could inflict more damage.

As the activity around us thinned, I spotted my cousin. He was sitting with his legs dangling over the pier, surrounded by a group of his admirers. Seicu let out an ear-piercing squeal as we approached, and he looked our way. When he saw us, he took the red and white candy stick from his mouth and grinned. My eyes flicked to the nearly empty bag in his hand.

"Don't worry, Little Rock Squirrel, I saved you some."

I scowled. "Don't call me that, Dog Fart." The other boys laughed, repeating my baby-name.

Seicu held out her hands to her brother, nearly falling off me in her eagerness. Samiqwas made a grab for her, giving her a kiss as he lifted her from my back and set her on her feet. Rolling my shoulders to ease their ache, I took a deep breath and stared across the lake, taking a moment to let go of my annoyance. The more fuss I made about him calling me by my baby-name, the more he did it. When I turned back to them, Seicu clutched her doll in one hand and held a long, striped candy stick in the other. She looked up at her brother with adoring eyes.

Seeing that look fuelled my anger once more. "It was me who saw the steamboat first, you know, not you. Why don't you tell them the truth?"

"Sure you did," Matoqwa scoffed, "Little Rock Squirrel." Matoqwa was sturdy and heavy shouldered like his namesake the bear. His eyes were sullen, his nose lumpy from an old break. A long white scar like a claw mark ran down his right cheek.

His younger brother Cohasi doubled over laughing, as if Matoqwa had said something very funny.

"What does it matter who saw the steamboat first," Tigali said. "It's the sharing among relatives and friends that truly matters."

Tigali's words hit me like a cup of ice water in the face. I hung my head. My Qwakaiva had given us this windfall, and a part of my Spirit wanted to be recognized for that fact. The other part of me was appalled by such a selfish thought.

When Samiqwas saw how upset I was, he put a reassuring arm around my shoulder. As he gave me my candy stick, he sang my praises to the others. "It's true. My brother-cousin saw the paddlewheeler with his Gift, so I could tell the Chamuqwani the news and claim the prize for all of us to share. He will be a great Qwakaihi someday, a treasure of the People."

Treasure of the People, eh? There was still a glint in his eye that let me know a trace of his earlier joking still lingered, but I could also taste the truth in his words. Samiqwas was proud of me. I was content, and so chose to ignore Cohasi's snicker and Matoqwa's snort.

I stayed talking to our friends for a time, but when they began daring each other to take a canoe out on the lake to explore the miners' rafts, I reluctantly took Seicu and left.

As I neared the store the bell on board the steamboat clanged three times, and then a man in a red coat blew a long horn that sounded like a mountain goat bleating. Everyone on the peer stopped what they were doing and stared.

As the sound faded, the line of soldiers standing at the end of the gangway straightened. A pale, big-bellied man with no hair on the top of his head paused to stare at the activity on shore, then started down. He was dressed in black wool jacket and trews. On his jacket a blue lightning bolt was stitched across the image of an ice-bear rearing up with its jaws open wide.

Two men in similar clothing, wearing the same picture on their jackets, followed him. The shorter one carried a leather trunk on his shoulder; the other, a man so tall and thin he seemed no more than skin and bones, walked just behind the fat man holding a large red umbrella over his head.

"There's no sun or rain in the sky," someone nearby murmured, "so why does he need to shelter his head at this time of day?"

"Crazy foreigners! A good coating of seal fat mixed with mint and tsami root to keep away the bugs would be a far better covering than that silly stick covered with cloth, pretty colour though it is," a woman said.

As the strangers neared the end of the gangway, the soldiers thumped fists to their chest in an honouring gesture. The man under the umbrella nodded his acknowledgement, then stepped forward to greet Jombonni.

Seicu giggled, distracting me. "Man got funny hat."

"It isn't a hat, it's an umbrella."

"How you know?"

"Kutima showed me a picture in one of his father's books," I said impatiently. "Hush now, I want to watch what they do next."

The chief trader shook hands with the man under the umbrella. Then he led his visitors to a nearby cabin. They all went inside and closed the door, spoiling my view.

"I want big umbrella like funny fat man," Seicu announced.

"Sure. Ask Uncle Tli or your father to get you one—tomorrow." Still puzzling over who these new arrivals might be, I paid her little notice.

"Little Rock Squirrel?"

"Hmm?"

Screwing up her face as if about to cry she tugged on my hand to get my attention. "Want umbrella now, Little rock Squirrel. Want now!"

I bent down to quiet her. "No. And if you cry I'll take you home to Grandmother. You want to go home?"

"N-no," she sniffed.

"Then don't cry," I warned.

Glancing around for a way to distract her, I happened to catch sight of Samiqwas's older sister, Esuli, standing with one of her admirers. Deciding I'd done enough babysitting for a while, I whispered to Seicu, "Let's go see Esuli. She might have a treat for you, too."

My bossy, older sister-cousin had recently returned to our home from her Shillsham ceremony. Upon the arrival of her first moon-blood she spent three moons alone in the mountains, praying and preparing herself for womanhood. Fending for herself hadn't done her any harm. Her lean brown body was strong, her black hair long and thick, her clear-skinned face bright and smiling. She had many suitors.

Seicu held out her hands and shouted her sister's name.

Hurrying over, I handed her to her sister, with a straight face. Tosgali, the young hunter she'd been talking with, gave me a knife-edged look. Trying not to laugh and spoil my joke, I climbed the porch steps to the trading post and flopped onto one of the long benches set against the wall. This quiet spot would be a great place to watch everything.

What kind of steel knife will Uncle trade for me?

Lost in my own thoughts I jumped when I felt something hard being slipped into my hand. I looked down at the small square of folded brown paper, explored the hard round lumps inside it with my fingers, and looked up, open-mouthed. My friend Kutima gave me a shy smile.

Kutima's mixed parentage gave his skin a pale golden colour. And because his father made him stay in to work on his lessons most of the time, his body was plumper than was common among the hard-working boys of our village. He was aware of his status as a trader's son, and could be bossy, but I still liked him.

"What's this for?"

Kutima blinked his brown eyes and shrugged. "Your brother-cousin claimed the prize, but I know it was really you who saw the boat first."

How had he known that? Samiqwas wouldn't have spoken so freely of my Qwakaiva to anyone living at the post. Kutima was supposed to be one of the Chamuqwani god's "Chosen", and not believe in what his father considered "primitive superstition"." But he'd told me once that he respected our traditions. Well, with a prayer for his good health, some of this precious stash would find its way into the lake as an offering to the Unseen Ones. I could do that much for him, at least.

I slid my hand a little closer to my side so no one could see the packet. It was an ongoing scandal among my relatives that his father beat him. Though I did like candy, I didn't want to be the cause of his receiving another harsh punishment.

"Thank you. Want some?"

He shook his head. "I have to get back before I'm missed."

"Wait, who was the fat man with the umbrella and the ice-bear on his coat that your father met at the dock?

Kutima glanced up nervously at the ice-bear and lightning bolt sign hanging over the trading post door. "He's some official from the trading company headquarters down south. The rich lords and the Father Emperor sent him north to check on how father is running the post."

Things are gonna change when the steamboat comes....

Feeling the cold hand of warning at the back of my neck, I blurted without thinking, "Are the bossmans angry with your father? Are they going to send him away?"

Kutima's eyes widened, then he shook his head vigorously. "No. I have to get back inside now. I have a lot of work to do."

"Can I help?"

Kutima paused as if considering, then shook his head. "They won't want any Za ... anyone from the village inside right now. Only those who can read can help with the sorting." He hurried towards the open door. "Thanks for offering, Tas. See you later."

Zaunk. Had that been what he'd been about to say? Mud-Grubbers, Slime-Eaters, and Zaunks: those were what the southerners called us when they wanted to hurt us, or make someone angry.

Hard, ugly words and so bitter a taste upon the tongue.

Chapter Five

When the temple bell rang the following day, an excited shout greeted its call. Finally the traders were ready. There was a ritual about the event that had to be performed in its proper order, however. The children all knew better than to rush to the store.

First of all, everyone had to gather at the Chamuqwani God's temple, with the priest leading us in prayer. I hated the ugly square building, because it always stank of sour sweat. As large as the post warehouse, the stone gather-hall was cold even in summer. It was also bare of furnishings save for the crude statue of the Mighty Djoven, holding a lightning bolt on a dais at the back of the room. Two thick wax candles placed on either side of the altar were lit for the occasion. At the statue's feet, a brazier wafted the thick smoke of resinous incense into the air.

It was a torture for everyone to stand silently waiting, but to my relief, on that particular trading day the priest took pity on us and made his prayers short. Maybe he was as curious as we were about the goods that would now be on display at the post.

As we filed from the temple, chief trader Jombonni, dressed in white shirt, black jacket and trews, and fine broad-brimmed black hat, led the procession of traders and villagers to the store to settle their accounts.

Everyone in the village as well had dressed up in their best clothes for the occasion. The men wore fine woollen shirts of red and blue trade-cloth, leather loin aprons, caribou skin leggings, and high-topped, rawhide-soled boots. Each man's long black hair was tied back in a thick club wrapped in leather strips.

The women wore their best blanket shawls with ermine trim and brightly coloured yarn fringes. Their long, tunic-style dresses were made from the same trade-cloth as the men's shirts, only much longer. High-topped boots trimmed with strips of beaver fur and dyed porcupine quills adorned their feet.

Their long black hair was greased and plaited with brightly coloured ribbons. The thick, shiny braids bound together hung down their backs. Framing their faces were masses of long shell- and glass-bead streamers, dangling to their shoulders from woven headbands.

I raced Samiqwas to the post, and for the first time that season I beat him. I was very proud of myself. Maybe I was growing after all.

Then, my happy mood soured. The fat official who'd arrived with the steamboat was sitting on a carved chair in the yard waiting to view the trading. Behind him his tall servant held the bright red umbrella above him.

Accompanying him were several grim-faced, dark-skinned soldiers. They spoke to no one, not even Jombonni. The menace they represented wasn't lost on anyone. They carried their thunder-weapons for all to see.

"I hope the fat man brought those soldiers here to protect us," an elder said. "If the miners should start more trouble...."

"Protect us? Not likely," someone in the crowd scoffed.

I glanced toward the tents that had sprung up overnight along the shoreline. Protect the miners, maybe.

Turning away from the soldiers, I grasped the otter claw around my neck and prayed, "Qwa'osi, keep us safe from all these bad men."

Where was Uncle Tli? Anxiously I searched for him among the approaching villagers. Uncle had powerful hands and the lean body of a hunting fox. He also had a temper that could ignite in a moment when he felt injustice threatened the Qwani'Ya people of our village.

When I found him he was glaring at the fat official and the soldiers. Then, he leaned forward and muttered something to Matoqwa's older brother, who laughed. I was too far away, but Shilshigua must have heard, because she hugged the baby she carried in the side-sling upon her hip.

Hoping to distract him, I hurried over. "Uncle, can I help you carry your trade goods?" My face must have betrayed my fear, because he smiled and tousled my hair.

"Don't look so worried, Nephew. Let's go trade for the knife I promised you." Motioning me to precede him, we climbed the porch steps.

The trading post always smelled good to me, a mixture of wood smoke, exotic spices, sweet candy, and saltfish. The room where the trading took place was a large rectangle, divided down the middle by a long, wooden counter about waist high on a man.

In one corner in front of the counter, an iron wood stove squatted, its grey hide caked with old grease and soot. A few benches had been placed around it, and on cold winter days some of the men gathered to talk with the traders and drink hot sweet tea laced with waskyja. But on that clear summer day the stove sat cold and abandoned. Only a few elders sat there to await their turns at the trading.

There were shelves nearly to the ceiling, stocked with all kinds of wonderful items on the traders' side of the counter. Further back, beyond the front shelves, extra goods were stored in the back warehouse. Jombonni and his men stood behind the counter and the people lined up in front. When it was a person's turn, he or she would point to wanted items on the shelves, and one of the traders would look in the post's black ledger book to see if the person had enough credits to pay for the desired items.

Chief trader Jombonni was a tall thin man with a sandy moustache and a funny little bald spot in the middle of his thinning brown hair. He was friendly, with a booming laugh. He'd lived among us for years, spoke our language well, and took an interest in the gossip of the clans. He drove a hard bargain, but no one complained over how much he cheated them.

Once inside, I dared not say anything to Uncle Tli. I knew better than to distract him from his trading, but each time he'd look around, I'd be at his elbow. Anxiety gnawing at my gut, I took note of the mounting pile of bright yarns, trade cloth, traps, and foodstuffs piling up at his feet. I hoped he wouldn't run out of credit before he got around to bargaining for my knife.

At last he ended my torture and pointed to the display of knives on the wall. Jombonni let out one of his booming laughs and gave me a knowing wink. Then, he took down several knives for my uncle's inspection. Expressionless Tli waited as Jombonni told him the price for each one as he set them on the counter.

"That one is five fox pelts. And that one, it's a fine blade, yes? That one is nine. And that one, a true wonder, that one would cost three wolf pelts."

Nine pelts; I liked that one. I glanced up at Uncle, hoping he could see the pleading in my eyes.

Tli shook his head sadly. "Knives are too much. My wife wants more oatmeal for the baby. Too much."

Jombonni nodded. "Food for a baby is important, but your nephew is a fine young hunter. With a good knife he could be a lot of help to you this winter. Then you could buy more food and pretty things for your family."

"Maybe, but he helps already; he's a good boy."

"I agree, but stone tools break so easily. With a good steel knife he could help even more than he does now."

"Mmm." Tli pointed to the knife I liked. "Three fox and one beaver."

Jombonni shook his head and my heart sank. "I can't do it—the Father Emperor's man is here. He would be angry with me for giving away his master's goods. Eight fox pelts."

"Too much. Four beaver pelts."

Jombonni held up another knife, that one smaller than the one I now wanted more than anything in the world. "I can let you have this one. Six beaver."

Tli studied the knife with slow deliberate movements, taking it from its sheath, testing its sharpness. Behind me impatient relatives, anxious for their turn, grumbled. My stomach clenched; I, too, wished he'd hurry, but I was also afraid of the outcome. What if he thought all the knives were too much and wouldn't trade for any of them?

"That one is no good for a hunter. It is only a toy, a baby's knife."

A baby's knife? Samiqwas and the other boys will laugh their heads off if he doesn't buy me something. I will be shamed—an outcast—forever!

They bargained for a while longer, at last settling on a knife with a blade about the length of my hand, with a slight curve to its tip. It had a ridged bone handle that would fit my hand well when I pulled it from its sheath. Uncle agreed on a price of seven fox pelts; I was stunned. It wasn't the one I'd wanted, nor the most expensive, nor the grandest of the knives on display, but it was a sturdy, serviceable tool that would help me in my work over the coming year. And, as I examined it more closely, I realized that it was a far better knife than the one I would have chosen.

I was so proud of that knife. As soon as Uncle Tli handed it to me, I ran outside and removed the blade from its leather sheath to stare at the silver metal in the sunlight. Samiqwas had been generous about letting me share the use of his knife, so when he came over to see my prize, I willingly handed it over.

He drew out the blade and nodded his approval. "Let's go down to the shore and find some driftwood to test its sharpness," Samiqwas suggested.

Smiling, I agreed and we hurried down to the lakeshore.

Absorbed in our own concerns, we'd been paying no attention to the activity at the trading post, until shouts and a woman's high-pitched scream alerted us to trouble. I slipped my knife back into its sheath and looked around. We'd drifted farther along the shore than I'd realized, and now a stand of willow and birch blocked the view. "What's going on?"

Samiqwas shrugged. "We better go see."

Fear goading us, we raced up the beach.

As we neared the post a Chamuqwani shouted, "Dirty Zaunk! Kill the bastard!" And in response, one of my Qwani'Ya relatives cried, "Greedy, ignorant foreigners, go back to your own lands and leave us alone!"

Samiqwas sprinted ahead and I soon lost sight of him among the jostling crowd. No matter how I tried to squeeze through the press and follow, a kick and a punch aimed at my head was all I got for my effort. Wiping blood from my nose, I backed out of the crush. Spotting Aunt Tuulah and Mother standing together on the trading post porch, I headed in their direction. Aunt Tuulah clutched Seicu close to her side, pushing the sobbing little girl's face into her dress. Mother stood wide-eyed, a hand to her mouth, staring at something going on amidst the milling people in the yard.

Hoping to see better from there, I leapt up the steps and joined the women. Tugging on her arm, I shouted over the noise, "Amima, what's happening?"

"Some Qwani'Ya men are fighting with miners."

"Where's Uncle Tli?"

Mother opened her mouth, but Aunt Tuulah spoke before she could get the words out. "Where have you been? Weren't you supposed to be helping him?"

Trade goods! A twinge of guilt tugged at my heart. I'd been so excited about my knife that all other obligations flew out of my mind. "Yes, Aunt Tuulah, I was. I-I forgot."

"You forgot, eh? Do you think your uncle will be happy when he hears your excuse?"

"No, Auntie. But where is he? I can help him now."

"The last time I saw my brother, Tli was accompanying Shilshigua and her mother back to the village."

Mother shook her head. "He's not there. He came back—with Mother."

Tuulah's eyes widened. "Mother's inside the store drinking tea. Where did he go after that?"

"I don't know. I wasn't paying attention." She stood on her toes peering into the haze of dust surrounding the brawling men. "Sister, can you see him? Is he there?"

"I don't see him. Oh, I can't tell."

I strained my eyes, but couldn't find my uncle. In the midst of the shouting people, a man with yellow hair appeared for a moment, then disappeared once again. He seemed somehow familiar, but I couldn't place the recollection. With their wide-brimmed hats and the hair growing all over their faces, it was hard to tell one miner from another. "What happened, Amima? How did the fighting start?"

"The trouble began when the Jomash brothers and their friends pushed their way into the store and demanded to be served ahead of everyone."

The Jomash brothers. Now I recognized the yellow-haired one.

Things are gonna change when the steamboat comes.

"Rude, dirty miners," Grandmother said as she joined us. "They demanded that Jombonni trade with them first, because they were better men than any of us." She snorted. "Without our help most of the miners, including those troublemaking brothers, would have died last winter. And how do they repay us? By destroying fish traps, and stealing our food, and invading clan-owned territories in search of pretty yellow rocks. Rocks! Those men have no sense."

I closed my ears to her complaints; I'd heard it all before. Something else far more disturbing had caught my eye. His face purple with outrage, the fat man was gesticulating to a group of soldiers. Off to one side his overturned chair and smashed red umbrella lay abandoned in the dirt.

While I watched, more soldiers hurried up from the pier. Bellowing "Give way!" and using their thunder-weapons like clubs, they waded into the crowd, bloodying anyone too slow to get out of their path.

The fight was over within moments after that. Miners and villagers alike backed away, and I got my first clear view of the combatants. On one side Chugai, Ko's brother Gagayii, Uncle Tli, and Matoqwa's older sister's husband from downriver were struggling amidst several soldiers. Not far from them, the Jomash brothers and three of their friends were being guarded by a similar group of grey-clad men. Though loosely confined, they continued to inflame our young men by shouting curses and nasty names, which the soldiers did little to stop.

Over the elders' and Jombonni's protests, the soldier's headman and the Father Emperor's official halted the trading for the day. "I'm sorry, friends," Jombonni said. "These men are concerned for everyone's safety. He feels everyone needs time to set aside their bad feelings, before we can resume the trading again."

Grandmother muttered under her breath, "That fat man is more concerned for his own safety than ours."

"When will we be able to come back?" an elder asked.

Jombonni turned back to the men for more talk in their language. "They will meet together tonight. They'll decide and let us know tomorrow." He held out his hands palms up. "I'm sorry, but I'm sure all will be well in the morning."

Muttering, the people started to drift away; then, realizing that the soldiers had no plans to let our young men go home without being punished for their part in the disturbance, they came back to see.

When he understood the penalty the soldiers intended, Jombonni protested loudly on our behalf. "A whipping for the men of the village is unjust and too harsh! The Jomash brothers are troublemakers. I've banned them from the post before for fighting."

"Go back inside now and tend to your business," the soldier in charge said. "These Zaunks need to be taught a lesson. Fighting with the Emperor's miners won't be tolerated, especially in times of war."

Jombonni folded his arms across his chest and glared. "If these men must face a whipping, then so should the miners involved."

"The miners will be dealt with in due time," the officer said. "But...."

The trading company's official smirked. "If you can't be counted on to obey orders without insolence, then you'll be replaced."

Jombonni's bravado deflated like a fish bladder poked with a stick. Without another word, he brushed past the women and went back inside.

The Jomash brothers and the rest of the miners involved in the trouble were sent back to their encampment with nothing more than a stern warning. Uncle Tli and the other men from the village were bound to the porch rail, stripped of their shirts, and flogged with a long whip until their backs were bloody.

Chapter Six

With the trading unexpectedly over for the day, the village defiantly went ahead with plans for a celebration. In preparation for this annual event, several fires were built on a grassy bluff overlooking the lakeshore, out of sight of the Chamuqwani buildings.

Two days before some hunters had killed a moose, a special treat at that time of year. When I arrived with Mother, the old women were roasting the meat on iron spits hung over the flames. As the meat browned, they cut off the cooked chunks, then returned the rest to the fires to cook some more.

Placing the roasted meat in flat reed baskets, younger women carried the trays to a plank table where mounds of flat griddle bread and bowls of fresh berries dusted with white store-bought sugar awaited the hungry people. Countless kettles of strong black tea, as sweet as birch syrup and nearly as thick, completed the feast.

After we ate, five of our best singers took their hoop drums from sealskin cases, and stepped to the fire to warm them. When the stretched hides sounded just right, the men formed a line at one side of the central fire and began singing. Old men and women, recognizing the song joined in, their high-pitched voices echoing across the lake in the twilight.

When the younger men and women began dancing, Samiqwas and I watched the snaking lines for a time. Soon enough though, we became bored and joined some of our friends down by the lake. Most of the children who were old enough to leave their mothers were doing the same.

It was a still night, the lavender sky above streaked with coral, the outlines of the grey peaks softened by an evening mist collecting far out on the lake. I could hear the drumbeats echoing off the nearby hillsides, before the sound was flung wide across the deep green water. The smells of woodsmoke, roasting meat, and rotting lake weeds mingled on the air.

I hurried as usual after Samiqwas. In a long, flat area near the water's edge, we joined some boys lining up for foot races. Further down the shore I could see another group engaged in a stone-throwing contest.

Most of the boys in the group we'd joined were older than I was. I'd no intention of joining their game and looking foolish. Samiqwas, however, feared nothing and stepped up alongside Slylum for the next race.

He didn't win, but he ran well, ten times better than I could have done. Tigali shouted ko'hey in praise of Samiqwas's attempt. My cousin beamed and lined up again.

I watched for a time, shouting ko'hey whenever anyone made a particularly good effort, but I was cold and bored just standing around watching. I wanted to do something to warm up and show my own skills. Waving to Samiqwas, I wandered further along the beach. Walking on logs and leaping over clumps of grass, I headed for the stone-throwing group.

I took in several deep breaths as the Qwakaiva of Earth and Water enveloped me. I lifted my face and sang a prayer song, just for the joy of it. High above the eastern peaks, pale ribbons of phosphorescent green light snaked in shimmering spirals across the violet sky. I shivered, wondering if I had inadvertently called them. This was the first time I'd seen the Spirit-Lights since the summer sun had paled the night sky. Summer was waning, but it was still too bright at night for them to be more than a ghost of their winter greatness.

Continuing down the beach, I blew into the hollow made by my clasped hands to call them closer. Then I sang a song to the lights as I picked up stones. I held them between my palms and felt a tingling power awake deep in the heart of each one before I put it in the pouch at my waist.

My hands grew warm; the stones would do my bidding. The evening felt charged with power. I laughed, feeling suddenly as carefree as willow blossoms blown on the wind. I leapt into the air and did a few dance steps in time to the distant drum as I joined this new group of boys.

Most of the stone throwers were my age or slightly younger. They greeted me warmly with teasing calls. All but Matoqwa, the oldest among them, who scowled and turned his back on me. I stuck out my tongue at his back, returning the insult.

When someone laughed, he mumbled something fierce under his breath and began throwing stones with a vicious intensity. His brother Cohasi shouted a praise call as one of the Bear's stones jumped four times before sinking. Then other boys began to throw, trying to match his feat, and the tension dissipated.

The heat from the stones' Qwakaiva nearly burning a hole in my pouch, I joined the shouting line. My hands moved as if the will of the Spirit-Lights guided them. I tossed stone after stone into the water. Three, four, five times they jumped. Again and again, my throws were impeccable, my Qwakaiva unbeatable. My arm, my whole body flowed gracefully with each movement. Ensnared in the power twisting and crackling through the world that I'd given a focus, I gave no thought to the other boys.

My mind spun with a storm of images: warm sandy beaches, and golden stones shimmering at the bottom of green pools, white fish leaping high, their silver scales bright in the sun, jump, jump, jump, splash.

I didn't notice the other boys had stopped throwing until harsh laughter smashed through my shell of concentration. When I dropped my arm and glanced around, they were all staring at me. Cohasi made the sign against evil when he thought I wasn't looking. My stomach heaved; I couldn't breathe, couldn't think.

I stared dumbly at Matoqwa, too shocked to speak. He curled his lip and spat on the ground. "Siyatli Boy, are those scales I see at the nape of your neck? Or maybe there's a lake seal's brindle fur under your hair, eh? Why don't you crawl back into the lake with the rest of your kin?"

Matoqwa might have said more hateful things, but Samiqwas, who'd come up unnoticed, decided at that moment to smack him on the side of the jaw. Matoqwa staggered, then, roaring with outrage, he charged his adversary. Grim-faced, my cousin met his charge with another bone-jarring punch. They fell to the ground, rolling over and over, each one trying to gain the upper hand.

Trembling, I stood watching, unable to think or move. A part of me wanted to race down the beach and keep on going. But the part of me loyal to my brother-cousin wouldn't leave him to face his enemy alone, in case Cohasi decided to join the fight.

I needn't have worried; the dispute didn't last long. Tigali and a few of the older boys heard our shouting and came over to break it up. Prying the combatants apart, the older boys asked no questions; they merely dragged both fighters to the lake and pushed them into the icy water. Amidst howls of laughter, Samiqwas and Matoqwa came up spluttering and dragged themselves ashore dripping.

Samiqwas grinned and slapped his opponent on the back.

Matoqwa wasn't as ready to forgive and forget, but under the watchful eyes of the older boys, he reluctantly let the matter drop.

When I was certain that Samiqwas would be all right, I fled. Soon after, a bedraggled Samiqwas trudged along in my wake. Behind us, the rock-skipping contest resumed.

The Spirit-Lights still gyrated in the violet sky. A low humming like the sound of angry insects whirled around inside my head. On the lake the mists were creeping ever closer to shore. The world about me felt brittle and as dangerous as a broken waskyja bottle smashed on the rocks. I shivered as if it had been me who had been dunked.

I kicked a stick out of my path and said without looking at him, "Aunt Tuulah is going to be mad when she sees your best shirt." He just shrugged.

I'd been moving aimlessly, only wanting to distance myself from the others. We'd nearly reached the place where Hot Springs Creek emptied into the lake before I was paying attention to my surroundings again.

An old spruce blown down in a winter gale lay sprawled along the creek bank. Its roots arched into the air, while its crown tip fanned out into the water. Sprinting ahead of me, Samiqwas began breaking off dry branches and laying them in a pile near the arching roots.

"Have you got your make-fire kit with you? Mine's wet."

I stared at him stupidly for a long moment. My mind still mulling over Matoqwa's words, I had a hard time making the connection. I finally nodded and reached for the hardened clay vessel covered with leather tucked into my belt. I crouched and placed a wad of dried moss on the sand, then struck the stone to the metal. When the red spark jumped into its fluffy nest, I blew on the smouldering ember until the whole mass burst into flames. Samiqwas added a handful of spruce needles and twigs. We broke off larger branches and kept adding them until we had a comfortable blaze going.

Taking off his wet clothes, Samiqwas draped them over the arching tree roots to dry. Going to the creek, he washed the blood from his bleeding nose. When he came back, he lay down by our fire with a big sigh, like a tired sled dog. I crouched on the other side of the fire, feeding it more twigs, and watched him. He closed his eyes. A trickle of blood still leaked from one nostril. "You'll have a nice bruise around your eye. He must have punched you good."

Samiqwas chuckled. Without opening his eyes, he said, "Wait till you see Matoqwa's face."

I looked away, concentrating my attention instead on the writhing patterns of gold and crimson within the flames. What was happening to me—to the world around me? Did everyone know some dark secret about me? Was I a Siyatli, one of the half-human creatures sired by a magical being living at the bottom of the lake? And why now was my cousin, my brother, my best friend, so silent? Why wouldn't he look at me?

I tossed the stick I'd been playing with into the flames with an angry gesture. The fire hissed a complaint, tiny red sparks shooting into the air with a snapping sound. Samiqwas opened his eyes and looked at me.

"What did Matoqwa mean?"

"I don't know what you're talking about. I didn't hear him."

"You didn't hear him." I jabbed the fire hard with another stick, and sparks shot up once again. "If you didn't hear what he said to me, why did you punch him in the face to stop him from saying more, hmm?"

Samiqwas sat up, picked up a twig, and began pulling its grey-green moss off, tossing it into the flames. "I didn't hear what he said, truly." I gave him a disgusted look. "And I hit him because ... because I wanted to, that's all. I just wanted to."

"Tell me, please."

Ignoring my plea, he jumped to his feet to check his drying clothes. Finding them still wet, he scowled, then leapt atop the log and began walking up and down its length with arms outstretched for balance. "There's nothing to tell."

Siyatli, is there a lake seal's brindle fur under your black hair? Why don't you crawl back into the lake with the rest of your kin.

No, no, I'm no Seal Man's child, no enemy! Qwa'osi, tell me it isn't so!

I watched him for a time, then my anger flared once more. Why was he lying? He'd never done that before. Picking up the nearest object I found by my hand, I threw it.

Samiqwas had reached the end of the log and was coming back towards me. The pinecone hit him square in the middle of his chest with a hard thunk. The log rocked, Samiqwas teetered, lost his balance, and then landed hard on his backside in the grass. He gaped, picked himself up and walked back to the fire rubbing his chest.

"Why did you do that?"

I glared at him, but refused to answer.

"I don't really know what Matoqwa was talking about," he finally said. As I reached for another pinecone, he held up a hand. "No, wait. I don't know much, but I'll tell you the little I do know. I don't think Matoqwa really believes you're a Siyatli. He was making it up, because he was angry that you were beating him at the stones."

"Maybe, but there has to be more to the story. Tell me."

He let out a long-suffering sigh, and busied himself with adding more twigs to the fire. At last he said, "I only overheard my mother and one of her friends joking about your mother having a Lake Seal Man for a suitor when she was young. That's all I heard, because they saw me and stopped talking. That's all I know, I swear it!"

Waves of ice pounded through my veins. My chest tight, I could hardly breathe. Spirit Stealer, fish thief, was I truly kin to one of Co'yeh's hated warriors? No, impossible!

"Your mother never talks about him, does she?"

"No. Does yours?"

"No, but she may know. When your mother was so ... ill, she may have confided in her sister. Amima might tell you if you ask her."

I'd already thought of that, but never found her alone to ask. "Maybe.... But why would anyone think my father one of Co'yeh's kin? What if one of those creatures heard that kind of joking and sent bad luck to us for a punishment?"

Samiqwas shrugged and reached for his shirt. "It is crazy talk, true, but everybody likes to gossip about a mystery. And your mother's lover is a big mystery—even you have to admit that. So people talk. So what? Matoqwa is a dog fart. What he says means nothing; just forget about it."

Samiqwas was fully dressed by the time he finished talking. His clothes were dry but dirty. Crouching by the dying blaze he shovelled handfuls of sand onto the fire to put it out. "I'm getting hungry; let's go back to the dance and see if there's any food."

I stood, pondering his words, but made no move to leave. "Why wouldn't people think my father was a Chamuqwani trader or ... a tribal refugee from the south? Plenty of those men come through our village. Mother could have taken a fancy to one of them."

My voice trailed off as Samiqwas began shaking his head. "There are times, like back there." He pointed with his lips up the beach.

"Sometimes...." He took a deep breath and tried again. "You're different, you know. Your Qwakaiva, it's special, like Grandfather's, and that kind of power can make some people uneasy."

The queasy feeling was back in my gut. "But...."

"I know. Just forget about it."

Chapter Seven

As we climbed the slope, Mother and Aunt Tuulah were standing near the cliff edge. "You boys get Seicu. We need to go home, now."

"Go home?" We looked at one another. Samiqwas shrugged. No one had ever called us to come home from the summer celebration, but the tone of their voices, and the spiky grey light outlining their bodies, stopped me from arguing.

"Something's wrong," I murmured.

"I'll get Seicu. She was sitting in a patch of crowberries near the base of the trail." Samiqwas said. "You go on. I'll be right behind you."

Slylum and two of his cousins were coming down, eating meat and griddle cakes. They gave me odd looks as we passed.

Siyatli. The new story of my strangeness was bound to be all over the village by morning.

Samiqwas and I hadn't been paying attention to the adults' celebration, but as we approached the top of the bluff, my eyes almost popped out of my head. A large group of miners and off-duty soldiers were standing to one side of the fire. They were passing large jugs of waskyja among themselves and joking about the People and the dancing. A few of the boldest of our young women stood nearby, giggling and whispering behind their hands.

As I watched, one dark-skinned soldier, with curly hair like a mountain sheep, smiled and held out the jug in their direction. None of the girls had taken the men up on their offer—yet—but they were considering it. Jombonni and the clan elders sitting by the fire had also noticed the strangers' advances and weren't happy. To make things worse, those of our young men who weren't dancing were passing around their own jug of waskyja and glaring at everyone.

I couldn't understand why no one as yet had asked the Chamuqwani to leave, but I hoped someone would soon.

Her mouth and cheeks stained purple with berry juice, Seicu complained, "Not sleepy. Want pick berries." From Aunt Tuulah's hip she held out her hands to Mother. "Auntie please take me berries."

As we trudged up the trail to the village and away from the celebration, the little girl's maddening whine filled my head to bursting. Finally, my aunt had had enough. "Noisy Gull, be quiet or the Ogre Woman of the Mountain will hear you. She will put you in her basket, take you home, and eat you."

"Tuulah!" Mother gasped.

Seicu cringed, buried her face in Auntie's shoulder, and started crying. Samiqwas gave his mother a reproachful look, picked up his sister and put her on his back. He bounced her up and down snorting like a buck deer, making her laugh. Pushing past the glaring women, he trotted towards the village. Seicu's delighted laughter floated back through the trees, growing fainter as he put more distance between us.

I would have liked to follow him, but I'd been lagging behind, not wanting to go home any more than Seicu. Now both Aunt Tuulah and Mother angrily faced each other on the path ahead, blocking off my escape. I considered disobeying and going back to the celebration, then decided not to risk being caught. I would be missed at home and get into trouble for it.

"You shouldn't have lashed out that way," Mother scolded. "The child already has too many nightmares as it is."

Tuulah sighed. "I know. Father will scold me for frightening her, too. He told me that ghosts in the lake are calling to my sweet girl."

Mother's tone softened and she took Tuulah's hand. "Don't worry about her so much. She's recovered fully from the coughing sickness. She's fine now; everyone says so. It's you I worry about more than my niece."

"Me? Whatever for?"

I crouched low as Mother turned her head and pointed with her lips back toward the dance. Tuulah made no comment. Quickening her pace, she punched deep holes into the damp moss with her walking stick.

"Will you go back after Seicu is settled?" Mother asked. "Ko was with his brother by the food table."

"I saw him too. But he was drinking, not eating."

"The old people are still there; nothing will happen." Mother's tone had been soft and reassuring, but the muddy swirls of worry in her Spirit-Fire revealed the lie in her words.

Tuulah let out a mirthless laugh, not believing her either. "Gagayii had another bottle under his vest. He'll share with his brother, as always. Mother will leave when the singing dies down and the drinking increases. And our father can't do anything. He isn't of Ko's lineage."

"Maybe Father can talk to Ko's uncle, and he can talk to Ko."

Tuulah gave her sister a withering look. "And, maybe Ko's uncle will be too drunk by that time to listen as well, then what?"

"I didn't know he was drinking again."

The women were stopped in the trail once more, facing one another. I eased off the path and crouched down behind a bush. They would be furious if they discovered me.

After staring for a while in silence, Tuulah stepped around Mother and announced, "I'm going back. With all those soldiers and miners barging into our dance, who knows what might happen. Now that the children are safe, I have to take care of Mother. I'll be back later."

"If you don't like what your husband is doing, Sister, put his things outside our lodge and be done with him."

"I can't."

"Why not, because of the children?"

"Yes. No. It isn't only that."

"What then? Tell me?"

"Forget about it."

"I want to help. What?"

Tuulah shook her head and started walking. "Off in your dreams most of the time, you don't understand anything, do you?"

"What do you mean by that? Come back here and talk to me." Mother shouted at her retreating back.

"Never mind, there's no point. Tell my daughter I'm sorry. I didn't mean to scare her."

Mother made a disgusted sound deep in her throat and started walking back to the village. I trailed as silent as a hunting lynx in her wake. By the time we reached home more families had left the dance and joined us.

Near our lodge I caught up to her and put my hand in hers. She must have guessed that I'd overheard, but she only gave me one of her sad smiles and ruffled my hair as we stepped into the lodge.

Later, when all was quiet, I lay on our sleeping platform and watched the patterns made by the grey smoke drifting up through the smoke hole. The drums still pounded, but mingled among their beats were shouts and the occasional peal of high-pitched laughter. Someone's tied-up sled dog howled, then other dogs joined in the song.

The night sounds made me feel incredibly sad, and I didn't know why.

"Amima?"

Something in my tone of voice made her put down her sewing. Coming over, she pulled back the furs and crawled in beside me. Making herself comfortable, she took me in her arms. "What is it, my boy?"

Inhaling the scent of poplar resin and bear fat that always clung to her hair, I shamelessly snuggled closer to her warmth. "Why are the old people always complaining about how bad things are since the traders came? I wouldn't have my new knife and you wouldn't have a copper cooking pot or a sharp silver needle if they weren't here."

She laughed softly and brushed hair off my forehead. "That's true, but other gifts aren't so welcome as cooking pots and knives."

"You're talking about waskyja and Ko's drinking, aren't you?"

She continued to stroke my hair as if it soothed her. "Yes, the Chamuqwani drink is very bad. And some people like Ko have a problem knowing when to stop."

"Then why don't the elders tell Jombonni to stop trading it to us."

I couldn't see her face clearly in the dim light, but there was no mistaking the frustration in her voice when she said, "Maybe because some of them like to drink waskyja now and then too. But the problem is more complicated than just the waskyja."

I thought about that as I listened to the night sounds outside, then I said, "I've heard Grandfather telling Uncle Tli that he's worried about the land. He thinks too many animals are being killed to pay for items we get from the post. He thinks the Ancestors and the Spirits might become angry with us if we don't stop."

"Hmm. Your grandfather is a wise man."

"Samiqwas said Uncle Tli tried to warn the traders, but they only laughed at him. Do you think Grandfather is right, Amima? Will the fish in the lake and the animals abandon us to starve?"

"I think you need to go to sleep now. Qwa'osi will protect us, my son." Mother kissed me, then rose and went back to her sewing.

My troubled thoughts had reminded me of yesterday's Spirit-Sending. I mustn't forget again. I would warn Grandfather in the morning. Surely with all his power, he could stop evil. He was a great Qwakaihi. He would know what to do.

Chapter Eight

After the old people came home and went to bed, Mother gave up on Aunt Tuulah returning before Ko finished his drinking. She banked the fire and crawled under the sleeping furs beside me. Her soothing warmth eased my heart, and finally I slept.

In my dream, a pack of unknown dogs chased a small herd of caribou far out onto the lake ice. Exhausted and unable to go any further, the caribou formed a protective circle around their young and faced the yammering pack with antlers lowered.

The dogs were massive creatures with shaggy yellow coats and glowing red eyes. In twos and threes they leapt in to snap at the caribous' thin legs, then darted back to avoid their lethal thrusts. The ice was stained red with blood, the buck and his strongest does failing as I watched.

I could hear the pack's triumphant howling ringing in my head, when suddenly the ice split wide. The hungry dogs and the wounded caribou forgot about each other, scrambling desperately to avoid the black water. Kunai raised his great head out of the lake. Green-gold eyes with vertically slit pupils contemplated the struggling beasts. Then he turned his cold, unblinking stare in my direction.

Fear clutching at my heart, I forced myself awake. Mother and Auntie were already up and making the morning meal. A big pot of fish stew bubbled on the iron grating set over the fire. The most delicious smell wafted throughout the lodge. Mother saw me watching her, smiled, and motioned me over to the hearth. Still muzzy-headed from sleep, I stumbled from the bed platform and headed for the privy.

Outside, the summer fog blanketed the village in damp woolly folds. When I returned home, a tendril of its mass followed me. It slithered inside on its belly, before I could get the inner door flap closed. I felt its clammy touch on my neck as I took my place by the fire, and pulled my wool blanket tighter about my shoulders.

Blinking a stray wisp of smoke from my eyes, I cradled the warm stew Mother handed me, grateful for its heat. The steaming broth contained big chunks of white fish, wild onions, lake lettuce, crowberries, and oatmeal. Trying to banish the uncomfortable feeling that cold green eyes were still watching me, I raised the spoon to my mouth.

Aunt Tuulah was cooking griddle cakes and spreading the golden slices with lake seal fat and honey. There was also hot black tea for those who wished it.

Mother served the old people still sitting on their bed platform, then went to sit beside Seicu with her own bowl. Ko sat alone across the fire from Samiqwas and me, drinking a steaming cup of tea. There was a large purple bruise on his cheek. He stank of waskyja and looked red-eyed and haggard. The smoke from the fire kept blowing in his direction, making him cough.

Offering him no food, Aunt Tuulah ignored him, her mouth a thin line, her movements sharp and angry as she moulded the soft dough into flat cakes and slapped them with extra vigour onto the hot soapstone griddle.

Everyone looked a little pale and worn out that morning. Seicu was fretful. She'd had a bad night as Mother predicted, crying out more than once in her dreams. Seicu's nightmares had increased after the miners began digging further up the lake.

I'd barely finished my first bowl of stew and was contemplating the next piece of griddle bread my aunt had just flipped, when the temple bell unexpectedly began ringing.

"Now what?" Grandmother grumbled. "Who is making all that noise? Some young men still celebrating, no doubt."

"That old priest jealously guards his bell. I doubt if he would let anyone from the village close enough to touch it. There must be a good reason for waking us so early," Grandfather said.

The adults glanced at one another warily. Finally Mother ventured, "Maybe there's some kind of trouble." Aunt Tuulah snorted and busied herself with her cooking.

While we were still discussing whether to go to the temple or finish our meal, we heard a crier coming round with news. "Come out," he shouted. "Come down to the temple, everyone, immediately! Trader Jombonni has important news for us. Come, come now!"

"Important news, bah," Grandmother said. "What could possibly be so important that Jombonni must rouse us from our warm hearth on such a dismal morning? The man has no sense at all."

Tuulah shot Ko a withering look as if somehow this unexpected summons was his fault. He returned her stare for a time, then dropped his eyes and sipped his tea.

"I think it isn't the trader who commands this but the soldiers or the Emperor's man who came on the steamboat," Grandfather said quietly.

I glanced up from the griddle cake I'd snatched from the pile, and saw the frightened look in Mother's eyes before she turned away to grab her shawl.

"Whoever has called for us to assemble, we'll know more if we go down to hear what they have to say," Grandfather continued. He reached out a hand to help Grandmother to her feet. She scowled, ignoring his hand.

"I'm staying right here. I'm no slave to come at this foreigner's bidding." Seicu whimpered and crawled up on the bed beside her. For once the old woman didn't rebuke her for whining. Instead she put an arm around the child and pulled her close. "You can tell me what he wants later."

The fog had retreated from the slopes around the village, but clouds still obscured the glacier, the grey water of the lake rough as tree bark. My blanket whipping behind me like a sail, I started running, hoping to warm myself with the exercise. Samiqwas sprinted to catch up.

We arrived panting at the temple, but even so we weren't the first. Some people were already there. But wary as a wolverine scenting a buried trap, they clustered in small groups outside the open door, talking in low voices, reluctant to enter. Ignoring the adults, I peeked inside. Some of the elders sat cross-legged near the altar.

Jombonni's son Kutima was also in there, crouching by the wall, talking to his elderly aunt. Unsure what to do next, I glanced back outside. Grandfather was engrossed in conversation with our headman Tsanqwati. Mother and Aunt Tuulah had been waylaid by a cousin and were involved in an animated discussion of Esuli's marriage prospects. Samiqwas looked in their direction and rolled his eyes, then motioned with his chin to a group of our friends bounding down the footpath.

I shook my head and stepped inside, heading in Kutima's direction. I didn't like abandoning my breakfast on such a dismal morning, but since I was here, I was determined to satisfy my curiosity. And if I waited for my family to stop talking, I might be forced to stand in the back, where I would see almost nothing.

"What's going on?" I whispered as Samiqwas and I squatted beside Kutima. He glanced at me, but didn't give me his usual smile.

"Nothing ... yet."

I made a rude noise and his mouth twitched. I waited. Finally he said, "My mother's been crying and my father's very angry."

But surely his parents' quarrelling was no reason to summon the whole village? Before I could think of a suitable insult, he dropped a bees' nest of news in my lap.

"There are more soldiers camped by the Socanna River. They're coming here, I think."

"More soldiers than were on the paddlewheeler?" Samiqwas asked.

Kutima shrugged. "Maybe, or maybe they just got off the boat before it got to the post."

"Why would they do that?" I asked.

Kutima shook his head, but wouldn't look at me. He kept his eyes focused on the floor between his knees.

Samiqwas and I exchanged anxious glances over his bowed head. The presence of more soldiers didn't sound good. "Kutima, why didn't they come openly into the village? Do you know?"

At the sound of his name, he jerked his head up. Receiving no response, I repeated my question. At last, he said, "I don't know. I didn't see them, but I heard the fat man talking to my father last night."

"Maybe they're here to make all those crazy miners go home," Samiqwas suggested hopefully.

Recalling my dream, I shook my head. "No, I don't think so."

"Well then, maybe the war that Jombonni and the priest speak of is coming closer. Maybe the soldiers are here to protect us."

"Protect the miners, you mean," Kutima muttered barely above a whisper.

"What?"

Kutima made a noncommittal noise. Then the priest, dressed in his ceremonial blue robe, came out of his little room behind the dais, stepped to the altar, and there was no more time for questions. Someone shouted, and the people outside filed in.

When everyone was settled, the priest tossed incense into the brazier. Turning to face the god he raised his hands and intoned a long, monotonous prayer. During the incantation Trader Jombonni and two other Chamuqwani entered, walked down the centre aisle, and waited with the people in the front row for the priest to finish.

Jombonni had on his black wool coat and trews, just as if it were a holiday. He must have buttoned his white shirt too tightly around his neck, however, because his face was a deep pink.

Carrying a scroll in one hand, the stout Father Emperor's official with sagging jowls was dressed in a similar black coat and white shirt.

On Jombonni's other side, a Chamuqwani soldier—and a high ranking one if the gold and black trim on his jacket was any indication—waited. This man's skin was so dark a brown that it looked almost black against his smoke-grey uniform. Under his thick leather helmet, I could see wisps of his black hair as tightly curled as mountain sheep wool.

Jombonni was speaking to his companions in a low-voiced murmur, but they ignored him. I glanced at Kutima, hoping he would enlighten me, but the look on his face silenced my question before the words left my lips.

Then I forgot about Kutima, because the priest had finished his prayer. Throwing up his hands in defeat, Jombonni followed the others to the platform and turned to address his waiting audience. The Spirit-Fire surrounding his head pulsed with pent-up rage, and his voice roughened with emotion as he began to speak.

"These men have asked me to translate the Father Emperor's words to you. These aren't my words that I'll speak. I want you to know that, my friends. I only do what these men require."

Jombonni nodded to the man wearing the ice-bear's insignia. The trading company's official took a pace forward and unrolled his scroll. He read the words in a loud voice, pausing now and then for Jombonni to translate. The speech was confusing, but finally he said things that were too terrible to contemplate.

"Your lonely isolation in this harsh wilderness is ended. Thanks to the beneficence of our kind Father Emperor, you will become loyal and productive subjects of the Empire at long last.

"As I'm sure your trader has already explained to you, The Empire is under attack from evil men to the east. We need the gold rock found in your land to help with the war effort. Lord Hiram, your trading company's patron, is angered by the trouble between your people and his miners.

"So to prevent further unpleasantness that would hinder the mining, you must accept the Father Emperor's judgment. You must all become good servants of the Empire and leave this lake for a new home we are preparing for you elsewhere in our vast land."

A stunned silence fell over the hall as he finished and rolled up his scroll. My chest emptied of breath as blackness swirled at the edges of my vision. What was that crazy fat man talking about? Samiqwas muttered a bad word in the Chamuqwani language and gripped a fist about the handle of his knife.

After a long wait in which the clan mothers whispered among themselves, a man arose from among them and stepped forward. Tsanqwati was our headman, the one chosen by the clans to speak for us with outsiders. He was a tall man for my people, who tended to be short and square of build as a rule. He wore his iron-grey hair in two long braids tied with leather thongs. Normally his angular face wore a gentle expression, but at that moment his beak of a nose and cold eyes reminded me of a bird of prey rather than a kindly uncle.

Rudely turning his back to the fat man, Tsanqwati said, "Trader Jombonni, explain to these arrogant strangers. This land was placed in our care by the Unseen Ones. Who told the Chamuqwani otherwise? Our ancestors' bones lie here. Who is he to say we must leave?"

Jombonni's face turned a deeper shade of red. "You'll have no choice. A treaty has been signed between the Qwani'Ya people and the Father Emperor. The soldiers will make you leave, and I can't stop them."

Hearing Jombonni's answer, a low muttering like the buzzing of angry insects began among the young men clustered by the door.

Tsanqwati conferred with the elders again, then, addressing the Chamuqwani directly, he tried a different argument. "We have heard the words of the great lord and the Father Emperor in the south, and we thank him for his interest in us. What we don't understand is how our leaving the lake will help him win his war. Who will fish for his soldiers? Who will trap furs to keep his people warm in winter if we go somewhere else? These foreigners, these miners, can't do that. They are bad hunters and fishermen."

Jombonni translated Tsanquati's words for the men and then listened to their reply. When he turned back to us, he had to clear his throat several times before he could get the words out. "They say that the gold is more important than fish and furs."

Tsanqwati stared incredulously at the fat man. Then he turned to the trader to translate. "A man can't feed his hungry children with rocks, no matter how pretty. Nor will these rocks warm his body on cold winter nights, but furs and smoked fish can keep people alive. Jombonni, tell him to set aside the imaginings of a foolish child and behave like a sensible man. Tell these foreigners to forget about yellow rocks."

Jombonni hesitated, but when pressed he rendered a halting translation. "They say that you don't understand the world outside these isolated mountains. With enough gold they can trade for all the fish and furs they need elsewhere."

"And what will happen to our land when all the yellow rocks are gone? Will these strangers just abandon the land wounded and bleeding? Who will care for the ancestors and the animals when we are far away? Who will restore the harmony that they destroy? Their priests? I don't think so."

Jombonni took a deep breath and continued, "They want you to leave this lake and go to a new place further south. The Father Emperor has promised that by signing his treaty everyone will have plenty to eat and lots of new clothing on this "Tribal Allotted Preserve" they're setting aside especially for you."

Tsanqwati frowned. "What is this 'treaty' that you speak of? I don't know that Chamuqwani word."

Jombonni glanced at the official, then took a deep breath. "They say there's a paper with Chamuqwani writing on it. The writing says that the Qwani'Ya Sa'adi people give the Chamuqwani their northern lands in exchange for new land further south in the Tribal Allotted Preserve."

Angry murmurs grew in volume among the villagers. Tsanqwati's face darkened with emotion, he made a cutting gesture with one hand, and the people quieted. "What Qwani'Ya people signed such a thing? No one from this village."

"I know," Jombonni said, "but they say it doesn't matter. The treaty has been signed and everyone must go."

"Will we be allowed to come home when they have taken all the yellow rocks they want?" Tsanqwati pressed.

"I don't know. But it'll be good for everyone on this Tribal Allotted Preserve, they say. The children will be taught the Chamuqwani magic of how to read and write in books like my black ledger book. They'll grow up to become good citizens of the Empire like all the other peoples of this big land. They promise it is a good place, and you'll be happy there."

"Happy?" Our headman's back straightened, suddenly as stiff as an arrow shaft. "How can these strangers know better than we do what is good for us? This is our home. Our ancestors' bones lie here. We can't go. We wouldn't be happy on another people's territory. Our Qwakaiva is a part of this land. We would sicken and die if we lose our Qwakaiva. No one from this village signed any Chamuqwani paper. We aren't going anywhere." With a stubborn thrust to his jaw, Tsanqwati folded his arms across his chest as if the matter was now settled.

Jombonni's expression conveyed pity, but his next words were spears of ice in our hearts. "Oh, my friends, you have no choice," Jombonni said. "The soldiers are here to see that nothing stops the mining. And after the trouble yesterday it has been decided—over my protests—that the only way to have peace is to make you leave. If you don't go willingly, they will kill you. Please, think of the children and don't do anything rash."

From outside someone shouted a warning and a soldier barked an order. As the young men rushed the door, they were shoved back inside by soldiers with long knives stuck on the ends of their thunder-weapons. Pandemonium suddenly took over the room. A woman screamed when a soldier knocked her husband to the floor. Children cried for their mothers. Men and women climbed over one another in a desperate attempt to reach the outside. Another man fell, before the crowd blocked my view. Jombonni and the old priest begged the People to stay calm, but no one was listening. The scent of fresh blood stung my nose. Tendrils of black fear writhed through the haze of the incense-laden air.

At the first sign of trouble, Samiqwas grabbed the dazed Kutima, and the three of us backed against the wall behind the altar, trying to keep out of the way. Now I wished I hadn't been so eager to be so near the front. I longed for the comfort of my family. I could feel Kutima trembling where his shoulder brushed against mine. Samiqwas was trembling, too; but it wasn't the fear scent I smelled on him or saw dancing in his Spirit-Fire. It was rage.

Then, to my astonishment, my brother-cousin grabbed Kutima by his shirt, twisted the fabric tight about his neck, and spun him around. "Stinking pile of fish guts! You knew this would happen, didn't you?"

Like his father, Kutima was tall—taller than Samiqwas—but he was soft and no match for my cousin's hard-muscled fury. Wide-eyed Kutima stammered something unintelligible. Samiqwas slammed him backward. His head bumped against the wall, causing him to bite his tongue. "Answer me, Dog Fart. You knew. Admit it."

Blood trickled out of the corner of Kutima's mouth and onto his chin. "Brother-Cousin, what are you doing? What's wrong with you?" I laid my hand on his shoulder, and he spun to face me snarling like a wolf. The hard, yellow eyes of his Guardian glared at me from the Spirit-Fire about his head.

"Wrong? Wake up, Tas. Pull your mind out of your dreams. Can't you see it? He knew the soldiers were going to make us leave, and he said nothing. If he had told us, we could have warned...."

Angry now himself, Kutima yanked free and faced us defiantly, eyes blazing with indignation. "Yes, I knew. I admit it. And what would have happened, if I had told you or Tas, hmm? Would things be any different?"

"We could have warned them." I said quietly. "I thought you were my friend."

Kutima brushed a hand across his face, wiping some of the blood onto his sleeve. He swallowed the rest and glared at Samiqwas. My expression must have revealed the depth of my feelings, because his voice softened when he said, "Oh, Tas, I'm sorry. But if I had told you what I suspected, would your family have believed you?"

Samiqwas and I looked at each other. The idea of being forced to leave our homeland was so preposterous I could hardly believe it even now. No, they wouldn't have believed it. They would have thought our wild tale no more than a childish game.

"The soldiers are too many and their weapons too strong," Kutima said, pressing his argument. "If your uncle Tli and the others try to fight they'll die. I couldn't tell; I didn't want to be responsible for their deaths. And my father...." Kutima's voice trailed off as he fought for control.

I let my bad feelings go and tried to think of what I might have done in his situation.

Kutima must have sensed Samiqwas's unrelenting anger, because he said, "I know you don't think much of me; I don't care. My father has arranged for my mother and me to stay with him, but I choose to go with my people. That's why I'm here today, instead of hiding at home."

While our attention was diverted, the soldier standing beside the trading company's official had removed the thunder-weapon from the sheath at his hip. Pointing it towards the ceiling, he fired. There was a bright flash, its roar nearly deafened me, and tiny rock chips pelted down among us.

The weapon had the desired effect; everyone stopped what they were doing and fell silent, facing the men at the front of the room once more. When the echoes of the shot died away and all was quiet again, the soldier spoke in a hard voice that made his words all the more terrible for their lack of emotion. Jombonni translated.

"Commander Mu'Dar says you must not fight his men or you'll be killed without mercy. Men, women, or children, it doesn't matter to him. You'll die if you don't obey."

When my people greeted his threat with angry words of their own, a ghost of a smile curved his full lips. He lowered his weapon to point directly at one of the clan mothers standing in the front of the crowd. The cold yellow eyes of a spotted cat watched me from the shifting colours of the Spirit-Flame above his head.

The commander wasn't afraid; he wanted to kill and would welcome our resistance. I followed the direction of his pointing weapon, and my eyes widened. How had he known Ina was our most precious lore keeper? Had he only guessed, or had Jombonni betrayed us? If we lost her.... My mind couldn't imagine such a disaster.

Unafraid, the wizened old woman never moved. Eyes as hard as obsidian pebbles, she met his stare. People around her froze. Someone shouted for the angry people in the back of the room to be quiet. The priest continued to mumble his prayers. Jombonni made an ineffectual protest of his own, but the soldier never wavered, and the trader fell silent.

"Since you choose to challenge my authority, you'll remain here in this hall until the steamboat is ready to take you south."

When Jombonni finished translating, Tsanqwati stepped forward again, and this time addressed the soldier. "It's true we don't have the weapons to resist you, but what of our family members who aren't here. What will you do with them? And what of our tied-up sled dogs, who will feed them? If we are forced to make this long journey, we will need our warm clothing, bedding, and food. Allow us to return to our homes to collect these things."

By that time, the priest was paying more attention to the proceedings. Ignoring the priest's protests as if they were no more than the drone of an annoying insect, Commander Mu'Dar kept his eyes focused forward and gave the headman another of his terrible smiles. "So you can run away into the mountains and make me waste precious time chasing you? I don't think so. You'll remain here. And as for your missing tribesmen, they are being rounded up as we speak. They'll be with you shortly."

Adding the truth to his words, I heard Grandmother's shouts and Seicu's hysterical crying as rough hands thrust them stumbling into the hall. Moments later other indignant people were also shoved into our midst.

Samiqwas pushed himself off the wall, but I clamped a hand on his arm and made him stay. He shot me an angry look, then relaxed. He couldn't possibly make it through the crowd at that moment. Other relatives were closer; they would care for his little sister. He must wait.

When he finished translating those harsh words, Jombonni angrily turned to the soldier. A heated argument broke out between the four men on the platform. When it ended, unshed tears of frustration welled in the corners of the trader's eyes as he turned back to face us.

"This soldier is a hard man. Believe me; he'll do what he promises, so don't anger him. But I have convinced him to let a woman from each family return to your homes to collect supplies for the trip. The soldiers will escort the women in small groups to get your things. Then they'll bring them back here to wait with the rest of the People. The dogs will be cared for. I know they are valuable animals. They'll be useful to the newcomers. You'll be paid for them; don't worry. I'm sorry. That is the best I can do for you."

As soon as he finished, the priest reluctantly spoke a blessing, and the four men started for the door.

Suddenly Jombonni became aware of Kutima. With a curse, he grabbed his son and shook him. "What were you thinking of to come here? I told you it wasn't safe and to stay at home with your mother."

"I wanted to be with my people—"

Jombonni slapped him hard. Blood trickled from Kutima's mouth again. "You stupid whelp! Your people? Who am I then?"

Their low-voiced conversation faded as the trader hurried to catch up with the others, dragging Kutima behind him. Once they were outside, the door was slammed and locked.

Chapter Nine

Without waiting for me, Samiqwas pushed his way through groups of distraught people as soon as the outer door closed. Yelling for him to wait, I trailed the best I could in his wake. Though the gather-hall was large enough to hold the entire village on a holiday, at that moment, with so many people milling about, the search for our family made it seem vast.

We found them at last, claiming a space against the back wall. Grandmother sat with Grandfather, his arm about her shoulders. She'd resisted the soldiers and they'd beaten her before hauling her to the temple. In spite of the bruises on her face, she managed to look as fierce as a mother bear protecting her cubs.

Aunt Tuulah had forgotten her quarrel with her husband and now huddled in Ko's arms, sobbing quietly. At her mother's feet, Seicu hugged herself, looking small and bewildered. She brightened and held out her arms when she saw her brother. Mother gave me one of her sad smiles when Samiqwas and I sat beside her.

I glanced around me then asked, "Amima, where is Esuli?" I thought I'd pitched my voice so only Mother would hear, but it was Aunt Tuulah who answered me.

"That Tosgali boy better take care of her good or...."

"Hush now," Ko soothed her. "He's a good young hunter. The soldiers won't catch them. Be at peace, my heart."

Grandmother snorted and sat up a little straighter, glaring at him. "How can my daughter be at peace? If they find Esuli and the young man, they'll be sent away like the rest of us. And if they escape into the mountains, Esuli will be lost to her clan forever. Carrion eaters!"

She made the hand sign for hexing someone with evil. My eyes flew wide. "Kunai, kill them all!" she muttered.

Grandfather seized her hand and held on to it, before she could conjure any more curses. "Enough woman, do you want to bring bad luck upon us as well? This is a dangerous time. Every word and action of ours has power. We must be careful, very careful, if we want to survive. The Chamuqwani will suffer for their crimes without your meddling. Let it be. Pray instead for the Unseen Ones to protect us."

Her face darkened with anger, Grandmother opened her mouth to argue, then she looked into his eyes and changed her mind and instead covered her face with her hands, trembling. Grandfather watched her silently for a long moment, his expression stern, then he relented and pulled her into his arms. To offer them some privacy, the rest of us looked away.

"Don't worry about your sister-cousin; she is a woman now," Mother assured me. "She would have brought Tosgali as a husband to our home soon enough. If he is as brave a hunter as Ko thinks, then they have as good a chance as any of us to survive. Once we're gone, I doubt if the foreigners will look very hard for the runaways. They'll be too busy digging in the dirt to care."

"And it's good that some of our people remain here to comfort the ancestors," Ko added. "They need to know that we haven't willingly abandoned them."

"True words, sister's husband, though sad ones," Mother said.

"Ati," Samiqwas said, "why didn't some of our Qwani'Ya men fight the Chamuqwani and keep them as hostages until the soldiers outside agreed to let us go?"

He considered the question for a moment, then said, "We have squabbles, like any large family, and sometimes those disputes are settled in blood, but such things are rare among us. Everything happened so fast, they probably didn't think of it."

"But if our young men...."

"Like an unhappy sled dog, they make a lot of noise, but rarely bite," Aunt Tuulah grumbled.

"Be glad of that, Sister," Mother said. "Violence only makes more trouble. Maybe it's good that surviving the long cold-time takes too much of our Qwakaiva to have any left over for making war."

"Too bad for us, then," I muttered, staring her in the eye. "Is my father a Warrior? Maybe you should have taken Grandmother's advice. Maybe he could have stopped them." Her mouth dropped open with shock, as if I'd slapped her.

"Tasimu," Aunt Tuulah cried. "Show some respect. What's a matter with you? Is everyone drunk or crazy today...."

"Are you all right, Mother?" a man's voice said. Startled, we looked up to see Uncle Tli standing over us. A long cut oozed a trail of blood down his cheek, and he held his arm awkwardly, as if it hurt him.

"Tli," Mother gasped, "Were you fighting?"

Uncle Tli waved her question away. "Mother?"

Grandmother rested her hands in her lap and looked up. "The soldiers hit me, but I'll survive. Don't trouble yourself on my account." Then, as if seeing him clearly for the first time, her mouth hardened. "Chamuqwani carrion eaters! What did they do to you?"

"It's nothing. I'm fine—"

"You don't look fine," she snapped. "how badly are you injured?"

"Forget about it, Mother. Didn't I say it was nothing?"

For just a moment I saw the hurt in her eyes, then she grimly nodded, accepting his answer.

"Your arm looks painful, Son, let me help you," Grandfather said.

"Maybe later. I need to go, my wife...." and with that he was gone.

Once the doors were closed there was little light in the hall, and no food, so we just sat with friends and relatives on the cold floor and waited. To pass the time, I took out the loop of leather cord I always kept in a pouch at my waist and began idly making string figures between my hands.

Seicu saw me and squealed with joy. "Story, story, make pictures tell me story, Little Rock Squirrel."

I made a face. Am I doomed to be always called that baby-name? With my stomach churning and my mind in turmoil, the last thing I wanted to do was make up stories for her.

Mother saw my look and patted my shoulder reassuringly. "Go ahead." She motioned with her chin to Samiqwas, who looked nearly as bewildered as I felt. "You both can play with her. It will help pass the time."

My voice was growing hoarse when Grandfather announced, "I'm going to walk around and see if anyone needs my help." He turned to me. "Do you want to come with me?"

Deliverance! I scrambled to my feet. "Oh yes."

A ghost of a smile curved his lips. "Come along then."

As we walked away, I glanced at his empty hands, and asked, "Grandfather, without your medicines what can you do to help the injured?"

"Not much," he admitted. "But talk can soothe a frightened Spirit, and my Gift can ease its pain somewhat."

"I wish my own special Gift was healing, like yours," I muttered. Seeing terrible visions and hearing ghosts isn't much fun or useful.

"Perhaps Qwa'osi will gift you with that power if you study harder the lessons I give you, eh?"

I nodded, unable to speak, a lump of hurt and frustration choking back my words. I wanted to please him—and I did try, truly I did. Like Fire and Earth, or Wind and Water, our Qwakaivas didn't exactly oppose one another, but neither were they compatible—or so Grandfather had hinted many times when I failed at a lesson he'd given me.

"I want to help; please will you show me again what I must do?"

"We'll see. You're a good boy."

As we threaded our way among the families, snatches of conversations caught my attention. "Those men running from the soldiers warned us. We should have listened and gone with them deeper into the mountains."

"And what would you feed your children, hmm? There's little game on those high slopes. Those people are probably all dead by now...."

"Pray, brothers, Mighty Djoven will protect us."

Derisive laughter, "I don't trust any Chamuqwani, even their god."

"True enough. The Chamuqwani know more about conjuring than they'd like us to believe. That old priest cursed us. He's a Malicer."

A Malicer? That was a chilling thought.

During our first day of confinement more relatives returned home, were captured, and thrust inside the temple with us. But not Esuli and her lover. I prayed they'd seen the danger and crept away into the mountains.

Shilshigua's maternal cousin's two young daughters were also among the missing. Her black hair tangled around her face, her shawl hanging by a loose end from her belt, the distraught woman pounded on the outer door with someone's walking stick, screaming.

"Let me out, let me out! Oh, please, I won't run away. I just want to find my children ... please."

Her pleas were collecting the interest of the young men huddled in their own council. Moving as of one mind, they approached the door, adding their own raucous shouts to the din. When Tli headed that way along with Shilshigua's brother Chugai, I touched Grandfather's sleeve, drawing his attention to the group.

Grandfather had stopped to converse with some clan elders and

Tsanqwati before heading back to our family. I didn't have to say anything. He could see the jagged spears of red lightning exploding in the young men's Spirit-Fires as well as I could. There was going to be trouble, and Tli would be right in the middle of it again.

Turning back to the headman, Grandfather murmured something that I didn't catch. The next thing I knew the elders were heading towards the door, their expressions grim. Grandfather had forgotten about me. I tagged along in his wake, trying not to draw attention to myself. I focused my mind on images of white hares standing perfectly still in drifts of new snow. I needn't have worried. Grandfather's focus was centred totally upon his son.

The elders had just convinced everyone to sit down without further trouble when the soldiers opened the door to let in an old man and spoiled their efforts. As soon as the door opened, Shilshigua's cousin saw her chance to look for her children and squeezed through the opening.

Once outside, she faltered in her headlong rush when she tripped on her shawl. Soldiers shouted and a big yellow-haired man with a scar on his cheek grabbed her and knocked her backward into the temple with his fist. Chugai hit the soldier, and he tripped over the fallen woman, crashing to the floor.

Uncle Tli shouted and lunged for the door, but Grandfather grabbed him, pulling him back. "Don't be a fool, my son, this is pointless."

To my astonishment, Tli cursed him and continued his struggle. The hair rose on the back of my neck as Grandfather's Spirit-Fire flared bright silver, and Tli suddenly went rigid, his mouth dropping open in surprise. Unable to move, he seemed caught in the mesh of an invisible fishnet.

"Let me go, Father," Tli growled.

"I will. When you calm yourself and once again have reason." Tli glared, but made no more attempts to free himself.

Cursing and lashing out with their weapons, the soldiers retrieved their fallen comrade and banged the door shut on the shouting people. Seeming not to be aware of her bleeding face, the weeping woman hurled herself once more at the heavy door, screaming.

Grandfather let out a long sigh and released Tli from his power. He stepped away rolling his shoulders. Trails of red stained the back of his shirt. "You're bleeding again from the whipping. Let me help you."

Tli turned, scowling. Grey-faced, Grandfather leaned against the wall and met his stare. Neither spoke for a long moment, but at last Tli dropped his eyes. He looked like he wanted to cry, but instead he snarled, "I don't want, or need, your help. So much power and your only thought is to use it to stop me from going to the aid of my wife's cousin. If you can do so much, why do you let them confine us in this stinking place? Why don't you use your Qwakaiva to help us drive them from our land?"

Grandfather rubbed a hand over his face. His Spirit-Fire shrank to a thin pale line, exhaustion blurring his features. "Though what I did may seem a wondrous thing to you, it isn't. I would need power many times stronger than I possess before I could turn back this evil. All I could manage was to save my son from possible death at the enemy's hands this day."

Tli snorted. "I don't believe you. And don't expect me to be grateful, because I won't thank you. You are a coward, afraid to use your power to help us. You shame me and your ancestors."

Grandfather blinked, as startled as I was by the venom in my uncle's words. When he was gone, I took Grandfather's arm. My presence startled him, then without a word, he allowed me to lead him back to where our family waited. When we arrived he sat down and covered his face with his blanket, leaving me to answer the women's anxious questions.

The light coming through the tiny windows near the ceiling faded into the long summer twilight. Shilshigua's cousin's hysterical pleading gave way to a monotonous sobbing that hovered at the edge of my awareness. Children cried themselves to sleep. Men and women talked in low voices, slapped at the black flies, or slept leaning against one another. The entire hall stank of feces, stale incense, and fear sweat.

Outside we heard the Chamuqwani celebrating, and feared the worst.

Chapter Ten

Once a day some strips of dry-meat and buckets of water were handed inside. Then the doors were relocked, and we were left to our misery. The temple didn't have a privy. In a gesture of defiance, people began pissing and shitting behind the statue of the Chamuqwani god. When I let my piss spray upon the god's robes, it made me feel a little better.

He was helping these soldiers take us away. I hated him.

Time passed, agonizingly slow. I thought I might die of boredom. I slept as much as possible.

Commander Mu'Dar kept his word and allowed a woman from each family to return to her lodge to collect supplies for our journey. But he waited until the second day of our confinement and by then the miners had looted the village, taking whatever suited them.

Their eyes moist with unshed tears, Mother and Aunt Tuulah stumbled back into the temple with only a few cracked baskets and some ragged bedding. Her face dark as a thunderstorm, Grandmother rose to meet them. "Was this all the soldiers would let you bring?"

Aunt Tuulah dropped her bundle and sank to the cold floor beside it. Tired from worry and a sleepless night, she had new lines of exhaustion etching her round face. "This was all that was left, Mother. Those filthy miners took everything else."

Ko briefly inspected her few belongings and swore a soldier's curse. "So much for the honour of Chamuqwani."

Coming over to hear the news and see our supplies, Auntie Qwatsitsa snorted with disgust and folded her arms across her bony chest. "My daughters tell the same story. And how, I wonder, do they expect us to survive on this journey without proper blankets, warm clothing and food?"

"Maybe they don't," Grandmother said as she looked into one of Mother's baskets. "Maybe they're hoping we'll all die along the way."

Seicu whimpered and crawled into her brother's lap. Samiqwas hugged her close, looking fierce. Then, plastering a smile onto his face, he bounced her on his knee to make her laugh.

I shivered, the cold hand of a foretelling touching the back of my neck. "Surely not, Ami!" I blurted. "Why would anyone do such a terrible thing?"

"I doubt if they want to, Grandson," Grandfather said, giving Grandmother a reproachful look. "The Chamuqwani are just short-sighted, like the beetles crawling among the tree roots. They don't take into account the consequences of their words and actions."

"Until it's too late," the old auntie said.

"Until it's too late," he agreed.

"Well, I'm going to tell Tsanqwati," she announced. "These Chamuqwani need to pay for what they've stolen."

Grandmother rose to her feet. "I'll go with you. The next time the door opens to allow in the returning women, we'll tell them we want to see Jombonni and the lord's man. If they want us to go with them they'll have to make it right."

"How far away is this new Tribal Preserve?" I asked.

Grandfather shook his head and spread his hands as he rose to follow the women. "No one knows."

"Maybe the Chamuqwani themselves don't know," Samiqwas whispered only loud enough for me to hear.

Mother watched the elders go, then she turned to her sister, and asked, "Do you think the soldiers or the trading company's man will make the miners give back what they've stolen?"

"No. But most families still have credit left at the post. Maybe we'll be allowed to buy enough supplies to last us on this journey."

I hoped so. In another two moons—maybe less—winter would touch our northern homeland with its icy breath.

On the fourth morning of our confinement, the soldiers passed in buckets of hot tea, pieces of hard flat bread, and a foul-smelling stew. It was the first hot meal I'd eaten since Mother's good fish soup the morning after the Dance. It tasted like boiled dog turds, but I choked it down anyway.

After the meal, the soldiers' interpreter announced that heavily armed soldiers would separate the young men like Ko and Uncle Tli from their families. He also warned us that if the men resisted, some of the children and the old people would die.

"How could anyone be so cruel?" Aunt Tuulah wondered.

"They are all Wannigua demons," Ko snarled as he stood. He glanced at the grim-faced soldiers outside the open doorway, and then back at his youngest daughter, holding tight to her mother's hand.

"You're right for once, daughter's husband," Grandmother said. "Only a monster could do such a thing." Ko gave her a grudging nod. He turned back to the doorway, smoothing out the angry expression on his face. As he walked outside, he held out his hands for the shackles without a protest.

The smell within the temple was unbearable, and I for one was grateful to be going anywhere. When I stumbled outside blinking in the bright light, I took in a big lungful of the cool air to clear my head. Nothing to me had ever smelled so sweet as the damp lake wind on that terrible day.

As Samiqwas emerged from the temple just behind me, he stepped boldly up to one of the soldiers and held his hands out for the chains. The soldier blinked, then burst out laughing. Samiqwas's face darkened, but he stood as straight as a fir tree, with his hands outstretched.

No one could deny Samiqwas was big for his age, but he was hardly a man. I dropped my eyes; why was he making a spectacle of himself? Then I happened to glance at the line of our chained men. Pride shown in Ko's and my uncle's eyes. Samiqwas looked so fierce, standing there defying the Chamuqwani. His age didn't matter to them. The courage of a hunter and warrior beat strong in my brother-cousin's heart.

Samiqwas. I wish I'd thought to do the same thing.

When it was clear that he had no intention of moving, one of the soldiers slammed the butt of his weapon into my cousin's back. Samiqwas let out a surprised grunt and sprawled in the dirt. I rushed forward to help him up. As I did, I made an obscene gesture the Chamuqwani traders used when they were angry at one another. I received a painful slap that bloodied my nose, which made me feel a bit better.

The dark-skinned soldier might have done me further damage, but Mother, normally such a quiet, gentle person, surprised everyone by punching him in return. Almost as astounded by her assault as he had been by Samiqwas's defiance, he stared open-mouthed as she shouted at him in the broken Chamuqwani she'd learned from the trader and his wife.

"Cowards, what kind of man you are to hit child? Your mother be shamed she bear you." Someone shouted a praise call, and the chained men stirred restlessly.

The situation might have progressed to further violence if an officer hadn't noticed and barked an order that soon put an end to the trouble. I took my place beside Mother. Basking in the admiring looks directed our way, Samiqwas and I grinned at each other behind the adults' backs, wearing our battle scars with pride.

When everyone was lined up outside the temple, they marched us in a long line down the path to where the steamboat waited.

"Slime-eating Zaunk." Grimy, foul-tongued men in dirty canvas trews, patched tunics, and wide-brimmed hats, the miners stood in small groups, passing round jugs of waskyja and yelling insults.

"Should'a got rid of'em a'for now, filthy Zaunks," someone called.

"You got that right. By Mighty Djoven's hairy balls, get a whiff of that smell!" a black-bearded man with a greasy vest shouted.

The soldiers cursed us too. "Hurry along, you lazy Zaunk bastards. We don't have all day. Move!" When the officer wasn't looking, some of them prodded us with their weapons to show off for the miners.

I glanced over my shoulder at my grandparents walking silently behind us, pleading for an answer. How could this be happening to us? Grandfather returned my look, but his expression remained impenetrable. He had no answers to give me, and perhaps that frightened me most of all.

Mother walked beside me, carrying a blanket roll of our possessions. She seemed unconcerned by the abuse. But no matter how I tried to ignore it, the men's animosity settled about my shoulders like a water-soaked blanket. "Why do they hate us so much, Amima?"

At her puzzled expression, I repeated my question. She thought about her answer for a few steps, then sighed and shook her head. "I don't know, but don't let it trouble you. They're very unhappy people. We should feel sorry for them and pray for them."

Incredulous, I jerked to a stop and stared up at her. "Pray for them? Feel sorry for them? How can you say that, Amima? After what they are doing to us, they deserve my hatred, my vengeance, not my prayers."

"Keep moving," a soldier snarled, and pointed his weapon at me.

Gently, Mother put a hand to my back, urging me forward. "If you let their evil fester inside you it'll poison your Spirit. Treat their words like water rolling off a lake seal's oily back. Ignore them."

Ignore them? Fingering the knife concealed by a fold of my shirt, I stole a look at the soldier walking behind us. "I can't do that," I muttered.

Retreating once more into her own thoughts, Mother likely didn't even hear me.

When we arrived at the dock with the onlookers in our wake, the paddlewheeler's engine was already rumbling. Its lower deck was piled high with cargo for the return trip downriver. Black smoke boiled out of its tall smoke stacks to mingle with the grey mists over the water. Snugged up tight against the boat's bow was a long barge made of rough planks, placed over a sturdy raft of logs. On either side of the raft, long cables were attached that ran back to winches on the lower deck of the steamboat.

I learned later that the cables and winches were there to help turn the unwieldy raft and keep it in the channel. Also to help steer, several crewmen with long sweep oars stood poised on the raft's rim, ready to guide the clumsy float out into the lake once we were loaded on board.

I wondered how the raft had arrived at the trader's dock without notice. Then I remembered the string of miner's flatboats and rafts the paddlewheeler had been towing this year. During the past four days, while we were confined in the temple, the Chamuqwani must have taken apart those floats and built this larger raft.

"What a stupid, sad joke," Samiqwas murmured as he came alongside me. "We're going to be the boat's main cargo this year, not the salted fish and furs."

The raft they forced us aboard was nothing more than a long float with a flimsy, waist-high wooden rail built around its outer edge to keep back some of the wet. Near the centre, a roofed-over cabin with tarpaulin sidewalls had been erected as a makeshift shelter against the weather. In front of it a large wooden box lined with rocks and filled with sand had been placed to hold a fire.

I stared in disbelief at the tarpaulins. The corner of one wall was already flapping sluggishly in the breeze. If the shelter managed to stand up to the next storm, it might protect a few old people and mothers with small children, but anyone else travelling on the raft would be completely exposed to the weather.

Our chained men were placed closest to the paddlewheeler's lower deck, where the soldiers could keep an eye on them. The rest of us were allowed to spread out as we pleased. When my family was herded onto the raft at weapon-point, we sat upon the damp planking, huddled among our few possessions, and watched the remainder of our friends and relatives being driven on board around us.

Like many of the younger children, Seicu was crying when her mother carried her aboard. Grandmother, right behind my aunt, stumbled as she stepped from the gangway to the moored raft. She gave Grandfather an angry look when he steadied her, as if our misfortune was somehow his fault. Then, ignoring him, she stalked off to sit by her daughters.

Before following her, Grandfather turned back to the people on the shore as if searching for someone.

"Who are you looking for?"

He gave me a sad smile and put an arm around my shoulder. "I was looking for Jombonni. I wanted to thank him for being generous. The warm blankets and supplies he bought us will help us survive the coming cold."

"Maybe he's too busy inside the trading post selling waskyja to the miners. I certainly see enough of them over there."

He sighed. "Perhaps you're right."

A lump of sadness formed in the back of my throat, nearly choking me. "I'll miss Kutima. He wanted to come, but his father wouldn't let him."

"I didn't know that. He's a brave boy."

Though Kutima, his mother, and the other traders' wives and children weren't among the exiles, many others in their lineages were going with us. Kutima's Aunt Ri and his grandmother looked so bewildered sitting among their belongings. Their tearful prayers to the Chamuqwani's new god hadn't mattered to the soldiers in the end.

When all were loaded, the paddlewheels churned up great frothing mounds of white water, and both raft and boat backed away from the dock. The crewmen stationed on the front of the raft took their long oars and pushed us out into the lake. Then the cables and winches turned the raft toward the mouth of the Socanna River.

As I looked back over my shoulder, smoke rose from the village in dark plumes. The icy hand of the Unseen Ones stroked the back of my neck. I shivered as sounds and images from my vision exploded in my mind. What they hadn't stolen from us, the miners were now destroying with fire.

Commander Mu'Dar was standing among his officers on the upper deck also watching the conflagration. Had he ordered the destruction? His dark features gave me no clue.

Gazing in the same direction, Aunt Tuulah let out a low, mournful cry. There had been no sign of Esuli and her lover. Nor had Shilshigua's cousin's daughters been found.

Staring at the smoking ruins of my home, I wondered about the fate of my sister-cousin. No one had mentioned the possibility of Tosgali dead and Esuli held as the hidden-away captive of some foul-smelling, hairy miner, but the thought lingered.

Chapter Eleven

When the steamboat reached the first settlement after we entered the Socanna River, I lost all hope of our rescue by other Qwani'Ya peoples. Samiqwas and I had gone with Aunt Tuulah to sit with Ko and the other chained men, when the stench of rotting fish guts and charred timber assaulted our noses. At almost the same moment, the blackened ruins of the Deer Clan's fish camp came into view.

"Oh, Holy Unseen Ones, what happened here?" Aunt Tuulah breathed. Quickly she turned Seicu's face into her chest, tempting her with her breast to distract the little girl from the gruesome sight.

In truth, there wasn't much to see from the raft. The wolves and other forest-dwellers must have seen to the disposal of the dead. Only scattered bones, charred lean-tos, and skeletal drying racks remained.

"All the clan members would have been in the camp, cutting and smoking tasty Red Wanderer flesh for the coming winter," Tli said. "Not expecting trouble, they would have been easy prey.

"The Deer Clan were our nearest neighbours," Ko said quietly. "My cousin Chugii's boy married into the band two winters ago."

"Is that so? I didn't know that." Aunt Tuulah glanced at him, then returned her horrified stare to the shoreline. "Who would want to hurt them?"

"Chamuqwani. Who else?" Tli snapped without looking at her.

"There weren't very many people in that lineage, were there, Appi?" Samiqwas said.

"Too few to fight off their enemy, that's for certain," Ko growled.

"But why would someone kill them?"

"Does a rabid animal need a reason to kill?"

No, it doesn't. I tasted the horror of their deaths and the Deer Clan's betrayal on the breeze. Turning my back on the river, I stumbled away to sit by Mother and the old people.

"What's going on?" Grandmother asked.

"I'm not sure; the Deer Clan's fish camp has been burned, the people killed maybe."

Mother gasped. "Oh, Amima, what about Da'wabin? Do you think he and his wife's family are dead, too?"

Grandmother's skin paled, then her mouth hardened and she glared at everyone. "Of course not. Your elder brother is fine. Don't say such a terrible thing—don't even think it."

Mother dropped her eyes and murmured barely above a whisper, "You're right. Of course he's fine. It will be good to see him again. I've missed him since his marriage downriver."

The old woman grunted. "I should've never let the clan elders talk me into such a match. But he's fine, I'm certain of it."

She didn't look certain; she looked frightened and exhausted. Suddenly a bell on board the boat rang, the sound echoing off the tree-lined banks. The bell clanged again, and the paddlewheeler slowed, and then stopped. The long gangway was winched out and a number of soldiers descended to the shore. They briefly examined the site. Then all too soon, they returned. With no further explanation, the gangway was drawn up, and the boat resumed its course down river.

The wailing of the Deer Clan's ghosts trailed in our wake, calling out to me over the chuff-chuff of the steamboat. Grandfather put an arm about my shoulder. "What's wrong?"

My eyes blurred with unshed tears. "I hear the ghosts. They're crying. They want me to help, but I don't know what to do."

He sighed and continued to watch the retreating shore until the river mists and the trees blocked the camp from view.

The ghosts still clamouring in my head, I faced him. "I hate my Gift. I wish the ghosts would leave me alone!"

For just a moment an unreadable expression crossed his face. Then it was gone, replaced by new lines of sadness. "I know it's hard for you, Grandson, but be patient. When you're older you'll know how to help ghosts and other beings that come to you. But for now," he squeezed my shoulder, "there's little we can do but pray for them. The Chamuqwani aren't going to allow us to do the proper ceremony."

"But Ati, how could the soldiers behave as if nothing's wrong? The Deer were our kin; isn't anyone going to tell us what they discovered about who murdered our relatives?"

Grandfather's mouth hardened. He glanced towards the soldiers lounging on the paddlewheeler's upper deck. "You have a point. We have a right to know what the soldiers learned on shore." Giving me one last pat on the shoulder, he headed to where some of the elders were sitting.

After a brief discussion, they decided Tsanqwati should ask Commander Mu'Dar for an explanation.

The soldiers' translator, Pete by name, was a small man who walked with a limp. He spoke with a heavy accent that marked him as being from one of the downriver villages. His hair was greasy and thin, his skin pale, bespeaking his mixed origins. He wasn't well liked by the soldiers. Even so, he chose to take up accommodations on the lowest deck with the steamboat's crew rather than be seen by the Chamuqwani as a Zaunk.

Tsanqwati positioned himself near the makeshift gangway that could be lowered onto our raft. He shouted in a loud voice for Pete to come. When the interpreter didn't appear after a time, the soldiers shook their weapons and told Tsanqwati to be quiet. Tsanqwati ignored their threats, refusing to leave until we received an answer. Finally one of the disgusted soldiers went searching for the interpreter.

Stinking of waskyja, Pete arrived at last, red-eyed and staggering. "What do you want?" he grumbled.

"The Deer Clan were our relatives. We want to know what the soldiers found when they examined the camp. Who killed them?"

By that time, one of Commander Mu'Dar's officers, a red-haired man with a broken nose, had come down to the lower deck to hear what we wanted. Pete turned to him and repeated the headman's request. The soldier murmured something and shook his head. "The soldiers don't know who killed them. Commander Mu'Dar didn't order it," Pete said.

"These deaths are the most foul of murders," Tsanqwati said. "The souls of the dead cry out for justice. What do they plan to do?"

Pete translated. The officer shrugged. His face an expressionless mask, Pete turned back to us, and said, "Nothing."

The rage flared in Tsanqwati's Spirit-Fire. When he spoke, bitterness coloured his voice. "Nothing? If we are the Father Emperor's children as you claim, then why isn't there any justice for us like the other peoples of his Empire?"

The officer reddened and looked uncomfortable when Pete translated that. Finally he said, "We have no time to investigate further. If we delay our journey longer, winter may catch us still in the mountains. And if that happens, more people will die."

Tsanqwati shouted more questions, but Pete went back to his bottle and the soldiers ignored us. The officer retreated to the gaming room on the upper deck, so he wouldn't have to listen.

The forest we sailed by was silent, but in my mind the ghosts whispered of blood and agony. A lump of incredible sadness swelled in my throat.

"Our dead cry out for justice!" a young man shouted.

Then a woman lifted her voice in a high-pitched keen, her lament soon joined by others. The sound tore at my heart, giving voice to the sorrow threatening to drown me. Tears streaming down my cheeks, I raised my voice with the rest of my people.

When the first cry of the women's lament rang out across the water, the soldiers and crew aboard the steamboat poured out of the cabins and flocked to the rail to stare down at us. As the eerie wail continued, however, the soldiers' expressions hardened. They shook weapons or their fists, demanding that the People stop.

We ignored their threats. Why shouldn't we grieve? What more could they do to us? Let them kill us if they dared. It was a good day to die.

Suddenly a red-faced soldier jumped onto the raft and pointed his weapon at my aunt, screaming at her and the other women to stop. Aunt Tuulah laughed in his face. Coming closer she unlaced her tunic and bared her breasts. Someone sang out the praise cry for her bravery. Then other women began removing their own clothing, taunting the angry soldiers with their nakedness.

A wild gleam shown in the red-faced Chamuqwani's eyes, and I tasted his fear, sour as vinegar. He was desperate, willing to do anything to make the unnerving sounds stop. I lunged forward shouting a warning, but my words were lost in the confusion.

With trembling hands the soldier raised his weapon and sighted down its barrel. Tuulah remained perfectly still, her eyes never leaving his face. Sensing the danger at last, others around her silenced their own cries and moved back. The man didn't seem to notice.

"Troublemaker! You're the one, you Zaunk bitch," the soldier snarled. "You made the voices come back. My head—it hurts. Make 'em stop! I'm gonna kill you for it...." He licked his lips. His finger curved about the trigger.

Just as his finger tightened, another soldier shoved the man's arm towards the sky. The weapon exploded with a flash of light and deafening peal of thunder. A tiny cloud of grey smoke discharged in its wake. Before the crazed soldier could react, the other man slammed a meaty black fist into his face. He toppled like an axed sapling to the planks at my aunt's feet.

Tuulah looked down at the prone man as if she wasn't sure how he'd arrived there. Then, taking in a ragged breath, she straightened and met the eyes of her rescuer. Like his commander, this man too was one of the dark-skinned Chamuqwani. He was tall and heavily muscled with full lips and the grey-green eyes of a lynx.

By this time, more soldiers had joined their leader on the raft. He barked an order, and two men picked up their dazed comrade, and half carried, half dragged him back on board the steamboat. The trouble removed, the black man's eyes flicked to my aunt's heavy, rounded breasts, and his lips curved into a smile.

Returning his gaze to her face at last, he said in a badly accented version of our language, "Fix your clothes. You'll get cold."

Tuulah's mouth dropped open in surprise. The man showed his teeth once more and repeated his words. Tuulah closed her mouth, her eyes flashing dangerously. When he continued to smile and admire her breasts, she laced up her tunic with a defiant toss of her head. By this time all the women were silent, watching them.

Seeing Pete hovering at his elbow, the officer addressed us in his own language. "I can't allow this display of grief to continue. The noise upsets my men. Such a disturbance won't be tolerated again. You have been warned."

Regaining her composure, Tuulah took a step towards him, her eyes still smouldering with anger. "Why are you here, and not among your own kin? Why do you obey these evil men like a whipped sled dog? Have you no mother, no sisters?"

The interpreter stammered, reluctant to translate, but the soldier knew enough of our language to catch the gist of her words anyway. His mouth hardened and he drew himself up to his full height. "I'm a soldier of the Empire. That is all you need to know in order to obey me."

My aunt looked like a small, round ptarmigan facing down a wolf, but she held herself with dignity. "I obey no man." Tuulah gave him a withering look and turned her back on him.

An unreadable expression on his face, the soldier stared at her back for a long moment, then he returned to the steamboat with his men. I let out the breath I hadn't realized I was holding and sank down to the planking. I felt drained and a little dizzy, but my aunt had made me proud.

Chapter Twelve

Day followed upon day as we continued to steam down the green Socanna River and its chain of small lakes. We paused only now and then to take on wood to feed the boat's hungry furnaces. There were no more burnt ruins, but we did pass other cold and lifeless villages. Samiqwas and I were staring at one such abandoned settlement, when Grandfather came up behind us. Without turning, I asked, "Ati, what village is this; do you know?"

He was silent for a time staring at the shore. At last he said, "I believe it is Broken Shell Mound Village."

Broken Shell Mound. Without pausing to consider my words, I blurted out the thought that came into my mind. "Where is Uncle Da'wabin, Ati?"

"I was wondering that myself," Grandfather said.

"Did miners or soldiers kill the people here, too?" Samiqwas asked.

Gazing out across the river, Grandfather took out his pipe and stuck it into his mouth. He told me he was hoarding the little smoking mixture he had left, but the comforting presence of his pipe helped him think.

"I don't know."

One of the hardest things to get used to while travelling on the raft was the constant clamour of men and machines aboard the steamboat. I never dreamed a mechanical thing could be so noisy. Men shouted, bells rang, the engine rumbled and chuffed, and the big wheels endlessly scooped up water and splashed it down again.

"It's no wonder the Chamuqwani are crazy; they never get a good night's sleep," Grandmother complained over and over. So stiff she could hardly move, she sat in the shelter by a tiny fire with the other old people, telling stories to the young children.

The steamboat's lowest deck wasn't very high above the raft. At meal times the small gangway was lowered so the women could board the boat to collect food for their families. The gangway wasn't left in place, but even so, it wasn't hard for an agile boy or girl to climb up to the deck and go exploring when no one was paying attention.

If the soldiers caught us, they would send us back with curses and a few well-placed kicks. The Sooties, the men who fed wood to the fireboxes that made the steam for the engines, were more tolerant.

The Sooties' faces and hands, as well as their clothes, were covered in soot, which is how they got their name. Mate and the officers who lived on the top deck were always yelling at them and making them do lots of hard work. The Sooties didn't like Mate much, but when he wasn't around, they let us come on the boat and help them. We didn't mind chopping or carrying wood for them, because in return they would give us some of their food, or let us dip our cups into the big barrel of strong tea they kept always simmering.

One evening as I dumped my last load of wood into the fire box and wandered over to the tea vat, Matoqwa said to Cohasi, "Someday I'm going to be like Steamboat Master. I'll have a big new paddlewheeler painted white and red with a brass bell I can ring whenever I want." Cohasi nodded, giving his brother an adoring look.

Dipping his cup into the steaming vat, Samiqwas laughed. "Do you think the Chamuqwani will ever teach us their magic? Maybe if you are a good little Zaunk they'll let you be a Sootie."

Matoqwa balled his fists. "Don't be stupid," Tigali snarled. "Mate's coming." Flinging the tea back into the vat, I hurried over the rail with the rest. Secretly I agreed with Tigali, but I had the sense not to scoff at Matoqwa's imaginings. It did no one any harm to dream. There was little else to do.

Not content to hide away or sleep, my restless brother-cousin was tormented to distraction by our confinement. When barred from the lower deck by an over-vigilant guard detail, he paced the edge of the raft like a caged wolf, snappish and irritable, his pent-up energies having no outlet.

One day he cut a few rusty nails free of the raft's planking and fashioned simple fish hooks for us. That afternoon we spent throwing out our lines and trolling for anything willing to snap at our bait. In the evening, the fish we'd caught for our family was a welcome addition to the porridge, hard-cakes, and nearly spoiled salt-meat that made up the bulk of our rations.

Our efforts hadn't gone unobserved. From their high aerie in the little house at the very top of the steamboat, both Pilot and Steamboat Master saw the nice fat whitefish we hauled in. The next morning Pete came to tell us that if we gave some of our fish to the man who cooked for the bossmans and the soldiers, the cook would give us extra food in return.

Uncle Tli overheard the interpreter speaking to us. When Pete finished, Tli put a manacled hand on each of our shoulders. His fingers squeezed slightly, letting us know to keep silent and let him do the bargaining.

"Even though they are still young, my nephews are both very good fishermen. They will fish for Cook, but not for more lumpy porridge. My family is cold. Most of our fine warm clothing was stolen by Chamuqwani miners. You pay one blanket for three nice fat whitefish, yes?"

"One blanket! That is too much."

Cook was called, and then other Chamuqwani joined in the haggling. By that time, other relatives had taken an interest in Tli's trading and came over to add their advice to the discussion. Some other men offered their own nephews' skills in exchange for trade goods, too.

At the first scent of trade, Tli sent us off to our fishing, while he took care of the rest. We were happy to go. A nice fat string of fish would go a long way to aid his bargaining.

As we neared the southern boundary of Qwani'Ya land, the river's channel suddenly narrowed. Rock walls loomed over its shallow, foaming water. Above the chuff-chuff of the engine and the splash of the paddlewheel, the distant roar of the rapids was an ominous sound.

We'd already passed through several short rapids, with little trouble. This stretch, known as Drown Canoe Rapids, however, was the last and worst before the Socanna widened out into the Blue Lake.

Even without being able to speak much of their language, I could feel the tension growing among the Chamuqwani as we neared this dangerous rapids. The winter before had been dry with little snow, and that summer the steamboat had missed the spring runoff. Unfortunately, there was no other way to reach the Blue Lake and the Fort beyond.

Being good fishermen all, the men of my village knew the river's unpredictability and feared for their families. Pilot and Steamboat Master must have had their own misgivings for, at the last moment, the boat changed course and headed for a quiet cove on the eastern shore. Once in the sheltered water, the paddlewheeler slowed, and the crew threw out the boat's heavy anchor to help us resist the strong current.

While the light remained good, Mate, Pilot, and two of the Sooties launched a small rowboat and headed for shore. When they landed, the Sooties stayed with the boat while Pilot and Mate walked into the trees. I was sitting near Uncle Tli at the time. I'd brought him some fish that Shilshigua cooked specially for him, hoping to cheer him up. When he'd finished his meal, I accompanied him to the privy hole cut through the logs. I helped hold his chain. He didn't need my help in such quiet water, but it was comforting to be near him. I hoped he felt the same about me.

"I wonder what they're doing,." I had asked with little hope of an answer, so I was surprised when Tli spoke.

"They go to check on the water. The river is very low. Maybe the boat can't cross the rapids so late in the year and we'll have to walk."

"Will they let us go home if the boat can't pass?"

Tli snorted and gave me a withering look. "We have no home, foolish boy, remember?"

I dropped my eyes, my skin heating. Tli was changing, his mood settling into a brooding silence that deepened the farther we travelled downriver. Grandfather was worried about him, but Tli still hadn't forgiven him for not using his Qwakaiva to stop our removal. He never spoke against his father, but the easy camaraderie between them had dissolved into a stiff formality that made everyone uncomfortable. Their behaviour was all the more puzzling to my female relatives, because no one but me knew why they were behaving like strangers—and I had been asked by Grandfather not to talk about it.

Deciding to move away from Tli and his sour mood, I said, "Amima is expecting me to catch another fish for the old people's meal. I have to go."

He smirked, then waved me away. "Maybe you should ask the Sooties to give you some of their stinking porridge, since you seem to have forgotten your duties to your elders, lazy boy."

It wasn't our way to beat a child, but shame can be as powerful a weapon as a birch switch when used effectively. Tli was very skilled at shaming me, with or without a good reason.

I hunched my shoulders and slunk away. He'd seen me fishing with Samiqwas earlier, and knew I'd caught plenty.

Chapter Thirteen

The boat with Pilot and Mate came back in the grey twilight, but no one told us until next morning what they'd decided.

When we assembled for morning ration of hard-cakes and tea, the black soldier who spoke our language told us, with the interpreter's help, "Steamboat Master has decided to risk running the rapids, even though the river is low. When we get underway, stay in the middle of the raft and don't walk about or you may fall in. We'll give you extra rope to tie down your belongings."

"If this crossing is going to be as bad as we all fear, then we are in the greatest danger here aboard the raft. Tell Steamboat Master to let us come aboard the boat for the crossing," Tsanqwati begged.

The soldier spoke to Mate standing nearby, then turned back to us. He shook his head. "No, we can't do that. With added people the boat might become too heavy to pass over the rocks. Also, there isn't enough room with the cargo on board for so many people. The boat will need lots of steam. We must go faster than the current if we want to stay off the rocks. The Sooties will be too busy feeding the furnaces to have extra people cluttering up the deck and getting in their way. It's better that you stay where you are."

"Stay where we are?" My aunt stood up, surprising everyone with her boldness. She folded her arms across her chest and glared. "So, a mound of dead furs means more to you Chamuqwani than children's lives? Come down here. Sit among us if you think it will be safe."

This dark-skinned soldier was the same man who had saved her from the crazy one. Sometimes when I'd been running errands for Cook, I'd seen him secretly watching her from the upper deck.

Some of our younger men laughed at her jibe, but most of the people on raft and boat stared at them in a stunned silence. The black soldier's face was too dark for me to see if he coloured at her insult, but for just an instant, his eyes flashed, then he controlled himself and gave her a predator's toothy smile. "I would love to come sit beside you, my sweet, but this isn't the time for such pleasantries. Maybe later."

He'd been speaking in our language, which made his banter with a married woman even more humiliating. For what reason I couldn't say, I happened to glance at Ko at that moment. His brother leaned over and said something to him. Ko glowered like a man with a bellyache.

When their leader's remark was translated by Pete for the soldiers, they guffawed loudly and slapped one another on the back. The soldier allowed the mirth to continue a short time longer, then he turned, and the merriment stopped abruptly.

As he was walking away, Tsanqwati called out to him. "Wait. If the worst should happen and the raft breaks apart, we'll have to swim. Our young men can't do that in chains. I have asked you before to release them. Our clan mothers have given you their word. There'll be no trouble; there's nowhere for us to run. Please unchain them so they'll have a chance. We can't survive in this new land without our young hunters to care for us."

All bantering forgotten, everyone remained silent while the soldier considered. At last he spoke to one of his men, who hurried up the stairs to the second deck. "What you've asked for is a reasonable request," he told Tsanqwati. "I've sent a man to ask my Commander. If he also agrees, I'll have my soldiers release your young men."

Giving Tsanqwati one of his predatory smiles, he said, "I'm not sure the sworn words of women can curb rebellious fires in the hearts of young men, but as you say, there's no place for you to run now."

Keeping the men shackled had fuelled a growing resentment among us. Tsanqwati had brought up the matter many times, but always before the answer had been no. The men would have to wait till we reached Fort Protection. This time, however, Commander Mu'Dar saw the wisdom in our request and unchained them.

The roar of the river seemed especially loud as the steamboat headed into the main channel. I sat next to Mother. Our family's baskets and bundles were lashed to the raft's planking around us. Aunt Tuulah had taken Seicu and gone to sit with Ko. Samiqwas was somewhere, maybe with Tigali and the older boys, planning something daring no doubt.

My grandparents sat together nearby. Eyes closed, Grandfather sang softly, his hand tapping his thigh in rhythm with his song.

Hai'ya, Qwa'o-o-osi.
Fast Swimmer.
Clever Hunter.
Follow us down these dangerous rapids.
Share with me your Qwakaiva.
Swim beside me, swift and silent, through the frothy green water.

I trembled, listening to his chant. The roar of the river increased, pounding in my head like a Qwakaihi's drum. The river narrowed, a ribbon of white water tumbling over dark boulders just ahead. Above its rocky walls I could see the trees on either shore, rushing by at an unbelievable speed.

As we entered the white water, the raft rocked from side to side. Then, it pitched high into the air and came down with a shuddering slap. Someone shouted on the deck above. A crewman holding a long oar at the front of the raft dug in his oar and pushed us sideways, avoiding a collision with a large rock. There was a terrible grating sound, the engine strained, and then the boat and raft shot forward.

Grandmother moaned, her skin paling like rawhide. A baby cried. Icy spray splashed onto my cheek. I wanted to call out to the Otter, as Grandfather did, but I couldn't choke the words past my lips. I swayed and placed my hands flat on the planks. I could feel the rocks' sharp teeth not far below the water's cold green surface. Once again, the raft grated against hard stone, bucked, slewing sideways off a boulder.

Suddenly a man cried out. His long oar splintering into kindling, one of the Sooties lost his balance and tumbled into the white foam. Women screamed. The raft hit another foaming wave, reared upward, then came down with a bone-jarring crash. Disaster hovered, so close, so close.

As the raft settled, a Qwani'Ya man rushed forward to take the dead man's place with a spare pole. We were deep into the rapids by then, smoke pouring in a heavy black cloud from the boat's two smokestacks. The raft's timbers creaked in protest as the men on board the boat winched the ropes tight on one side, then the other, in answer to Pilot's bells. At the front of the raft the crewmen with long poles pushed us off the boulders whenever a turn was too close.

I feel the power surging within me, Grandfather sang.

I lay my hands on rough wood.

Power glides like an eel below me.

Qwa'osi, float the wood over sharp rock teeth.

Hai'ya 'eh!

I was so frightened. There was water all about me; I was soaked in it—nearly drowning in it—and yet my throat was too dry to swallow. I prayed that Samiqwas was safe, wherever he was.

Unfazed by the chaos erupting about him, Grandfather sat with eyes closed and fingers splayed flat upon the planks, still chanting. I could see his mouth moving, but the sound of the water was a deafening roar in my head. Nothing could penetrate its clamour.

The Chamuqwani manning the steamboat might be skilled at travelling atop such dangerous waters, but skill in the physical world alone might not be enough. The river was angry. Their appetite for fresh human souls whetted by the drowned crewman, I sensed hungry Water Spirits and the ghosts of the drowned, following us down the rapids in the hope of causing more misery.

We were a long way from the Big Ice Lake. So far from its source, I wasn't certain that Grandfather's power alone was strong enough to save us. Determined to help him, I reached for my Qwakaiva. My lips moved silently in prayer, but to my horror, no image bloomed in my mind to aid my summoning. This absence frightened me more than the fast water. Was my Qwakaiva, too, diminished by our long travel?

An ironic laugh bubbled up in my throat, nearly choking me. I had begged the Unseen Ones to take away my Gift. What a cruel joke it would be, if at that moment they chose to answer my prayer. Gathering all my strength I prayed again, harder....

"Unseen Ones, hear me. Save my family, my people, and I'll make a Give Away. I freely offer you my life, my Qwakaiva, whatever you want. Only guide us down these terrible rapids and I'm yours forever!"

"Mine?" a deep voice in my mind rumbled a laugh. "Forever is a long time. Do you swear it, young one?"

I had no idea who I had summoned, but we all might be dead in the next moment. "Yes."

"Then I will send someone to aid you."

Relief flooded over me; help was coming. Yes, now I could sense it. Another being approached, though the newcomer remained a shadowy blur to my inner-eye. "I'm coming. Open yourself to me."

"Open myself? I don't understand!" I resisted out of instinct the newcomer's first attempts to bond with me.

"Foolish boy, banish your fear! You prayed for help; accept it."

I wanted to, but in the next moment a heavy wave drenched me with icy water, breaking my concentration. I choked, clawing for air. People screamed. Then without warning, pain exploded in my brain, blotting out the world about me, ensnaring me in a net of agony.

"Pay attention, young one! Focus!"

"Who are you?" I cried.

"Never mind that—it's not important—open yourself."

"Can you float us over the rapids?"

The being growled in frustration. "I can only taste your strong emotion; I can't see through the Veil what's happening to you. Now stop wasting time."

"I don't know what you want me to do."

"Ah, now I understand. Just focus your Qwakaiva on my image and I'll do the rest then."

As I concentrated, the being I'd seen only as a blur of light resolved into the luminous violet eyes and brindle fur of a Lake Seal.

A Lake Seal!

Hysterical laughter threatened again. I was speaking to one of Co'yeh's Hated Kin. Qwa'osi and his warriors were always on guard to protect us, my grandfather assured me. That was why I wore the Otter's charm. My hand fumbled for the otter claw under my tunic.

It was gone!

In the back of my mind a deep voice laughed, reminding me that I had asked for help from anyone, hadn't I? I'd sworn an oath. Shouldn't I accept what was offered? I took in a shuddering breath and willed my fears away.

"That's right, young one, relax, and don't be afraid. I would never hurt you, my son, believe that."

My son. Wonder and dismay tangled in my awareness, then the brindle seal opened his mouth wide and swallowed my spirit whole.

I caught the impression of sharp white teeth, and then my being was sliding into a warm moist blackness. Panicked, I writhed like a hooked fish. "Stop." the voice soothed. "Be easy and trust. Look through my eyes and we'll swim together."

As the voice promised, in the next moment the moist darkness was replaced by other sensations. I now swam the river's icy water, buffeted by the current, my flippers tucked close to my oily fur. Blurred images in black and green sped by. The ghosts of the drowned raised white talons of dripping foam, calling me to join them. Scaly, blue Water Spirits laughed and, feeling playful, slammed me hard against a rock. I pushed myself off the stone and bared my teeth.

Sucking in a great mouthful of the river, I allowed Water to flow into every part of my being. The next boulder they tried to dash me against, I floated easily above it and spun on. Their howls of anger echoed in my mind as the current whisked me away. I barked a laugh.

Catching the current, I allowed it to spit me out onto the surface. When my head cleared the water, I looked about me searching for the steamboat. The boat was racing fast, trying to outrun the current. I sped after it, my back flippers whipping the green water to milky foam. But when I came up to the raft, I sensed my enemy, Qwa'osi, nearby. I bared my teeth, ready to fight. Then I realized he was linked to a Qwakaihi; his power harnessed to aid the people on the raft. For once, we were allies. Ignoring him, I focused my superior Qwakaiva.

Calling upon Air and the essence of the Spirit-Lights, I opened my mouth. A stream of violet light flowed out from between my teeth. The Qwakaiva fanned out, sliding under the raft, lifting it a flipper's breadth above the rocks....

Boat fly.

Raft fly.

Sail high on the surface of the water, my human voice sang.

Flying, flying.

Over the rocks, over the waves.

Flying, flying.

No harm will come to me and my kindred.

No bad Spirit can curse me.

Flying, flying, over the rocks, protected.

Ya hai'ya ho'a aiya.

As the steamboat battled the rapids, my awareness seemed split in two. I was conscious of my body drenched by spray, slumped in my mother's arms, while at the same time I swam the rapids with my father the Seal, feeling Qwakaiva coursing through my furry body at every twist of the channel. I lost all track of time.

As the current finally spat us into the calmer waters of the lake, my awareness changed focus once again.

"It is over, young one, rest now, you'll be safe," the Seal Warrior assured me.

As he withdrew, I cried, "Father don't leave me. I need you. Mother and my people need you. Please—"

"I can't stay, my son. Kunai has lent me his Qwakaiva for only a short time. My power in your world is linked to the Big Ice Lake. I can't follow any further. When you return to your village, I'll come visit you. Kunai told me I had a son with the Gift among the humans. I should have come earlier—I didn't believe—but it is time to see to your teaching. Yes, more than time. I'll come when you return home."

"But we aren't going back home. The Chamuqwani—"

I had no more time to explain. With the last of his strength, the Lake Seal spewed me from his mouth in a spray of crimson light. His violet eyes still focused upon me, he sank back into the Spirit-World from which I had unknowingly called him.

The magical being had called me his son. So, Matoqwa had been right when he taunted me. Siyatli, go back to the bottom of the lake where you belong. Tears pouring from beneath my closed eyelids, I lay shivering in my mother's lap.

Fish thief, Spirit Stealer, beware of Co'yeh, Grandson.

All along, had Grandfather known about my Lake Seal father, and the deep voice of Kunai in my mind, the one who was to be my Spirit's Companion? All these years, had he been lying to me?

Part Two

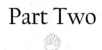

Chapter One

At the bottom end of the Blue Lake, we came to a Chamuqwani settlement with a number of log houses encircling a stone temple dedicated to the Chamuqwani god. Two stone warehouses and a trading post had also been erected near a long pier.

"What is this place, Grandfather?" Samiqwas asked in a low voice.

"The people living here call it Fort Protection." He pointed with his chin to a massive walled structure I hadn't noticed until then.

The fort itself was a long rectangular enclosure of upright logs built on a small hill above the settlement. On each of the fort's corners a taller, roofed platform had been attached to the walls. Soldiers with thunder-weapons stood on the platforms surveying the water and the portage trail beyond the lake.

"So many people," I murmured. "This place is so much bigger than home."

"Yes. This is where the steamboat spends the winter each year."

The boat's whistle sounded several long blasts as we approached. People on shore paused in their tasks and hurried down to the pier. The soldiers not on duty flocked to the boat's rail, waving and calling to friends and family members on shore.

"Welcome, welcome home!" People shouted as they hurried to the peer. Quite a crowd had gathered by the time the steamboat chugged into the shallows by the dock. The Sooties tossed mooring cables to the onlookers as the paddlewheeler eased alongside the pier. The raft bumped against the planking with a hard thump. The jolt caught me off balance, and I fell backwards against Grandmother.

"Pay attention," she grumbled.

I straightened and murmured an apology.

"Thought you were gonna winter upriver with the Zaunks and hunt for gold," someone shouted to a crewman on board the steamboat.

"Nah, Cap'n couldn't get this pot-boiler ta' run wi'out me."

These strangers laughed and talked among themselves, calling to the men on board, while continuing to point and stare at us. The word Zaunk was repeated many times.

There were soldiers and traders among the onlookers, but there were also many women and children. All wore the Chamuqwani style of clothing. The men who weren't in uniform were dressed in canvas trews and black wool coats or leather vests, the women in dresses with long, full sleeves and pleated skirts that hung down to their toes.

Many of the women and children had the golden skin that told of their mixed parentage, but a few of the women had the pale pink faces of the true Chamuqwani. Those women held themselves apart, shading their pale faces with wide-brimmed hats.

"No friends or family are here to welcome us," Samiqwas said. "Grandmother, where's Uncle Da'wabin?"

"He lives with his wife's relatives nearby, doesn't he?" I asked

Grandmother shook her head. "I don't know where he is, but I'll find out as soon as I can. He should've been here to meet us."

We had damp blankets and tangled hair, and we were all wearing dirty clothing. I huddled with the rest of my family among our belongings. I wished there was somewhere to hide. No one felt like talking much.

Grandmother placed a gnarled brown hand on my shoulder, steadying me. I looked up, startled. "Don't let them frighten you," she murmured without looking down at me. "These people are nothing—chattering gulls, filthy carrion left for the ravens to devour. You're one of the Qwani'Ya Sa'adi; be proud of that. Ignore what they say or do." Like an old bear, Grandmother faced the unknown with chin high, boldly staring into the eyes of anyone who dared to gawk at her.

Seicu was crying, a soft monotonous drone against her mother's shoulder. Samiqwas was trying his best to distract her by making funny faces and tickling her feet, but for once, neither he nor Aunt Tuulah was able to calm her. I glanced around looking for Ko. The little girl loved her father; if anyone could settle her I figured he could. "Amima, where's Ko?"

Startled out of her thoughts, Mother glanced about, then pointed with her lips. "He's sitting with his widowed mother and his brother Gagayii's family," she murmured.

Mother hadn't spoken much above a whisper, but Grandmother must have heard her. Or perhaps her patience just chose that moment to snap. "Give that child to me, and go get your husband. He should be here—with us."

Aunt Tuulah blinked in surprise, glanced in Ko's direction, then rose, handing Seicu to her mother. Grandmother settled her in her lap and spoke to her quietly. To my surprise Seicu's noise subsided.

Ko followed Aunt Tuulah back to us, looking irritated, but he sat down beside his wife without complaint. "Appi! Want my Appi." Seicu brightened when she saw him and held out her arms. Ko gave her a smile and settled her on his lap.

When Grandfather returned from speaking with Tsanqwati, Grandmother asked, "Well, what are they going to do with us now?"

Grandfather shook his head. "Our headman knows no more now than what we've been told already. We'll stay at Fort Protection until it's time to journey on to the Tribal Preserve."

Grandmother made a disgusted noise in her throat. "Fort Protection, and who does this fort place protect? Certainly not us."

A new group of soldiers, led by a yellow-haired man with one ear, met Commander Mu'Dar on the pier. They exchanged fist-to-heart salutes and talked for a time, then the yellow-haired man barked a few orders and the unloading began.

"Filthy Zaunks!"

"Hope the soldiers take 'em south soon!"

Just like when we were herded on board the steamboat, we passed through a gauntlet of staring and name-calling strangers. The soldiers marched us up the hill, but we passed by the log fort we had seen from the boat. Behind Fort Protection was another stockade, not as high, but just as large. Along its outer walls, armed soldiers paced the walkway.

The soldiers leading our procession shouted a command to one of the guards on the platform by the gate. The door of bound-together poles opened. "I see no room for us here. Where are we to stay, and for how long?" Aunt Tuulah muttered.

"Where?" Ko said, "I don't think these devils care as long as it's inside there."

The people walking ahead of us balked at entering the enclosure, stopping just in front of the open gate. A murmured protest grew louder as news of the stockade's conditions passed down the column. A low-voiced conversation ensued between my grandparents, then Grandfather left us and pushed his way through the people to join Tsanqwati and the elders at the head of the column.

Samiqwas motioned with his chin at Grandfather's retreating back. When no one was watching, we slipped past our female relatives to follow in his wake. Peering between the adults, we got our first good look into the stockade's interior.

Numberless gaunt and ragged people stared, as a sickening stench wafted out to greet us. People coughed, and babies cried. The enclosure reminded me far too much of the temple back home that had become our prison. Roused from their misery, most of the captives seemed apathetic, but others were angry, cursing the soldiers and shaking their fists at us.

Oh, Unseen Ones, protect us! What are we going to do now? I swallowed hard, my mouth going dry with fear.

"Ayah," Samiqwas said. "It smells bad in there."

Looking with my Spirit-Sight, I could see the sour green cloud of disease hovering above the walls, and I shuddered. "I can get used to a bad smell," I said. "But there's more to worry about here than a big stink."

Grandfather must have been looking with his Qwakaiva as well, because he said to the headman, "There's sickness here. We must ask the soldiers to let us stay somewhere else."

When Tsanqwati repeated Grandfather's words to the interpreter, the yellow-haired Commander seemed surprised that we knew, then anger flushed his pale features. "Who told you that? It's a lie."

Tsanqwati said nothing and only waited, staring him in the eye.

A flush darkening his face, the soldier growled, "The sickness is unimportant, a few children coughing, nothing to worry about."

"Perhaps, but it would be better if we stayed in some other place, so that our own children won't fall ill as well," Tsanqwati said.

"That isn't possible. I don't have enough troops to guard two encampments."

Tsanqwati continued to stare unblinking. The man gripped the butt of his holstered weapon. "And besides, you'll be leaving soon for the Preserve. You'll wait with the others until it's time to go."

"If we give you our word that we won't run away, will you allow us to camp outside this place? Our clan mothers will swear by the sacred bones of our ancestors, and all the Holy Guardians of our land. We'll obey your orders, but please don't force us in there."

The soldier's mouth hardened into a thin line. "Oh you will obey, no question of that. Swear by whatever you like, it means naught to me."

Refusing to become angry, Tsanqwati said, "Believe us or not, we've sworn it, and we'll cause no trouble, only let us stay outside."

The soldier sighed. "You have to remain within the stockade, for your own protection."

Samiqwas and I glanced at one another. "Our own protection?" he murmured. "Who's going to hurt us, a bear, a mountain cat?"

The hair on the back of my neck rose as a chilling thought came to mind. "Maybe these new settlers like to steal women and children for slaves." Samiqwas's eyes widened.

Samiqwas might have said more, but the Commander chose that moment to lose his patience. Threatening us with the points of their long knives, his soldiers shoved us inside.

With an ominous thud, the gate closed behind us.

Chapter Two

The stockade was only a large space surrounded by high, upright log walls. Those who had arrived before us made themselves shelters of blankets, bits of canvas, and saplings, propped up against the stockade's walls. Those not fortunate enough to claim such a desired space crouched in the centre area under similar flimsy shelters.

"Children, use your sharp eyes," Grandmother murmured. "Do you see Da'wabin among these people? He'll help us if we can find him."

We saw no one that looked familiar, nor did anyone step forward to greet us with a happy smile. It'd be a sweet blessing to have a relative in this terrible place, I thought as I scanned the crowded enclosure. "I can't see him, Ami."

"He must be here. Keep looking."

I thought I might grow roots and sprout leaves, we seemed to wait so long, but at last a delegation of men arose and came forward to greet us. To my surprise, a thin, young Chamuqwani man wearing blue robes with a silver lightning bolt hung on a chain around his neck, led them.

"That Chamuqwani priest has no business here," Ko snarled.

"You're right," Grandmother said. "Are these people trying to insult us?"

"We're ignorant of their customs, my dear, but I don't think they mean to give offense," Grandfather said.

Each group stared at one another with no one speaking. Finally, going against custom, it was the young priest who took the initiative and stepped forward to greet us.

"Welcome, brothers and sisters. I'm Intercessor Raymonel. May Djoven the Mighty One's blessing be upon you." He held up his hand in the blessing gesture I'd seen the old priest at home use on special occasions. "You look weary from your journey. Have you come all the way from the Big Ice Lake?"

He spoke in a badly accented but understandable version of our own language, and he called our home by its proper name, rather than calling it Lake Socanna as most foreigners did. I was impressed.

"Yes," Tsanqwati said, "we're the People from the Big Ice Lake."

The onlookers including the priest seemed relieved. "Good. You're the last. We've been waiting for you."

"Waiting for us?"

Next to the priest, a man with golden skin and short grey hair like a Chamuqwani explained, "The soldiers put us in this place while they waited for the people from upriver to arrive. They wouldn't let us leave for the new Tribal Preserve until you came."

"We've waited a long time, too," another man with stringy grey hair and a sour face grumbled.

The priest heard his comment, and rebuked him gently, "Now, now, Believer Mathin, I'm sure we'll all be leaving for the new Tribal Preserve soon. Lets help our brothers and sisters get settled so they can rest, before the meal cart comes."

Some of our villagers were lucky; they had relatives by marriage already in the compound. When these people were located, our friends and neighbours went with them. The rest of us were squeezed in among strangers, who at the priest's insistence grudgingly made room for us. Eventually everyone was settled, to no one's satisfaction.

During the initial confusion, Grandmother grabbed me and told me to accompany her while she searched for Uncle Da'wabin. Spying some women she knew from Broken Shell Mound Village, she hurried over to ask them where we might find my uncle and his family.

The first woman she asked shook her head. "I'm sorry. I don't know a man named Da'wabin." The woman turned away, making a big show of scolding a crying child.

Grandmother frowned, refusing to leave, but the woman continued to ignore her. Finally we moved on.

We asked several other people we encountered, but no one would admit to knowing Uncle's whereabouts. Grandmother became angry at last and stepped in front of one old woman with stringy grey braids, demanding an answer. "Kumla, we've known each other since our girlhood. You know my son. You were present at the marriage negotiations. Where is he?"

Kumla placed her hands on her hips and glared. "Yes, I know who your son is. But I also know he isn't in this stockade."

Her tone was so hostile that Grandmother took a step back as if the woman had struck her. She took a deep breath trying for calm, but her voice was still shaky when she asked, "What's happened? Where is he? Has he been injured?"

Kumla dropped her eyes, and muttered, "No. I don't know. He's just gone."

"Gone? But where?"

"He's gone to the Preserve," another woman with a red sore on her face shouted. "We don't want to talk to you. Go!"

"Preserve? When, how long ago? Why didn't he wait for us?"

"Go away! Leave us alone," she screamed and shook her fist.

We left. The women's behaviour was unsettling. "Ami, what's a matter with those women?" I asked when we were out of earshot. "Why wouldn't they tell us about Uncle?"

"I don't know. Shush now. I want to think."

Because we were latecomers with no relatives, our camp was in the back of the open area, too near the privy for our liking. Samiqwas and I begged some poles from a neighbour and helped Ko set up a small shelter for the old people and Seicu. Completing that chore, there was nothing to do but sit outside the shelter and glumly watch the activity going on all around us.

"Matoqwa and Slylum are heading for the front gate," Samiqwas whispered. "Let's follow them and have some fun."

I nodded my head ever so slightly and his lips curved in the barest shadow of a grin. When the women of our family seemed occupied with their own concerns, we rose slowly to our feet.

"Where you go?" Seicu cried. "Want go, too."

"Sit down!" Grandmother barked. "You boys aren't going anywhere."

Aunt Tuulah stuck her head out of the blanket shelter and glared. "Grandmother's right. You're staying right here and taking care of your sister, and Tasimu can help you amuse her."

Seicu, her eyes moist, held out her arms to us. "Want story, story. Get string, Little Rock Squirrel. Tell story 'bout Qwa'osi."

Samiqwas opened his mouth to protest, but just then a crier shouted for the women to come forward with their buckets. Aunt Tuulah thrust her daughter into Samiqwas's arms. "You and Tas play with her while I get food."

The soldiers opened the gate and brought in the evening meal. Mother and Aunt hurried with our cooking pail and water skins to join the line of women forming in front of the cart.

The stink of the privy made the porridge even less appetizing than usual. I ate it anyway, but it lay like a rock in my stomach. I hoped we wouldn't be here long. I hated it here already.

After our meal, an old man wearing a dirty blanket over his ragged trade-cloth shirt approached our tiny shelter. Grandfather, recognizing him as a Qwakaihi of his acquaintance from downriver, greeted the man warmly and invited him to sit with us.

A bit flustered with nothing to offer our guest, Mother reached for one of the water skins. The old man waved it aside with a faint smile. "Thank you, but I'm not thirsty. And you'll need to save what you can for your own use. The soldiers only bring food and water when it suits them."

Her face reddening, Aunt Tuulah said, "There's always enough if people share."

"How long have you been in this place?" Grandfather asked hastily.

The old man grimaced, then shrugged. "A moon at least, I think. It's easy to lose track."

"Do you have any idea how much longer they plan to keep us confined?" Grandfather asked. "There's sickness in this place."

The old man shrugged. "Who can understand the minds of such people? But I thought you might recognize the taint without being told."

"Do you know the cause of this disease?"

The old man met and held Grandfather's eye. "Yes, I do. The evil is the fault of the priest, his women, and his Qwani'Ya converts."

He turned his head and pointed with his lips to a group of people clustered around a large canvas tent erected in the favoured position by the gate. At that moment, the priest's followers were singing a loud Chamuqwani hymn. No one looked our way, but I felt a shiver run down my back all the same.

The old man may have felt the chill, too. He pulled the blanket tighter around his shoulders, his mouth compressing into a thin line. "I came to warn you about this priest and his followers, because there are impressionable children among your band who might be sickened, or hooked by his lures for new converts."

"But why would the priest conjure a sickness?" Mother asked.

"As you all ready know, I'm no follower of the Chamuqwani god," Grandfather said. "But I confess I've sensed no harm in the young priest. I detected only his concern when he came forward to help us."

"Yes, he's a sly one in that way, all gentle and kind, but under the surface of his lake, he's as corrupted as a seven-day-old corpse in summer, and as treacherous as a Talav Quake Monster, lurking in the black waters under the earth."

He fixed Samiqwas and then me with a long, penetrating stare, lingering for an extra moment on my face. I felt the cool touch of his power in my mind and shrank away, surprised and a little frightened.

"The priest will seem mild enough at first, to gain your confidence. He'll talk sweetly to your children, give them extra food when he can, but don't trust him. He's a child stealer. If you let him bathe them in his holy smoke, and give them Chamuqwani names, their souls will be lost to this land and our ancestors forever.

"Don't look at me so sceptically, honoured Clan Mother. I speak the truth. The Chamuqwani-appointed headman, the one named Royston Fish Spear, the follower of this priest and his thundering god, was one of those headmen who sold our land to the Chamuqwani.

"It's because of these accursed Converts that all of us are being forced to leave our homes. The traitors signed their treaty paper, sold our land, then the Chamuqwani took them south with their booty, before the rest of us arrived."

He's gone to the Preserve, there was a pounding in my head and my vision blurred. Was this true? Had some of our Qwani'Ya relatives traded away our land for their own gain?

After a long silence, Grandfather said, "This news is very troubling to me, honoured man of the clans."

The Qwakaihi laughed, but there was no mirth in the sound. "Troubled? Yes, you should be, since it was your own eldest son that was one of the men who signed and took the Chamuqwani's gifts."

Grandmother stiffened; her look could have frightened even the Great Aseutl Kunai at that moment, but the old Qwakaihi never batted an eye. "My son is an honourable man. He would never trade away his own sisters' inheritance to any Chamuqwani!"

"Oh? Are you sure? How long has it been since you've seen him?

"You said earlier that the people from the lower villages were gone when you arrived," Mother said. "How can you know who did what?"

Showing his teeth, he merely gave her a smile, as predatory as a hungry wolverine. "Ask the priest if you don't believe me. He was here at the time. Your brother has converted to the new religion, along with the rest of his wife's family."

Staring directly into Grandmother's eyes, he continued, "Your son changed his name; he took the name of one of their holy men. He calls himself Royston Fish Spear now, instead of the good Qwani'Ya Sa'adi name you gave him at his naming ceremony. He's your son nonetheless. You'll see when we arrive at this new land."

"I don't believe it," Aunt Tuulah muttered. "There's some mistake."

I tasted sour stomach juices in my throat and glanced about our family circle. Not being of our lineage, Ko looked away, refusing to meet my eye. Muddy colours of bitterness swirled in the old Qwakaihi's Spirit-Fire, but I sensed that he wasn't lying.

Go away. We don't want to talk to you! Did everyone in this place know of our shame? That would explain the old women's reluctance to speak of my uncle when Grandmother asked about him.

Her face flushed, my aunt cried, "Why should we believe you or this priest? If the priest was here then, why didn't he go with them?"

"Because, rude young woman," the old man snapped, "the priest is throwing out his nets for more converts to ensnare for his god to gobble up. That's why he stayed, not to help us as he claims."

For the first time in my life my grandmother seemed old and vulnerable to me. Tears pooling in her eyes, she covered her face with her blanket. The old Qwakaihi saw her tears, too. And maybe he was shamed, because he dropped his eyes.

Grandfather put an arm around her shoulder. She stiffened, but he persisted, and at last she leaned against him, still hiding her face. With her resting against his shoulder, Grandfather returned his attention to our guest. His voice was cool, as he said, "You've given me much to pray about. It grows late, but I'll speak to our headman and our clan mothers after the morning meal tomorrow, be assured. I'll pass on your warning about the children to those I think should hear of it."

The old man heard the dismissal in Grandfather's voice and rose. Refastening the twig he was using to hold his blanket upon his shoulders, he offered one last tart piece of advice. "Guard your dreams. The Chamuqwani god's converts work their evil while the unprotected sleep."

"Have no fear for me and mine. I'll be vigilant. Against all who wish us harm," Grandfather assured him.

After our visitor left, my relatives laid out their blankets, getting ready to sleep. I sat shivering, unable to move, the growing evening's cold seeping into the marrow of my bones. Mother called to me; I said something to her in return, but remained where I was. Finally Grandfather came over and sat down beside me.

I leaned into his warmth and he settled his blankets around us. "Old Chumco had many distressing things to say, but don't let them trouble you overmuch. The truth might not be as bad as that one made it appear."

"Who is he, Grandfather? He frightened me."

"He's a powerful Qwakaihi. But in all honesty, you should also be aware that his reputation is 'many layered', though he mostly does good for people. Treat him with respect, but don't go looking for him either. He's been known to use his Qwakaiva to benefit his relatives, or wish ill upon others who have crossed him."

Horrified, I stared up at him. "He's a Malicer?"

Nestled against his chest, I could feel his soft rumble of a laugh as he settled the blanket more comfortably about my shoulders. "I don't know him well enough to say that. I've no proof, and people are often too quick to judge before understanding all the facts. No, let's not accuse him of being a Malicer. It would be better just to say, he's a person with flaws and praiseworthy traits like the rest of us."

"But if he's doing bad things...."

"Whether something is good or bad often depends on who's telling the story, eh?"

"Yes, I know but...."

"It's like the stories they tell of Qwa'osi the Otter and Co'yeh the Lake Seal, isn't it?"

He chuckled at my expression. "Most people in our band praise the Otter Warrior and curse the Seal, thinking one our protector and the other a thief. But the relationship between the forces of the universe isn't that simple. Otter and Seal are often uneasy rivals for the same school of fish, but they aren't enemies. Each has its own place in the balance of life." He brushed the hair off my forehead. "So intense, you can't puzzle out the mysteries of the world tonight. Go to sleep now and don't be afraid. I'll keep guard over your sleep."

Thinking of fried mushrooms, wild onions, and roasting meat, I drifted into sleep to the sound of Aunt Tuulah singing Seicu a lullaby.

Chapter Three

During the grey twilight that passes for a summer night in the Northlands, clouds rolled in from over the mountains, bringing with them an icy downpour. I woke later, thoroughly miserable, my teeth chattering, to a cold wind and rain stinging my face.

Pulling my dripping blanket around me, I crawled under the soaked blankets of our shelter. There I huddled with the rest of my family and waited for the storm to pass. The waiting seemed endless. This time we suffered the rain, but in another moon cycle—or less—similar weather would mean snow. My chest ached from so much shivering, and my hands and feet grew numb.

"I wish someone would make a fire, and let us sit by it," I said to no one in particular.

"Maybe this new land in the south won't be so bad," Samiqwas whispered to me. "It should at least be warm there. Hot sun, all the time, mm-mm warm." I bared my teeth in an attempt at a smile.

Grandfather continued his low chanting. He was using his Qwakaiva, draining himself, trying to help us survive that terrible night.

The rain stopped as the sky lightened, but the daylight brought no warmth. Boiling clouds still hid the sun. Wind from the northeast knifed through my wet clothing. Emerging from our shelter to walk to the privy, I saw about me a colourless world of dripping shelters, mud, and miserable people. I splashed through puddles, my feet numb, listening to people coughing and small children crying.

The pit dug for the privy was nearly overflowing with water and floating excrement. I gagged as I spouted my own stream of urine into the foul mess. When I finished and looked around, the priest was standing beside me. The storm had made its mark upon him, too, though he was more comfortably housed in his big tent than the rest of us. His blue robe was wrinkled and mud stained, his face blurred with fatigue.

He'd been gazing into the flooded privy as well. When he sensed me looking at him, he turned and smiled. Suddenly shy, I dropped my eyes. I couldn't help recalling the old Qwakaihi's warning. I should go back to my family, yet I was unable to move.

"You're one of the new boys, aren't you?"

I nodded.

He looked back at the pit then at me once more. "This is very bad, isn't it?" His priest's power seeming to hold me in place, he kept watching me with those unnerving blue eyes, waiting for an answer.

Finally, I stammered, "Y-yes. It is."

"The soldiers will have to do something about this before it gets worse. I'll go and speak to them. Does your family need anything?"

Need anything? We needed everything: shelter, dry bedding, warm clothes, something besides oatmeal and rock-hard cakes to eat. The list was endless. "Fire," I heard myself say, before I could sensor my tongue. "Cold, so wet and cold."

His voice was low and determined when he agreed with me. "Yes, fires to dry out clothes and bedding are definitely needed on a day like this. Commander Magoss will have to send us wood for fires or there'll be more deaths. And we must go soon, or we'll be trapped here with no shelter or supplies adequate to survive the coming winter."

I started to edge away from him, wanting to return to my family, but he caught my movement out of the corner of his eye and spoke to me again. "You're a smart young man. What's your name?"

My face grew hot. My name, give my name to a stranger? "I have to get back to my family," I mumbled.

He seemed puzzled by my refusal, then he nodded. "All right. Forgive my rudeness. I'd forgotten for a moment how sensitive the unconverted are to giving strangers their names. Your parents aren't among the Mighty Djoven's children, are they?"

I looked away, embarrassed and uneasy, yet still I was unable to break away from the intense stare he was giving me. At last I heard him sigh. "Yes, I can see the way of it. Your family still cling to their primitive notions. No matter. Come visit the big tent. We have singing there in the afternoons and evenings. You'd be welcome to join us. We often share hot tea and flat bread, so do come. You'll be welcome. And tell your father that if your family needs anything, he should come talk to me. I'll try to help."

I nodded and hurried away. My father? Once out of his sight, I doubled over, not sure if I wanted to laugh or throw up. I was so intent on keeping my Spirit from shattering, I wasn't paying attention, and I bumped hard against someone. Startled, I looked up, choking on an apology. Chumco was glaring down at me. His eyes were fierce black pools, seeking to ensnare my Spirit in their depths.

"What did the blue robe say to you? What did he want?"

I blinked—another adult stranger wanting to hear my words. As if he had sucked the voice out of my throat, I heard myself say in a rush, "He said he would speak to the soldiers about the privy. He wanted to know my name, but I didn't tell him. He wanted my father to come talk to him."

Chumco's eyes widened at this last revelation, releasing me from his power. "Your father?" He barked a mirthless laugh. "Don't looked so shocked, boy, of course I know who your father is."

He rapped his finger hard against my chest. "I see you've discarded that fool otter charm. Come talk to me when you want to learn the Gifts that are your birthright." He chuckled softly at my startled expression and allowed his hand to trace the line of my jaw, then brushed it across my hair in a suddenly possessive caress. Power sizzled through my skull. I trembled, my breath coming in ragged gasps.

"How do I know these things? Because like you, my Qwakaiva comes from the dark water under the earth where only the Great Aseutl Kunai and his allies can swim."

Images of cold, scaly bodies brushing against my flesh choked the breath from my lungs. Unable to speak, I shook my head in denial.

"Why look so frightened? Kunai offers power and great wisdom to the man who isn't afraid to suffer the tests needed to reach his hidden lair and claim them. One of Co'yeh's kin may have sired you, and one of Qwa'osi's Qwakaihi may try to shield you, but only Kunai can bless you. Master of enigma, of light and dark, it's only the ancient Aseutl who knows your Spirit. And only I can teach you the true meaning of your Gifts."

He studied my face for a long moment, then shook his head. "Perhaps you're still too young, but you will come to me, or another whom the Great One favours. Yes, you will come someday for our teaching. You cannot deny your nature forever."

Then he turned away from me chuckling to himself. "So the young fool of a priest wants to meet your father—what a laugh."

Siyatli. Once more Matoqwa's taunt echoed in my mind.

I walked the long way back to our camp, trying to warm my blood and stop shivering. But more than the cold now chilled my bones. I wasn't like him; Kunai wasn't my Spirit's Companion. Maybe the Chamuqwani priest wasn't the only fisherman tossing out his net.

Returning to our shelter, I completely forgot about my strange encounters with the priest and Chumco. Standing outside, their faces flushed and angry, Aunt Tuulah and her husband faced one another. "I need you here, not running off somewhere," Tuulah was saying.

I froze, hoping not to draw attention to myself. Grandfather was nowhere to be seen. Samiqwas was gone. Grandmother was lying in the shelter with a blanket over her head. Also inside the shelter, Seicu sat on my mother's lap, her thumb in her mouth, her eyes round.

Ko let out a longsuffering sigh. "I'm not running off somewhere. I'm just going to see how my mother is doing this morning. Why is that so unreasonable?"

Aunt Tuulah folded her arms across her chest still glaring. "Your brother Gagayii can see to her. Your place is here with us...."

"My mother is old; Gagayii has his own family, and I've no sister to take care of her. Why do you begrudge her the sight of her son?"

"I don't begrudge her the sight of her son," Aunt Tuulah said, her voice rising. "You aren't being fair!"

"Oh? Then what exactly is the problem?"

"The problem is that your mother isn't the real reason you're going," she snapped. "You're going because you like sitting around with your brother and his friends, gambling and drinking waskyja—"

"Waskyja?" Ko's voice was becoming louder too. In the shelters around ours, people were stopping what they were doing to look our way. "Have your wits melted in the rain?" he spread his arms wide, showing off his ragged and dirty clothing. "Look at me, woman. Where would I, or any of us, get money for waskyja?"

"You got some on the steamboat—"

Ko threw up his hands and gave her a disgusted look. "You're barking at shadows, sled dog. I'm not going over there to drink."

"You'll be gone all day and I might need you."

"What could you possibly need me for? There's nothing for any of us to do but sit in the mud and watch the soldiers walking along the outer wall—and you don't need me to help you do that!"

"I'm not looking at the soldiers. I care nothing for that black man!"

"Oh? That isn't the way my mother heard it."

Tuulah's face darkened. "I don't care what your mother said. He means nothing to me!"

"Then why is he always watching you whenever he's around, if you aren't encouraging his interest?"

"I've no idea, and I could care less."

"Well, I care. You're my wife!"

"Then act like my husband."

"Enough. I'm going to visit my mother."

"Go then; I don't need you. Stay with your mother if you want."

Ko made a disgusted noise deep in his throat and moved his hand in a cutting gesture. "Woman, that isn't what I want and you know it. Don't try to put words in my mouth. I won't be gone all day." With that, Ko brushed past me and stalked away. Aunt Tuulah stared after him, dabbing at her eyes with a dirty sleeve.

I looked down at my feet, unsure what to do. Samiqwas appeared out of nowhere and touched me on the arm. Seicu perched upon his shoulder. He motioned with his chin. "Come on, Seicu has to pee. Let's go look around." I gladly fell into step beside him.

The wind had blown away the clouds at last, the sun now giving off a little warmth. Light reflected up from the mud puddles, and tendrils of vapour floated above the drying shelters. People were emerging, talking to neighbours and setting out their possessions to dry.

"Seicu isn't going to like the privy. It's a mess," I warned.

"I know. I took her earlier. I used that as an excuse."

We shared a smile to celebrate his cunning. Then, leaving out my talk with Chumco, I told him about my earlier encounter with the priest.

"I wondered what he was saying to you. I saw you both earlier.

And what did the old Qwakaihi say to you afterward?"

My brother-cousin was an observant wolf all right. I felt my face heat, and hedged. "He just wanted to know what the priest had said to me."

Chapter Four

After the ground by our shelter dried, I took my damp blanket and curled up in the sun's heat to doze. My belly was full, I was warm and dry, and it was hard to keep my eyes open.

When the sun disappeared below the stockade wall, the afternoon's chill roused me. I woke stiff and sluggish, my mind still fogged with sleep. Over by the priest's big tent a fire blazed. People were laughing and singing hymns to their god.

I drank a bit of water from one of the water bags, then glanced around our camp, looking for Samiqwas. No one was there but Aunt Tuulah. She was sitting by the shelter, stitching up a hole in one of the blankets with a piece of copper wire Ko had broken off something on the steamboat and sharpened into a crude needle. Her mouth was set into a thin angry line as she jabbed at the cloth with unnecessary vigour.

Pulling my blanket about my shoulders, I called, "Auntie, I have to pee; be back later." She waved at me, never looking up from her work.

Breathing a sigh of relief, I went to find Samiqwas, but didn't see him. The singing coming from Intercessor Raymonel's campsite sounded nice; I decided to go over there instead of looking for him. I was hungry.

By the priest's tent people were sitting by the fire on blankets. Intercessor Raymonel, in a clean blue robe, stood with his hands upraised, leading the singing. The silver pendent worn on his chest flashed as he moved, reflecting back the flames like lightning come down from the sky.

On a log near the fire, several people with musical instruments sat and accompanied the singers. A man and a woman had what I first thought were small hoop drums. When they played them, however, they slapped them against their thighs or palms, making the tiny metal disks strung along the rim ring in time with the music.

The older man sitting between them held an even stranger instrument upon his lap. With one hand he stretched a part of it in and out, while using his other hand to press little pegs. The thing gave out a moaning sound along with a high-pitched melody that mimicked the song the people were singing. I had never heard or seen the like, and it fascinated me.

I moved in among the standing people at the edge of the circle, my attention split between looking for Samiqwas and watching the musicians. I kept my head down each time the priest turned in my direction, hoping he wouldn't notice me.

As I watched and listened, I also saw for the first time up close the priest's green-robed Mercy Women. They were the women Kutima said were dedicated to the goddess who was Djoven the Mighty One's compassionate sister. He'd shown me a picture once in one of his father's books.

The two women tried to keep the lower portion of their faces covered with their white veils, but the cloth often slipped. One was young, her pale face quite pretty; the other was much older, middle-aged, with hard lines around her nose and mouth.

When I arrived, they were standing behind the musicians, helping with the singing. Later as more people gathered, they went inside and came back with large baskets balanced on their hips. The crowd quieted, seeming to know what came next. Everyone bowed their heads and put palms together over their chests.

I knew this gesture as a sign that it was time to pray. The old priest at home had taught us how to do this. Feeling uncomfortable, but not wanting to draw attention to myself, I copied what the others were doing.

The priest raised his hands in a blessing and intoned a long monotonous prayer, punctuated now and then by praise shouts from his followers. When it was over, his women took their baskets and walked among the people, handing out to everyone more of the hard-cakes we were given at mealtime.

As the older of the women drew near, I forgot about my hunger. She gave off a foul odour, and I didn't like the muddy colours of her Spirit-Fire. Her eyes were grey, her expression contemptuous when she thought the priest couldn't see her. I would've liked to move away, but I'd waited too long. The people standing behind me were eager for her handout and pressed forward, preventing my escape.

Then, she was right in front of me, impatiently holding out one of the hard brown cakes. Her hand was red and square, with thick fingers with dirt encrusted under and about the nails. It was an ordinary Chamuqwani hand, save for the slimy green film of sickness I saw with my Gift, that was covering her fingers and now the food that she held out to me. My heart leapt into my throat, choking off the air from my lungs.

In badly accented words in my language, she snapped, "Here, boy, take it." I shook my head and stepped back, stepping on someone's foot. A sharp blow in the back propelled me forward just as she held out the cake again. Her hand hit me in the chest, the hard-cake dropping on the ground between us.

"What matter you? Bad boy, pick up eat."

I stared down at the hard-cake. It had broken in two when she dropped it. The green slime crawled like a living creature across the corrupted biscuit. Unable to look away, I stared, mesmerized. I didn't know if the priest and his women had started the sickness, but the old Qwakaihi was right when he claimed they were now spreading it.

"Pick it up, boy; are you stupid?"

I shook my head, my breath coming in ragged gasps. I raised my foot to grind the corrupted food into the dirt, but I was too slow. A big-bellied woman standing beside me guessed what I planned and shoved me roughly aside. I staggered, nearly falling with the force of her blow. Her blotchy face contorted with anger, she yelled at me, "What's a matter with you, foolish boy? Haven't your relatives taught you how to behave?"

The pregnant woman picked up the cake and proffered it to the Mercy Woman. She gestured for the woman to keep the broken hard-cake. Thanking her, the pregnant woman gave a piece each to a small boy and girl holding on to her skirts.

Horrified at this turn of events, I righted myself and stammered out an explanation. "Please, don't let your young ones eat the cake. It's tainted with sickness...."

The people around us murmured, some making the sign against evil. The priest's woman hadn't followed everything I'd said, but she had understood enough to make her face turn red with anger. When someone who could speak the Chamuqwani language better explained to her, she glared at me. "Sickness? Nonsense."

"You ignorant brat, how dare you!" the woman who had pushed me yelled. "This woman is one of the Compassionate Goddess's Mercy Women. She tends the unwell; she doesn't cause illness." She pointed an accusing finger at me. "Maybe it's you who have caused this evil."

I was so startled that I forgot my manners, and rudely blurted,

"Me? But my family just got here. How could I be responsible? The illness was here long before we came."

I could almost taste the fear swirling in the air around me. I took a step backward, my eyes scanning for an escape route. Out of the corner of my eye, I saw Intercessor Raymonel heading in our direction. He called to the Mercy Woman. When she and the others turned at the sound of his voice, I ducked under someone's arm and bolted.

Once away from the big tent, I slowed my pace so as not to excite attention. My body trembling, my thoughts in chaos, I didn't want to go back to my family's shelter. Damn Samiqwas anyway; why isn't he ever around when I need him? Fear and frustration blurring my vision, I wiped a hand across my eyes. I wouldn't cry; I just needed a quiet place for a moment.

But in such a crowded enclosure, there wasn't anywhere I could go to be alone. I wandered aimlessly for a time, then I headed for the privy.

The ditch the soldiers and our men had dug earlier had drained off much of the watery mess to somewhere beyond the stockade wall, but the sight facing me was still a loathsome mess.

As I stepped away and walked around the log partition set up for privacy, four boys confronted me. All about my own age, they blocked my path, making me step backwards as they moved in a solid wall towards me.

"Look, brothers, see what we've found," the tall boy standing in the middle said. He was a pale boy with brown hair cut short to hang just below his ears. His clothes were as dirty and nearly as patched as mine, but they were cut in the Chamuqwani style, made of canvas and wool rather than trade-cloth and caribou hide. Two of the others were also golden-skinned, but the fourth boy was as dark as any other child of the People.

"What we have is a stinking demon-worshiper who's just crawled out of the shit-hole." the darker boy said.

I blinked, and bit my lip. Speaking would only goad them further.

One of the others laughed. "Maybe we should send him back where he came from. Maybe teach him to be more respectful when talking to one of the Mercy Women, eh?"

So they had been at the singing. Their leader gave me a nasty smile. "Maybe you're right, brother. This little brat needs to learn some manners."

Without warning his hand shot out, and he gave me a shove, nearly knocking me off balance into the pit. I flung my arms wide, clawing for balance and at last my foot dug in. I pulled myself up right and glared. "Maybe it's you who should learn manners. You come at me like starving dogs. Four against one, do you fear me so much?"

The dark boy's eyes opened wide. Their leader tried to shove me again, but I was ready this time and stepped sideways, causing him to lose his balance and nearly fall in himself.

I needed to get out of there, before they jumped me all at once. "Why are you doing this?" I moved sideways. The pack followed.

Stalling for time, I took another step and said, "You aren't rabid animals. Why?"

"Because I hate mouthy, shit-eating Dog Farts from upriver," the leader said and aimed a punch at my face.

I dodged, the blow connecting with my shoulder. "I only spoke the truth. There was sickness on the food. You were there. Couldn't you see it?" One of the other boys hesitated. Then his friend said something to him too low for me to hear, and he moved with the others toward me.

"Come ahead then, Convert Carrion Eaters." I braced myself as best I could. "But if you think I'm going into the shitter alone, think again."

Sensing movement out of the corner of my eye, I risked a glance in that direction. Matoqwa and Cohasi stepped up beside me. I almost fainted, but quickly got my wits about me. Someone else had come up behind and slightly to my right. I dared not take my eyes off the boys in front of me to see who it was, but I prayed it was a friend.

Matoqwa made a point of cracking his knuckles loudly. He balled his hands into fists and twisted his broken-nosed face into a hideous grin. "Need a hand, little brother? These Convert boys already stink like rotten fish, so if we dump them in the shitter, their relatives won't know the difference." The leader scowled, but the odds were evened up now, and Matoqwa was big for his age.

Blows might still have been exchanged, but just then, two men I didn't know stepped behind the wall to use the privy. "You boys have a problem here?" the older of the two asked. The Convert boys' leader mumbled something, then he and his friends left without looking back.

Breathing a sigh, I turned to see that the third presence behind me was Samiqwas. As the four of us left the privy in the opposite direction, Cohasi muttered, "Stupid Convert brats. Guess us boys from the Big Ice Lake better start peeing together from now on."

Matoqwa saw the expression on my face and laughed. "Don't look so confused, Tas. We aren't going to let any dog-farting Convert push you in the shit-hole. You're from home; all us boys from the Big Ice Lake have to stick together in this place. No, if anyone is going to push you in the shitter, Siyatli, it will be me."

I smiled, showing my teeth. "You can try—anytime."

"Maybe I will." Matoqwa raised his fist and took a step towards me.

"Oh let him be," Samiqwas grumbled. "I'd have to sleep next to him if you did."

Matoqwa laughed. "See you later, Little Rock Squirrel."

Samiqwas watched them go, then shook his head in disgust. "You never learn, do you Tas? Bear baiting is dangerous."

"Me, bear baiting? Look who's talking."

He grinned. "Matoqwa called to me to follow him just now. What a surprise to find you going to war in the privy."

Chapter Five

Our evening meal concluded, I lay down with my head resting on Grandfather's leg. The adults were talking, but I paid them little attention. Too weary to find my bed, I must have dozed off, because some time later a low-voiced argument awakened me.

The women of my family were trying to keep their words from carrying to the neighbouring encampments, but the tone of their voices was plain enough. A disapproving frown curving his mouth, Grandfather was silently watching, but took no part in the discussion. I'd seen that look before. He wanted to say something, but felt it wasn't his place to interfere in what he'd decided was our clan's business.

"Call him back to us, my girl. Why be so stubborn? He has the power to help us," Grandmother snapped.

Mother shook her head, silent but determined. "No, he doesn't have that kind of power. It wouldn't do any good to call him."

Him? I wished my tired brain would wake up.

"We should've killed those crazy miners. If we had only known; if they had only waited 'til the boy was grown...." Aunt Tuulah broke off, tossing more sticks on the fire. The sparks swarmed upward like angry insects. "Look around you, they're taking us from our homes. Do you want your son to die? Do you want us all to die? Your Star Swimmer can save us. With his peoples' Qwakaiva empowering us, we can kill these foreign monsters...."

"He won't help us kill our enemies." Tears were in Mother's eyes now. She shrank within herself, her Spirit-Fire lying tight against her physical body, its colours dulled. "You don't understand. Even if I could summon him, he wouldn't help us in the way you want."

"Even to save you or his son?" Grandmother said. "I find that hard to believe, my girl."

I didn't. He never came to see me before. Grandfather's hand lay heavy on my shoulder, cautioning restraint, but I shook his hand off and sat up. Not being of our lineage, he might feel it wasn't his place to interfere, but those restraints didn't apply to me. "Leave her alone!"

"What do you know about such things, rude boy?" Grandmother said.

Grandfather's hand squeezed tight on my arm, another warning. I took a deep breath before answering. "He's bound to the Big Ice Lake."

"Be quiet, rude boy," grandmother snapped. "You don't even know who your father is."

"Are you so sure of that?"

Leaning forward, she stared at me with narrowed eyes. "Just what do you think you know? Tell me."

"I-I know my father can't help us," I stammered. My resolve was wilting under the intensity of her regard. Desperately I turned to Grandfather for help. "You saw—in the rapids— didn't you?"

He patted my arm, offering comfort, giving me strength. "I saw," he said quietly. "You're right, my boy."

"What's the child talking about?" Grandmother demanded.

"During our passage down Drown Canoe Rapids, our grandson summoned his father. He combined his Qwakaiva with mine to help us survive. We would have died otherwise."

Grandmother and Tuulah exchanged triumphant glances. "I knew it," Tuulah murmured. "Didn't I tell you?"

Grandmother folded her arms across her chest, looking smug. "Well then, Tasimu—"

He shook his head and continued, "No, he can't. We're too far from the Big Ice Lake now. But even if we weren't, the children are right, my dear one. The Seal Man wouldn't, or couldn't, interfere in our world in such a big way."

"But why not?" Aunt Tuulah asked. "The magical people in the lake are our relatives, aren't they? Don't they care what happens to us?"

"They do, and then again, they don't. It's complicated. They aren't a part of our world or living in the bottom of the lake as the stories say. That image is only a convenience, something for our human minds to cling to."

"Where do they live then, Ati?" Samiqwas ventured to ask.

Grandfather's eyes met mine. What words could we find in our human language to explain to them? He took in a deep breath. "They live in a place 'outside'. Their home is a place of Spirit, but it also has substance to those dwelling there. They can see past, present, and future. And because of this different perception, they rarely interfere in the Physical World. They fear destroying the balance of the universe in ways that might bring about more harm than good...."

By the time he'd finished his explanation, Samiqwas looked a little glassy-eyed. The others seemed less confused, but thankfully let the subject drop.

But I couldn't.

Following Grandfather to the privy before we retired for the night, I put a hand on his arm to stop him on our way back. Taking a deep breath, I said, "If you knew so much, why didn't you tell me about my father when I asked you before?"

He didn't speak for a long moment, and when he did, I was startled by the bitterness in his voice. "Co'yeh's kind damage whomever they touch, even when they don't mean to. I'd no wish to lose another that I love to the Seal Man." Pushing past me, he said over his shoulder, "I would have never told you. And one thing for which I'm grateful is that you'll never see him again. Every day we travel south I thank the Unseen Ones for that blessing."

I stared after him, my mouth agape. Father had helped us survive the rapids. We might have died without the Seal's help. Who had Grandfather lost to a Seal's unpredictability?

Later, as I lay in the blankets next to Mother, I wasn't able to sleep. Thoughts of what Grandfather had said tumbled and whirled about in my mind. Then, unbidden, the image of Chumco's weathered face appeared before my inner eye.

"Come to me, young Warrior. I will teach you. Would you like that?"

"Teach me?" my heart leapt at the notion. Then Grandfather's warning about the man deflated my excitement. I couldn't be Chumco's student. He would be angry with me.

"I can't."

I tried to push his insistent summons away, but I was only partially successful. Chumco's presence lay atop the skin of my mind, red and swollen, like an insect bite, demanding to be scratched.

Sensing my restlessness, Mother finally asked, "What's wrong, Little Rock Squirrel? You should sleep now."

I made a face. "Don't call me that. I'm not a baby any longer. I hate that name."

She drew her hand out from under her blanket and brushed

my hair in a soothing gesture. "No, you aren't a baby," then more hesitantly, "I was very proud of you tonight."

I squirmed with delight under her praise, and yet another part of me was angry. I wanted suddenly to hurt her. "And will my father the Seal Man be proud of me, too? Amima, you should have told me. Why did I have to learn about him first from the taunts of my friends. Why did I have to discover the truth on my own?"

She dropped her hand. "I'm sorry. I didn't know. You should have told me you were being teased."

Her words shamed me, threatening to put out the fire of my anger, but I hardened my resolve, and said, "Would you have told me if I had?"

She was silent for a long time before answering. "I don't know."

Well, at least she was honest. "Do you hate him now, like Grandfather?"

"No. I would leave my family and go with him—to the bottom of the lake, or wherever—if he would come for me. But he won't, not ever."

Trying to keep the note of desperation out of my voice, I said, "Amima, please, tell me now that I know something about him? Why did you lie with one of the Seal Men?"

"You've been thinking about this for a long time, haven't you?" I nodded. "I wanted to tell you, Tasimu, but it's complicated."

"Complicated? What's so complicated about it?"

"It just is. I'm sorry."

"I don't believe you! You're just like Grandfather, always keeping secrets!"

She let out a long sigh, securing the blankets about us to ward off the night's chill. "I keep my secrets to protect you."

"Protect me from what?"

"From his enemies—and maybe other magical beings of his kindred."

Her answer made little sense, so I focused on the one part I could understand. "And what about our enemies? He might not want to help us, but if he had given me his power, showed me how to use mine, maybe I could've done something to help our people when the Chamuqwani came to take us away."

"You were too young—still are—to use such Qwakaiva wisely."

"Is that your decision to make?"

Goaded to anger at last, there was a noticeable chill in her voice, as she said, "It isn't for you to judge me. When the time's right, maybe he'll speak to you in your dreams. Maybe he'll even take you away with him, as Mother wants, I don't know."

"But if his power is rooted in the Big Ice Lake, as he told me, how will he find me in this new land so far from our home?"

"There's dark water under the Earth everywhere."

"What do you mean by that?"

Ignoring me, she turned her back and pretended to sleep.

I closed my eyes, but I couldn't relax. Inside I seethed with resentment. In one moment she praised me for being a fine young hunter and fisherman, and then in the next she was treating me like a child again.

I'd show her, and Grandfather, too. I'd find a way; I had a right to know.

In my dream, Chumco held a glowing crystal in one hand, while with the other he beckoned to me. "Come closer and tell me what's troubling you, Little Seal."

I hesitated, thinking of Grandfather. "Have no fear. You're under my protection while in the dream. No one, not even the Otter's Qwakaihi, can hear you. Tell me."

Power sizzled and crackled in the ether between us. Before I could stop them, words poured out of my mouth. "Grandfather lied to me and Mother won't tell me about my father. I have a right to know, but they're keeping secrets, treating me like a baby."

"Baby, eh?" he chuckled and urged the crystal upon me. "I agree; you do have the right to know about your father. This crystal is one of Kunai's treasures. If you think you have the strength to pay its price and master it, then look into its depths. You may discover the truth you seek."

The crystal pulsed with a rainbow of bright colours as it sang; the talisman was so beautiful. Never in my life had I wanted something so much, and yet once more I held back. "Take it, young Warrior," Chumco urged, holding it out once more. The singing grew louder and more seductive in my mind

For a moment longer I resisted, and then Grandfather's cruel words echoed in my mind. I would've never told you. And one thing for which I'm grateful is that you'll never see your father again.

Heart aching and desperate, I banished all caution and reached for Chumco's gift....

But as my Spirit-Hands closed about its fiery curves, white-hot pain exploded in my mind. I screamed and looked down at the charred shadows of my hands. I tried to let go, but couldn't. By my elbows and then my shoulders, I was being sucked into a vortex of agony. Betrayed! "Elder, why have you done this to me? Merciful Unseen Ones, save me!"

"My aim is only to teach you, foolish boy. Pay its price and focus. A Lake Seal Man's blood flows in your veins, I know you can do it. I have faith in your power, you're stronger than you think," Chumco shouted as I fell headfirst into molten fire.

Chapter Six

Exhausted from last night's ordeal, I remained in my blanket long after everyone else was up, thinking about the warrior from the bottom of the lake who had changed our lives.

Though much of my consciousness remained within the crystal's protection, it had allowed a part of my being to merge with my mother's younger-self when she lived alone during her First Blood Ceremony. I tasted the love that grew between them after she rescued the wounded Star Swimmer from the enemy who followed him into our world. And when they were pursued, I marvelled at her cunning, as she used her woman's blood to hide her lover's scent, so they could escape those unnatural hunters.

I also now knew why Grandfather hated my father so much. The lovers had been desperate enough to ask for his aid in making the magical portal that would allow Star Swimmer to go home. Grandfather had reluctantly agreed, to get rid of his daughter's unsuitable mate. Then I saw with a saddened heart how Mother had remained befuddled in her mind long after the Seal Man left, because in order to help him heal, she'd gifted him with much of her life's Qwakaiva.

As Chumco had promised, I had uncovered what they'd kept from me, and now it lay like a heavy weight upon my heart.

"Tasimu, are you ill?"

Startled, I sat up, blinking. "No, Amima."

"Well get up now. We'll be eating soon."

Dark circles rimmed Mother's eyes; she seemed tired herself. Grandfather too looked as if he'd had a restless night. He watched me eat my porridge with a single-minded intensity that made the hair on the back of my neck bristle in alarm. But he never said a word to me.

After breakfast, Ko sauntered off to his mother's shelter and Grandfather left soon after. Aunt Tuulah ate hurriedly then took Seicu and stalked off to visit other relatives. Then Mother went to visit with Shilshigua and Grandmother returned to the shelter for a nap. That left Samiqwas and me listlessly sitting by a dying fire with nothing to do.

I was considering rolling in my blanket for a nap, too, when Samiqwas poked me in the ribs. Startled, I opened my mouth to call him a bad name, then I saw Slylum and Matoqwa motioning for us to join them.

I scrambled to my feet. Samiqwas grinned and took off after our friends. "Be back later, Ami," I called as I hurried after the older boys.

"Where are we going?" Samiqwas was saying to Matoqwa as I caught up to them.

Matoqwa shrugged. "Who cares? Anywhere away from my mother's nagging will be fine with me."

Restless and bored, we wandered among the shelters of people we knew from home, joking and challenging each other to feats of strength. But when Cohasi tripped over a sleeping child who sat up crying, a woman shook her fist at us and told us to go away. Chastened, we apologized and moved on.

"You could have gotten everyone in trouble, clumsy moose," I said to Cohasi. "Watch where you put your feet from now on."

Cohasi's face darkened and he balled a fist. "You're the one that had better watch it, Little Rock Squirrel. You're the one who pushed me."

"Yeah, Little Rock Squirrel," Matoqwa echoed.

"Did not. You're just clumsy."

"So, now what?" Slylum said.

His face still red with anger, Cohasi growled, "Lets find some Convert boys and have some fun."

Matoqwa grinned and cracked his knuckles. "Sounds good to me."

Tigali shook his head. "No, too risky. The elders wouldn't like it."

"The elders wouldn't be mad if the convert boys started fighting us first. We'd be just defending ourselves, right?"

"Maybe.... Let's go to the gate instead and see if we can go out to pick berries or fish," Tigali suggested.

"Great idea. I want to get some fresh air more than I want to fight Convert brats," Samiqwas said.

"If they let us out we could rummage through the midden behind the fort," Slylum added.

"Also a good idea," Matoqwa said. "Those lazy Chamuqwani in the town probably throw out lots of neat things."

When we arrived at the gate, four soldiers were smoking and

lounging on the platform above it. The two dark-skinned ones
I recognized from the steamboat, but the other two men's dirty
uniforms had a different identification badge on their shoulders.
They were probably from the nearby fort. One was a short man
with greasy yellow hair; the older man, the one in charge, had
no hair on the top of his head, but a mass of curly grey and black
covering his chin.

When we approached, they glared down and asked us what
we wanted. Slylum held up a roll of nettle twine and a rusty nail
made into a fish hook. "Hey Sold'jah, I hungry," he said in the
Chamuqwani language. "You let us out. We go fishing. Maybe bring
one for you, eh?"

The older man in charge shook his head. "You brats get out o'
here."

"Nice fat one," Samiqwas wheedled. "You like? I good fishmans."

The yellow-haired one seemed to be considering my cousin's
offer, but one of Commander Mu'Dar's men growled, "No, get out o'
here!"

"You got candy, maybe?" I whined, deciding to join in the
bantering. "I very, very hungry. No like lumpy oatmeal."

Samiqwas made the praise call for my quick wits, then he started
to dance in a circle chanting and waving his hands. "Can-dy, candy." Eyes alight with mischief, all my friends followed him.

We were making quite a noise, attracting the attention of many
onlookers. Sensing excitement, other boys and girls hurried over to
join the fun. Finally the one in charge had had enough.

"Quiet!" he roared. "You brats go back to your shelters right
now."

"If you no got candy, maybe you got smoke, eh?" Matoqwa called
out boldly. "If we no can go fish, we want smoke."

Cohasi made a loud praise call for his older brother and began
chanting and dancing, but before many could take it up the soldier
shouted, "No fishing! No candy! No smoking mix! Damn you all, get
out of here or we'll put you in our jail. You brats want that, eh?"

We didn't, so we left laughing and punching each other on the
arms.

At that point Cohasi repeated his suggestion to walk among the
Converts' shelters. This time no one counselled against the plan. I
trailed along with them, because I could think of nothing better to
do.

Samiqwas noticed my brooding and needled me, "What's a matter, Little Rock Squirrel, are you sad because you didn't get candy?"

His teasing got everyone laughing. My face grew hot and I took a swing at him. I missed, which made them only laugh the harder.

Humiliated beyond reason, I stepped close and in a voice too low for the others to hear, I said, "Don't call me that baby name again or I'll make you sorry."

"Oh yeah, Little Rock Squirrel?" he said loud enough for the others to hear. He raised his fist. "What are you going to do, hit me?"

Before he could throw his punch I smiled in a mean way. "Have you forgotten what you heard last night? Go ahead and hit me—if you dare."

His skin turned the colour of bleached rawhide. He lowered his hand and stepped back. Horrified at what I'd just done, I stammered, "I-I'm sorry—I'd never—I'm sorry!"

Not understanding what we'd said to one another, Cohasi jeered, "What's a matter, Little Rock Squirrel, afraid to come with us?"

Suddenly I felt the breath choke in my throat. I couldn't just wander around this camp with the rest of the boys anymore. I needed to talk to someone who could understand what I was experiencing; I needed to find Grandfather.

"Do what you want, you're all Dog Farts! I'm going back to our shelter." I yelled.

"Run back to your Mother, Little Rock Squirrel," Matoqwa taunted. "She may need you to sew up a hole in your uncle's shirt."

Cohasi doubled over laughing and the others followed.

Hands trembling, stomach churning, I turned my back and fled.

Chapter Seven

When I arrived out of breath at our shelter, no one was there but my sleeping grandmother. I hung around digging furrows with a twig in the dirt, hoping Grandfather would return. When he didn't, I left to search for him.

"He's gone to the priest's tent with the elders to talk about conditions in the stockade," an old auntie said. I thanked her and left.

Feeling sorry for myself, I wasn't paying attention and bumped into someone carrying an armload of firewood. The woman let out a startled cry, dropping much of her load on the ground.

Am I doomed to do everything wrong today? "I'm sorry, I wasn't watching where I was going," I stammered. I picked up the wood, and offered, "Can I help?"

This stranger was a pretty young Qwani'Ya woman. She had a round belly, full breasts, and a kindly smile. "Thank you." She straightened, rubbing her back. Giving me another warm smile, she led the way to her family's shelter.

When I finished stacking her wood and turned to go, she stood by her fire with a tin cup and battered pot in hand. "Thank you again." Setting the pot at the edge of the fire, she held out the steaming cup to me. "It'll be so nice when my own children are old enough to help with chores." She patted her belly. "This one is my first, so I'll have to wait a few years yet. Please sit." She waved me to a place by the hearth.

"My Uncle Chumco will be back soon. He's a great Qwakaihi and I'm sure he would enjoy meeting such a nice boy as you."

Chumco! My stomach lurched. What have you done, foolish boy! Grandfather is going to be furious with you. "Thank you for offering tea, but I should go, my mother—"

"Please. I've already poured it." She proffered the cup again. "It would be a shame to waste it. Surely you aren't needed so soon?"

It's only tea. Don't be rude. Drink it, then go. Feeling suddenly daring, I crouched by her fire and took the cup. Its resinous heat felt good on my dry throat. "Thank you."

As I sipped my tea, an older woman with pox scars on her face and a boy of about three on her hip nodded as they passed into their shelter. A man, who might have been the younger one's husband, trailed a hand lovingly across her back and poured himself tea from the pot. He drank it in several quick gulps, then left again. A shy girl of about my own age peeped out from the shelter to study me when she thought I couldn't see her.

"I can tell by your accent that you must be from the Big Ice Lake," the young woman said. "I've never travelled so far up the river, but I've heard from my uncle that it's beautiful."

"It is," I agreed.

"Won't you tell me about it?"

"What would you like to know?" I drank more tea and felt the knot of unease in my gut untangle. Chumco's relatives seemed no different than other Qwani'Ya families. And it eased my heart to talk about my home.

When the young woman rose and excused herself, I was surprised to see Chumco crouching and drinking his own cup of tea just to the left of me. He pointed with his lips to the empty cup still in my hand. "Come inside the shelter so we can talk in private."

My surprise must have shown on my face, because he laughed softly and motioned once more for me to set down the cup. "You wanted to talk to me, didn't you?"

I put down the cup before I dropped it. I wasn't consciously aware of calling him, but I certainly had been searching for someone.

Well, why not? I put down the cup and followed him.

To my surprise, the shelter's dark interior was empty. I hadn't noticed the people leaving. Chumco built up the tiny fire, then sat cross-legged on a rush mat, motioning me to join him. I sat and looked down at my hands nervously twisting a fold of my dirty shirt in my lap.

When I stole a glance at him, Chumco was watching me with a slightly unfocused gaze. I knew that look meant he was seeing me with his Spirit-Sight. It made me nervous.

At last, he said, "Last night's conjuring only one of your special lineage could have attempted. Were you successful?"

Startled, my head snapped up and I stared him in the eye. "Didn't you see? Surely I didn't imagine everything."

He shook his head. "No you didn't imagine seeing me. Your dream was real, a true gift of power. But it was your Qwakaiva and yours alone that insured the success of your conjuring."

Recalling Mother's intimate dream about her lover, I felt my face heat. "Yes. I learned what I wanted." Maybe more than I wanted to know.

"Start from the beginning and tell me."

And, so I did—everything. I told him about the argument between my female relatives, and what I had discovered about my conception.

"Wounded and dying, the Seal warrior who was my father fled from another world to the lakeshore near our home. Alone on her moon-blood retreat, Mother found him and nursed him.

Star Swimmer was still weak, so they risked all and came to Grandfather for help. He was angry, but agreed. Mother wanted to go with her lover, but that wasn't possible. Together the Seal Man and Grandfather created a portal and the Seal escaped."

Chumco nodded gravely. "You did well. Your conjuring confirms much that I'd already suspected. Kunai has favoured you. Be grateful that such a wise and powerful benefactor has agreed to be your lifelong Spirit Companion."

Any Spirit emerging from the depths of the lake to claim a human for its Spirit Companion would be more curse than blessing...

Taking a deep breath, I said in a halting voice, "Is Kunai's favour truly a blessing? Grandfather doesn't think so. And," I had to finish, "this morning I threatened Samiqwas with my Qwakaiva when he used my baby-name in front of our friends. He was afraid of me. Am I turning into a Malicer because of my father's Qwakaiva and Kunai's protection? Will I hurt people whenever I'm angry?"

"Neither having your father's inheritance, nor having Kunai's regard, will turn you into a Malicer." He chuckled and shook his head. "What a crazy notion."

"People say—"

"Only the ignorant speak such nonsense."

"But—"

His expression stern, he held up a hand to stop me. "Your family and friends should learn to treat you with respect. You were right to be angry with your cousin, but you wouldn't have hurt him. Your sense of honour protected you from giving power to that evil—as I'm sure it always will. Your concern is commendable, but I have seen your Spirit. You're a good person, so be easy in your heart."

"What if—"

He dismissed my fears with a wave of his hand. "These insecurities will pass. The power you've inherited is like learning to hook a fish, shoot a bow, or any other skill. As you practise and learn to trust in your Qwakaiva and the Benefactor who guides you, your thoughts and feelings will sort themselves out. You'll know in your heart what is right for you to do with your Gift, and what isn't."

"But I may have hurt my mother with my meddling—"

"As for your mother, I don't believe you caused her any harm. You may have induced her to relive her time with her lover, but I suspect she allows herself to fall into that temptation quite often on her own. The argument with her mother probably helped trigger the memories the vision showed you."

He laughed and ran a hand through my hair. "Don't look so sad, young one. Untrained as you are, you still had the Qwakaiva to overcome your fear and insert yourself into her dream and move with her throughout the events of that wondrous time. That shows the great potential of your lineage, so be content."

Content. Easier said than practised. Knowing more about my elusive father made my longing for him all the stronger. So far from the Big Ice Lake, was I doomed never to see him again? My heart pounded within my chest. Grandfather would never help me, but Chumco.... "Can you summon my father?"

He shook his head. "No, I can't do that for you. And don't look so disappointed. I haven't a link to him, but you do. I can teach you how to summon him yourself—in time. I'll make you my apprentice. Would you like that, eh? I could begin teaching you while we wait, and we can continue your lessons as we travel south. Are you interested? Are you willing to assist me in return?"

Make me his apprentice? Had I actually found someone who would—and could—teach me? Then the icy water of reality dashed my growing excitement. "I'd like you to teach me, but my grandfather wouldn't permit it," I said. "He hates my father, I think. He doesn't want me to learn about him or his power."

"And yet, the Otter's Qwakaihi himself can't teach you. Isn't that so?"

I nodded reluctantly, my mind recalling all the times Grandfather had tried—and failed.

As if echoing my last thought, Chumco said, "Your grandfather is a wise and good man. I respect him, but I also think it's unfair of him to deny his gifted grandson the opportunity to learn how to use what the Unseen Ones have bequeathed, because of a personal grudge against his daughter's chosen mate."

I had to agree. I had a right to know and learn about my heritage. "You said a moment ago that you wanted my help in exchange for the teaching. What did you mean? What service can I possibly do for someone so powerful as you?"

Chumco visibly relaxed and smiled. "Do you remember in your dream if the Seal Man spoke of the 'mirroring of the worlds' and his war with those unnatural creatures who seek our destruction?"

I thought about it for a moment, then nodded. "I didn't understand much of what he told Mother— something about many worlds being linked— and what happened in one would be mirrored in the others."

"Yes, that's right. Oh the time lines aren't always the same, but the wickedness and devastation that succeeds in one will be felt in the others. Your father is a warrior who battles evil in all its guises, as am I. Would you like to join us?"

I smiled eagerly. If I agreed to his terms, I would be helping my father, and maybe saving everyone. "Oh yes, I want this more than anything. What must I do for you?"

He caressed my cheek with a possessive gesture. "Well, as to that, I must swim into the Great Kunai's cave to seek the answer. What I do know for certain is that your deed will benefit us all, my brave little warrior."

Dismissing thoughts of payment, I agreed to become his apprentice and sat in front of him as he bade me. To my surprise, Chumco untied the thong around my braid, and began combing out my long dark hair with a finely carved wooden comb. As he worked, he sang a low chant under his breath. I closed my eyes, leaning into the pleasure of his gentle hands. The song brought back memories of my babyhood, Mother sitting me on her lap, untangling my hair with a brush made of poplar twigs. I smiled, feeling relaxed and safe for the first time since the steamboat came north that summer.

"You like this, hmm? That's right, relax and don't be afraid, my beautiful Little Seal. You are safe with me now. In time I will teach you many wonderful things."

When my hair ran in a smooth shiny river down my back, he cut off and gathered small clumps of the longest strands, weaving them together into a thin, four-ply braid.

Startled out of my trance-like lethargy, I sat up, suddenly nervous again. Ever since my babyhood I'd been warned about people who practise harmful magic using someone's hair in their conjuring.

"Why did you do that?"

He ignored my question while he worked with his prize. Then he held out the braid again to show me. It was now woven together to form a circle. He smiled at my surprise, placed the loop over his two hands and stretched them apart. "Why did I do this? I needed some part of you to aid me with our secret communications."

When I stared in confusion he left the braided loop to hang on one arm, rose, and rummaged in a leather sack propped against the shelter's wall.

He returned a few moments later with a finely woven loop made of leather, plant fibres, and grey hair. Sitting in front of me, he handed me the string. "This one is now yours. That string is made from fibres of powerful plant medicines, and the rawhide is from my guardian-animal, the lynx." He pointed to a coil of grey wound about the ends of the cord to hold it together. "The hair is mine and will help you form a link to me when you have need."

Not harmful conjuring, then. Still puzzled, I took it and automatically looped it over my hands as if I was going to make a string figure to amuse Seicu.

"Yes, that's right. I see you already have guessed my meaning."

I looked down at my hands and felt my face heat. "Not really, I just couldn't think of anything else to do with such a loop, but make the string figures like running dog and the raven's nest—the ones every child knows."

"Ah, but that is exactly what we're going to do with our strings, my Little Seal. We're going to focus our Qwakaiva on the loop, twine our fingers in special patterns through the string, and create the symbols of power that will teach you." He chuckled at my expression and held up the loop he'd made of my hair.

"Don't you see? I may not speak to you often in person, that's true, but by creating symbols in the loop made from your hair, I can open a communication between us. I'll see you in the centre of the pattern, and you'll hear my voice in your mind or see me in your dreams."

He tangled his hand through the loop, twisting it expertly into a simple pattern of intermeshed diamonds. "This one is called the Seer's Pool. It is how we will communicate." Then he dissolved that one and created another, more complicated pattern. "And then, there is this one. Let me show you one of its uses."

Chumco pulled on one of the pattern's cords. I took a ragged breath and looked into his face, my heart pounding in my ears.

He let go the cord and the pleasurable sensation died. "Did you like that, my Little Seal?" Seeing my expression, he laughed softly. "Yes, I believe you did. Such a simple thing, a woven cord, a child's toy; who would suspect its many wonders, hmm? There is no barrier between us now, and if you're careful, your grandfather will be none the wiser."

I dropped my eyes to the loop I held, experimentally draping it over my hand in the familiar pattern known as the Aseutl's Teeth. I wanted a moment to gather my wits, and that pattern was one of the easiest I knew. "Will I be able to speak to you with the aid of this string, or another person, like my father?"

"Me, yes. But as to your father? Perhaps. If you concentrate on the tasks I'll give you, and your Spirit-Gift is strong, then you may be able to communicate with him. But don't expect too much at first. That skill will take time to master. It isn't easy to pass into the timeless world where the magical peoples dwell."

My face must have shown my disappointment, because he patted my arm. "Be patient, young one. You can't learn it all in one afternoon."

Be patient. A lump of unbearable sadness rose in my throat and I swallowed hard. "But, Elder, soon we'll be gone from our homeland. I may never be able to talk to him—tell him—I-I have to do it soon."

Chumco shook his head. "Our leaving can't be helped. But always remember, as your skill increases, you'll be able to pass through the barriers of place and time within the dream. You will find him."

"But how can you be so sure," I cried, feeling a little frantic.

"Trust me, you will. Now pay attention. Our time together grows short." He brought my focus back to the cord looped about my hands. "More important than a talk with your father right now, is how you and I will communicate.

For the rest of that afternoon I sat by the Qwakaihi's side, learning the figure of the Seer's Pool and practising how to focus my Qwakaiva into the patterns I created. People came and went from the shelter, but they were only a blur in my awareness. All my attention was focused on mastering this new skill.

I thought of my cousin, and in the Seer's Pool I watched him and Matoqwa throw mud balls at a group of Convert boys. I brought up an image of Mother's face, and saw her picking berries with Aunt Tuulah on the hill outside the fort, while the black soldier and his men guarded them. My heart sang for joy of it. I was learning—yes, my new teacher said so.

Chapter Eight

Since that first afternoon with Chumco, I'd made a point each day of finding a quiet spot to innocently—so I hoped others assumed—make string figures for my private amusement. More and more I longed for Chumco's comforting presence in my mind, but he was stern with me and wouldn't always answer my insistent pleas.

Once, when my pestering became too much, he sent a searing burst of pain through our link that left me shuddering and gulping for air. In the next moment, he soothed me again, but the lesson was taken to heart. In future I would be more respectful.

I comforted myself with the knowledge that, being a great Qwakaihi, like Grandfather, Chumco was busy. He had little time for an untrained boy. Though cautious during the day, I often sensed him coming to me in my dreams. I had no conscious memory of what we said or did, but on the morning after such an encounter, I felt listless and drained of energy.

Suddenly a fiery pain stung my forehead and Chumco's loop slipped from my hands. Thinking it was a bug of some kind I slapped at my face without looking round. The next time I felt the sting I was quicker. When I pulled my hand away from my neck, a small round mud ball rested in my palm.

Muttering a Chamuqwani curse, I sat up looking around for my adversary. All was quiet near our shelter; no one in the surrounding camps seemed to be paying me the slightest attention. My ears straining for any hint of movement, I felt around in the dirt by my knee and loosened a pebble from the soil.

Hearing a rustling off to my left behind our shelter, I threw my rock just as Samiqwas lifted his head and aimed his blow-reed. He laughed and we both slapped at our bodies as the missiles struck. "Why did you do that?"

"To get your attention," He smiled, but when I scowled, not wanting to joke with him, he came a little closer. "What's wrong with you these days, Tas?"

"Nothing's wrong with me. I don't know what you're talking about." I turned my back.

"Ever since the rapids you've been ... different. And lately, like a love-sick girl, you disappear to play with your cord." He pointed with his lips to the loop still dangling off my arm. "You don't want to go with me and our friends, and you don't even speak unless asked a direct question. Everyone is worried; don't lie to me. Are you sick? Or in love? Who is she?"

"No, there's no girl! And I'm not sick—I just want you to leave me alone." Fear goading my anger, I aimed a punch at his head. He laughed and sat down beside me.

"Don't be cross with me, please. You know I was only teasing." Suddenly shy, Samiqwas dropped his eyes, tracing patterns in the dirt with his blow-reed. "Tas, just because I know now that your father was a Seal Man doesn't change anything. You're still my relative—my friend. Is that why you're so...?" he broke off, words failing him, a flush colouring his face.

I took in a deep breath and let it out slowly. Deep down, perhaps there was a seed of truth in his words. I did worry how people would behave if they knew I was a Siyatli. My real reason was my apprenticeship, but Samiqwas's concern was a warning I needed to heed. Refusing to answer his question, I asked one of my own. "What did you want?"

Going against custom, he rudely stared at me, hoping I would say more, but I met and held his gaze and at last he dropped his eyes. Instead he pointed with his chin to the soldiers pacing along the platform above the outer wall.

"See that soldier with the big red nose?" Puzzled, I nodded. He smiled. "I bet he's recently won at their gambling games."

"So?" I snapped up his bait. "How do you know that?"

His smile widened, showing lots of teeth. "Easy. See how he's laughing and joking with the others? He's very proud of himself. He must have won—and a big pile, too."

"Who cares?"

All serious, Samiqwas clicked his tongue in reproof. "What, can't you find it in your heart to wish him well? Rejoice for him; be happy."

"Why should I be happy for that Chamuqwani? He has a warm bed, good food, and games to amuse himself, while I'm cold and hungry," I grumbled.

He clicked his tongue in sympathy, looking sad. "Poor, poor, Little Rock Squirrel, so very, very hungry. Do you think if we go to the gate and ask him he will give us candy to ease the pain in your belly? Won't that be nice, eh?"

He was baiting me, hoping to make me mad. I laughed instead, slapped him on the back and stood. I put away my loop, resigned. "Let's find our friends and try."

The rains held off for the most part, but the season was turning. On our guarded forays outside the stockade to gather wood and wild foods, we could see the willows and aspens along the creeks changing from green to gold. The days dragged on, and still we remained in the stockade while the soldiers and Lord Hiram's agents argued over which of the troops were going with us, how many supplies to send, and the route we should take through the mountains.

When I woke in the night to people coughing and the Converts chanting, I prayed the agents and soldiers would hurry and make up their minds, before the bad Plague-Spirits found one of my relatives.

Traditional and Convert alike, all were growing anxious to leave. Many didn't want to go to the new land, but the thought of trying to survive the winter in the stockade was unthinkable. Tempers were short. Mothers snapped at children, husbands and wives argued, and sometimes a shouting match between two or more men ignited into a fistfight without warning.

That's how both Ko and my uncle Tli ended up in chains again and spent several days in the soldiers' jail. It shames me now to admit it, but their prolonged stay was due in part to me.

Aunt Tuulah suspected her husband was drinking waskyja, but no one could figure out where or how he was getting it. The couple fought constantly and always about the same things: the dark-skinned soldier's interest in Aunt Tuulah, and Ko's spending his days at his brother's shelter instead of his own.

Gagayii's encampment was always noisy; many men gathered there, not just Ko. To pass the time, the men resorted to the Bone Game and other forms of gambling. It seemed harmless enough, because no one had anything much to lose. But sometimes when the priest was gone, off-duty soldiers joined the games.

"What does a ragged Qwani'Ya man have that could possibly interest a Chamuqwani soldier?" Grandmother muttered loud enough for her daughters to hear. "They have no furs to trade, no

131

fish, no meat, nothing, why would the soldiers bother visiting Gagayii's shelter? They aren't doing it because they like Ko and his brother. That's too fanciful to believe."

The next afternoon when Aunt Tuulah took Seicu to play with some cousins, Ko saw his chance and went off as usual. Not long after he left, Samiqwas ran back to tell Grandmother that the same off-duty soldiers were heading over to Gagayii's wife's shelter.

"Go find your Uncle Tli, my boy," Grandmother said. "Tell him it's important he come to see me right away."

"What are you planning?" Mother asked. "The trouble's between Tuulah and her man aren't Tli's worry. Shilshigua's family won't like Tli getting involved."

Grandmother folded her arms across her chest and glared. "I don't care what the woman's family likes or dislikes. Tli still has obligations to his mother-clan."

"I don't think this type of "obligation" is what our ancestors had in mind when they gave us that teaching. Maybe Tuulah should just go over there herself," Mother said.

"Maybe she should just give the man's things back to his mother and be done with it—but she won't—and we both know that, too, my girl."

Mother let out a long suffering sigh and added some spruce needles to the embers of the morning fire. "I wish you'd let them settle their own quarrels in their own way."

"And I wish you had more respect for your elders, instead of trying to tell me what to do." Grandmother turned to go in the shelter and saw Samiqwas standing as if frozen to the spot. "What are you waiting for? Go get your uncle."

Samiqwas jumped as if stung by a bee and raced off. Not long afterwards he returned with a worried and grumbling Uncle Tli. "What is it, Mother? My nephew says it's important."

"It is important. Ko has gone to his brother's wife's shelter again."

Tli snorted and folded his arms across his chest. "That's nothing new—hardly a reason to drag me away from my own family."

"We're your family too, or have you forgotten that? Don't you care about your sister's happiness and the wellbeing of your nephew and niece?"

Tli glanced at Samiqwas standing with downcast eyes by the fire and sighed. "I do care, and you don't have to always be reminding me about my obligations. What do you want me to do about Ko?"

A ghost of a self-satisfied smile curved the corners of Grandmother's lips. "I want you to go over there and find out what's really going on."

Tli laughed. "I don't have to barge in where I'm not wanted to know that. They're gambling."

"Ah, but why are Chamuqwani soldiers gambling with them, eh? Tell me that, my wise and all-knowing son, tell me that?"

"Soldiers?"

"It's true, Uncle," I said. "Samiqwas just came and told us he saw them heading to that encampment."

Tli fixed his stare on Samiqwas, who reluctantly nodded. "And it's not the first time," Grandmother continued. "Every time the priest and the elders are busy elsewhere they come."

Uncle Tli accepted a cup of spruce-needle tea and drank it slowly as he thought about his answer. When he'd finished he set down the cup and rose. "All right, I'll go. Your news is troubling enough to need investigating."

"Be careful," Mother called after him.

He grunted a reply and without looking at us walked off in the direction of Gagayii's wife's shelter.

Not wanting to be left in camp with the women while something exciting was brewing, I said, "Ami, let Samiqwas and me follow him, so we can bring you news quickly."

"You boys are staying right here, out of harm's way." Mother said. "Tli will tell us when he finds out what's going on."

Ignoring her, I begged, "But Ami, Uncle may not come back right away. First he'll want to go check on his wife and baby, and once he's at her shelter, Shilshigua or her mother might want him to stay with them. It could be tomorrow before he gets time to come tell you. Please?"

Grandmother thought about it for a moment, then waved us off in a shooing gesture. We left quickly before she changed her mind.

Giving Tli time to make it to Gagayii's and join the game, Samiqwas and I crept close to a ripped spot in the shelter's cover to watch and listen.

All the men were sitting in a circle, taking turns shaking a leather cup containing little square rocks with painted dots on their sides. The soldiers had stacks of small strips of paper laid out beside them with some Chamuqwani writing on them. When one of the Qwani'Ya men won the throw with the rocks, he received a mug of waskyja, poured out from a clay jug. When one of the soldiers won, the loser made his mark on a strip of the Chamuqwani paper the soldier held out to him.

At first Ko wasn't happy to see Tli crouching in the shelter behind the players, but when Tli made no outcry and only continued to watch the game, he finally lost interest in him, and went back to playing.

As the afternoon wore on, many of the men were getting very drunk. Ko and Gagayii were drinking, but they were also losing more than winning. They seemed almost sober in comparison.

"I think the soldiers are cheating," Samiqwas whispered, "but from out here I can't tell how they're managing it."

I nodded. "There's some kind of cheating going on, true enough. Whenever a Qwani'Ya man gets angry at how much he's losing and threatens to quit, he always wins the next throw and a cup of waskyja, which keeps him playing and quiet for a while longer."

Samiqwas frowned, worried. "What should we do?"

I shrugged and turned back to watch. "There's nothing we can do. It's up to Uncle now."

At last Tli grew tired of just watching the game. Deciding to play a round for himself, he took a place among the players. Grandmother hadn't said anything about him playing. The sharp scent of danger stung my nose; maybe Mother had been right. I wanted to warn Uncle Tli, but he was sitting across the circle from where Samiqwas and I hid. I didn't dare draw attention to myself by calling out to him.

When it was Uncle's turn, a Chamuqwani with a long scar across one cheek smiled and held out the leather cup to him. Tli took it and shook the cup, then tossed the rocks down on the blanket. He won, and the soldier poured out a large amount of the amber liquid into another cup and handed it to him. Tli took the cup, drank, and made a face at the taste. The soldier laughed, urging him to drink more.

Tli occasionally had a drink of the Chamuqwani fiery liquor with Jombonni or some of the other men at the trading post, but he rarely got drunk. He took another drink, draining the cup, and handed it back.

"Want to play again, me bucky?" the soldier asked.

"Depends. What else you got to trade besides waskyja?"

Startled, the scarred soldier glanced at his companions, then he asked, "What else you want?"

Tli thought about it for a moment, then pointed to a long, black-handled knife in a sheath at the man's hip. The soldier laughed. "Nah, we can't play for my knife—Commander's orders. You buckies aren't 'pose 'ta have weapons."

Tli smiled when this was translated for him by one of the men from downriver who spoke the Chamuqwani language better. "All right, we will play for the stack of papers there."

To my surprise, when the soldier heard that, he became angry. Tli sat quietly, just staring at him as if he was stupid and didn't understand much. I'd seen that look before when Uncle was doing some of his most cunning trading. He was up to something, but I couldn't figure out what.

When the man quieted, Tli asked, all innocent, "Is only piece paper, eh? I can use to make fire. Why you no want trade?"

"Because I don't. Now, do you want to play or not? You're holding up the game."

Still not willing to be rushed, Uncle held onto the cup and the little rocks. He turned to the man of mixed parentage who'd been translating. "What's written on these pieces of paper? What do I truly forfeit when I make my mark on one of them?"

The man shrugged. "Nothing much. The piece of paper says that when we get to the Preserve you will give this Chamuqwani some of the treaty money owing to you and your wife."

"Me and my wife, eh? Not my sister's or my mother's portion?"

The man shook his head. "It isn't the Chamuqwani custom. For them, the man rules his home, not his wife or his mother."

Gagayii belched and slapped Tli on the back. "It's a good system, eh, brother of my brother? In this new land there'll be no more bossy women to tell us what to do. A Chamuqwani man can even beat his wife and no one will care." Gagayii turned to the mixed-blood. "Isn't that true, cousin?"

The man nodded sagely and took a drink of his own waskyja. "Yes, it's true. No more bossy women. The Chamuqwani god says so."

"Are you Zaunks going to stop jabbering and play or what?" the scarred soldier growled.

"I'll play," Tli said. "If I win you give me that pouch." Tli pointed to a fine leather pouch that probably contained smoking mix hanging on the soldier's belt.

"All right. But to play for such a big prize we need some new dice." He reached out for the cup. Tli handed it over. The soldier took out the old set of rocks and put in another set that looked the same. As he handed them back, he said, "If you win I give you this fancy pouch here." He removed the pouch from his belt and laid it on the blanket. "And if I win, you put your mark on ten of these papers." He laid the stack of papers beside the pouch.

Tli shook his head and held up three fingers. The soldier laughed. They bargained for a time, finally settling on five. Over the soldier's protest, Tli picked up the cup and tipped the dice out onto his hand. He held them up one by one before tossing them back into the cup. When he finished, he smiled, displaying his teeth. "Dice no good. I want play with other ones."

The soldier's face grew red, and he gripped the handle of his knife. "Are you accusing me of cheating?"

"Why you so angry? I just like other rocks. Are you cheating?"

"No! of course not. You shut up or I'll—"

"Kill me?" Tli held up his empty hands for all to see. Then in Chamuqwani, he said, "Would kill unarmed man? Commander Mu'Dar or yellow-haired headman no like that, maybe. How you explain to priest what you do in here, eh?"

Tli turned to the men around him and resumed talking in our language. "Brothers, can't you see what these soldiers are doing? They are stealing from you. For a few drinks of waskyja you are selling away your children's birthright. Is that what you want?"

"What are you talking about, brother-in-law of my brother?" Gagayii shouted. "We play for only some of the Chamuqwani waskyja. If we lose we mark their paper; it is nothing."

"Get out," Ko cried. "You're spoiling everything!"

His voice dripping with contempt, Tli said, "It's nothing? Only paper? And what will you do in this new land when you hear your daughter cry, how will you sleep at night knowing you traded away the paper needed for food to feed your children? Will you care? Or will you just find another bottle, get drunk, and forget about them?"

"I'll hunt to feed them, of course, you stupid meddler. You needn't worry about my family," Ko shouted, his face now also red as a berry.

Tli looked at the soldiers and then at Ko, his expression pitying. "And what are you going to do if there's no game to hunt, or the soldiers won't give us weapons to hunt with?"

"Did my wife send you here to spy on me?" Ko demanded. "No one asked you to come here. Get out."

"You pitiful piece of dog shit, I knew it was a mistake when my sister married you. But you've a sweet way when you want something, don't you? What did you like more, my sister or the good trapping territory that came with the match?"

Ko and Gagayii got to their feet, Tli rose too. They squared off glaring at each other, crimson sparks shooting from their Spirit-Fires. I glanced at Samiqwas; his face was ashen, his eyes wide with fear. I wished Grandmother hadn't interfered; someone was going to get hurt, maybe killed. Probably Ko or Tli.

Soon everyone in the shelter was taking sides and yelling. To my surprise, the soldiers seemed as frightened as we were. Maybe not everyone guarding us was a part of their thievery.

"Now, boys, settle down. Everybody have a drink on us. Make peace and then we'll get back to the game," the scar-faced soldier shouted. I doubt if anyone heard him over the din.

I didn't see who threw the first punch, but the next thing I knew, Ko and Tli were rolling around on the ground pummelling each other. Most of the men, being half drunk, became angry and confused by the yelling. Many other fights broke out. The shelter rocked dangerously, threatening to tip over. Scar-Face and his friends cursed, trying to snatch up their waskyja and papers without getting their hands stepped on.

Adding to the uproar, Ko's mother and some of the nearby women in her lineage were screaming at the men to stop fighting and get out of their encampment. No longer trying to hide, Samiqwas and I rushed to the shelter's opening to look in. I heard a shout from up on the wall and looked up. There were more soldiers running along the walkway, heading for the stairs by the gate.

"The soldiers are coming," I shouted. Tli glanced round, and Gagayii hit him hard in the stomach. He doubled over, disappearing in the brawling mass of men.

Then we saw one of the soldiers inside cutting a slit in the shelter's back wall and forgot about my uncle. "They're getting away. We have to stop them!" Samiqwas shouted.

The first man through the hole I hit with a heavy piece of firewood, knocking him backwards into the fray. As Scar-Face climbed through another cut a little further away, my cousin leapt onto his back, pounding him with his fists and shouting for someone to come help. Dropping his jug of waskyja, the soldier whirled round and round cursing, trying to dislodge him.

In the confusion that followed, I snatched up as many of the fallen papers as I could gather before a soldier saw me and aimed a kick in my direction. By that time, the soldiers from the wall had arrived, the black soldier who watched my aunt among them. I shouted for Samiqwas to let Scar-Face go. My cousin jumped away. And as I'd hoped, before Scar-Face could go anywhere, two of the soldiers grabbed him.

"Take your hands off me," he roared.

"You weren't on duty," one of the newcomers growled. "What you doing here?"

"When I heard all the noise I come down to help, and some Zaunk brats attacked me."

"Here to help," another scoffed. "Not likely."

"Bugger your mother! I was."

I thought they were going to haul him away in chains like they were doing to the rest of the brawlers, but after more shouting his comrades believed him and let him go.

Fists balled at my side, I watched helplessly as Ko, Uncle Tli, and the rest of the gamblers were marched out of the gate. Ko's face was bloody, his expression sullen. Tli's eyes when he turned in my direction had the bitter, haunted look in them I'd seen on the steamboat, when he'd been kept for so long in chains. They were going to someplace bad, I could feel it. Standing beside me, Samiqwas was breathing heavily. When I stole a quick glance at his face, I saw tears glittering in the corners of his eyes.

After the gate closed behind our relatives, we slunk back to our shelter to make our report. Grandfather had returned, looking stern. Grandmother motioned with her chin for us to follow her into our tiny shelter. Once we were all crowded inside and away from curious onlookers, she demanded, "Tell us what's happened."

Between us, Samiqwas and I managed to stammer out an account of the afternoon's events. By the time we'd finished, Grandmother's face was dark with anger and my aunt had buried her face in her hands sobbing. When Mother pulled her into her embrace Tuulah began to cry all the harder.

Grandfather let out a long sigh and rose to his feet. "I'll talk to Tsanqwati; we'll find out what they plan to do to our men. They shouldn't be punished for these soldiers' trickery."

Grandmother snorted but kept her opinions about the soldiers' justice to herself. When he was gone, she listened to her daughter cry for a time, then snapped, "Stop that."

Startled, the sisters looked up.

"I warned you about that man a long time ago, Tuulah, but you refused to listen. Now I give you one choice. You get up now and pack his things and return them to his mother's lodge. If you want to pack your own and go live in the Chamuqwani fashion, that's up to you, but I won't have that man in my household any longer."

"No!" Mother cried. "Can't you see how upset she is? Surely this isn't the time—"

"It is precisely the time. Tuulah, make up your mind."

Undaunted, Mother said, "Such a big decision can wait a while, 'til everyone has calmed down. Think of the children. They love their father."

Her attention drawn to them, Grandmother glanced at the trembling Samiqwas, and Seicu, sucking her thumb and looking frightened. Her eyes softened for a moment, then her mouth thinned into its hard line again. "Better to have no father, than a father like that one."

Mother gaped, then her eyes flashed in anger. "That was a very cruel thing to say...."

"Don't talk to me like that, Qwadalah," Grandmother said. "I am still your mother; show some respect—"

"I will when you deserve it!"

I had rarely seen Mother like this, and I trembled to see her so.

"Stop it, both of you," Aunt Tuulah said. She opened the door flap and crawled outside.

"Where are you going?" Mother called after her.

"To pack Ko's belongings. Mother is right. I should have done this a long time ago."

"Tuulah, wait—think. We'll need a strong young man to take care of us when we get to the new place. We're no more than women, old people, and children without him. The Chamuqwani won't listen to us—or care for us. We need a hunter in our lodge."

Standing in the doorway Tuulah put her hands on her broad hips and glared. "Then maybe it's time you find a husband of your own. You're right; we will need a strong hunter, but why is it always my responsibility to find a man to provide for us? Always refusing suitors, grieving for your lost Seal Man. Maybe I would have returned Ko's things to his mother a long time ago if you hadn't been so selfish." Without waiting for a reply, Tuulah turned her back on her startled sister and walked away.

Staring at the closing door flap, Mother's face flushed. She opened and closed her mouth several times, but no words came out.

"Never mind her harsh words. They mean nothing," Grandmother said. "Da'wabin, Tli, and your father will take care of us in this new land if we need men to hunt and protect us."

Mother gave her a pitying look and followed her sister out of the shelter. "I doubt if it'll be quite that simple."

Chapter Nine

Grandmother wasn't the only mother-in-law displeased with her daughter's choice of a husband that day. Not long after the news of the arrests got around, Tli's wife and some of his in-laws showed up at our camp. Carrying her baby on her hip, Shilshigua looked unhappy and maybe a little frightened. The heavy features of her mother and aunties were flushed and angry.

"Meddling old moose cow, my daughter's husband has been taken to the fort and it's all your fault," Shilshigua's mother raged.

"My fault?" Grandmother cried. " How dare you accuse me—it was the soldiers who—"

"It was you, chattering crow, who sent him spying and gambling in the first place. What's wrong with you?" one of her auntie's cried.

"Tli is a good son, who has a responsibility to his own mother-lineage. I merely asked him for help his sister."

"His sister should keep her own marital difficulties to herself. Tli's main responsibility is to my daughter and her baby."

They hadn't brought back Tli's things, but Shilshigua's mother had a lot more to say about Grandmother's selfishness and meddling in the shouting match that followed.

When it was over and the intruders were gone, I huddled by the fire pit with my blanket over my head, feeling miserable, my stomach twisted in knots. I wished I knew where Samiqwas had gone. I was worried about him. But he had taken off with his little sister on his shoulders at the first sign of trouble.

Her mouth set into a stubborn line, Grandmother stalked into our shelter and hung a blanket over the entrance so she wouldn't be disturbed. Mother glared at the shelter, but made no move to go after her. At last she sighed and threw some spruce twigs onto the dying fire, in hopes the smoke would clear away the bad feelings hovering about our campsite.

One look at Grandfather's face when he returned at mealtime told me his news wasn't good. As we scooped out handfuls of thick porridge from the large tin can we were using as a cooking pot, he said in a voice drained of emotion. "The soldiers have whipped Tli and put him in jail with Ko and the others."

"Whipped him?" Mother gasped.

"The Chamuqwani are all devils," Grandmother muttered and lowered her head to continue eating.

"Why did they whip our men?" Mother asked.

"In this case, the men were drinking and fighting. They caused a disturbance. That's against Chamuqwani law, and so they were punished."

"What about the soldiers who gave them the waskyja and tricked them?" Aunt Tuulah wanted to know. "Were they whipped and thrown into the jail, too?"

Grandfather shook his head, his expression grim. "No, they weren't."

"Why not?" Samiqwas cried "They were there and brought the waskyja. Tasimu and I saw them!"

Grandfather sighed and rubbed a hand across his face. "We all know what you boys saw is true, but Scar-Face and his friends tell a different story."

"They're lying," I said.

"Yes, I'm sure they are," Grandfather said. "But there is no proof to say otherwise."

"And just how does this commander at the fort explain the waskyja?" Mother asked.

"The commander doesn't know, but he believes some of the women who have been allowed out to forage got a jug from one of the traders. They hid it in their clothing when the guards were distracted."

"That's stupid," Grandmother said. "What Qwani'Ya woman would conspire to get her husband drunk?"

Grandfather turned up his palms in a helpless gesture. "True enough, but the men at the fort don't see it that way. No argument Intercessor Raymonel or the elders offered swayed their decision."

"How long must they remain in the bad place?" Tuulah asked.

"The fort's commander isn't saying."

"What does Commander Mu'Dar say?" Mother asked.

"Nothing. In this place it is the yellow-haired one with one ear cut off who's in charge. The ones who are lying about their part in the matter are his soldiers. He chooses to believe them, not us."

"And just what do you plan to do about all this?" Grandmother said, glaring at her husband. "Your own son is in that terrible jail."

"And who caused him to be there?" Mother said. "You have no one to blame but yourself. Stop glaring or expecting Father to work miracles."

"You keep a respectful tongue in your head, my girl, or I'll—"

"Enough!" Grandfather said and emphasized his command with a flick of his power. The women fell silent, staring. "These accusations and angry feelings have got to stop! It won't help our relatives if we fight amongst ourselves. No one is to blame, and everyone is to blame. We must be of one mind, working together to resolve this."

A little calmer, but still angry, Grandmother repeated her earlier question, "What do you and the headman plan to do?"

Grandfather rubbed a hand across his face. When he dropped his hand to his side, I could see how exhausted he truly was. "Nothing more now. They've locked us in and won't open the gate again tonight. Tomorrow is a new day. We'll meet once more with the soldiers, and we'll find a way to resolve this."

He stood and held out a hand to Grandmother. "Come, my dear one, let's go to bed." She rose without a word and followed him into the shelter. The rest of us went to our beds not long after the old people were settled. I lay by the fire, wrapped in my blanket, and stared into its amber depths. Now that the sun abandoned the sky for longer periods of time, the nights were once more dark—and growing colder.

The Spirit-Lights snaked across the darkness in twisting patterns of green and violet. At the edge of my awareness I could hear the droning hum of their singing. I took a deep breath and closed my eyes, allowing my spirit to follow them away into the sky.

In my dreams, Chumco found me swimming among the stars and snagged my Spirit in a net of luminous fibre. I wanted to stay among the lights, but he forced me to come with him.

"The stockade is in turmoil over the arrests and your family's part in the incident. Tell me what you know about this."

I told him about Ko's drinking and Grandmother sending Uncle Tli to spy on the gambling games and what I'd witnessed. "Please save my uncle, Elder."

"Why do you need my help, young warrior, when you already have the means in your power to release your relative?"

"Me? I don't understand. How can I help?"

"You'd know exactly what I mean, if you would allow yourself to be guided by your Qwakaiva, instead of feeling sorry for yourself and your family."

"How can I rescue them? I'm no great Qwakaihi, like you!"

I was afraid for my uncle, angry with the soldiers for lying, and worst of all, I was heartbroken because Chumco wouldn't help.

"Be at peace, young one," he soothed. "Calm your mind and the answers will come, you're a smart one, I know you are. Trust me."

Still ensnared in his net, I tested the strands of my confinement, feeling ashamed and restless. Chumco loved and trusted me; why couldn't I trust myself? So many people were counting on me. Why couldn't I calm my fears and solve the riddle?

He was silent for a long time, thinking. At last he said, "This injustice is but another example of the enemy's power, another victory that will be mirrored in that other world where your father battles. Such a pity. I'll pray for his safety."

Even within the dream I felt the icy hand of dread close about my heart. "Isn't there anything we can do to help him?"

"We can help him best by defeating the enemy that threatens us in this world."

"How? I want to stop the Chamuqwani."

He smiled. "So young and yet you're so eager. Brave boy, there might be a way, but it will be dangerous."

"Tell me. I'm not afraid."

"Very well, I'll tell you the idea that has just now come to me. Because of my reputation, I can't approach the priest or the soldiers as openly as your grandfather, but perhaps I can do something in secret to defeat our enemy. I'll pray for our Benefactor's help. If Kunai favours me, I'll make the charm. You'll be my messenger. Would you like that, Little Seal?"

"Yes, I'll do anything to help you and my father."

He released me from his net. "Good. Then we shall see if we can snatch the victory from out the enemy's closing jaws."

I pressed him for details, but he refused to say more. "When I'm ready, I'll call you to me, little warrior. At that time, we'll test your courage, and you can discharge some of your debt to me."

Over my protests, Chumco sent my Spirit back into my body, plunging me into deep and dreamless sleep.

Chapter Ten

Grandfather's opinion that the situation would be quickly resolved the next day was too optimistic. The day passed with our relatives still in the soldiers' jail, in spite of endless hours of pleading and talk between our representatives and the men at the fort.

When word got out that the fight between Uncle Tli and Ko was the cause of the arrests, there was a lot of bad talk going round about our family. People gave us black looks as they walked by. After one name-calling incident ended with me and Samiqwas getting our noses bloodied, we sat around our cook fire looking glum. Our female relatives also spent most of the day by our fire, since they weren't welcome in the camps of our relatives and friends.

Just before the evening meal when there was still no word of the men's fate, Samiqwas whispered to me as we came back from the privy, "Do you think the dark-skinned soldier that's always watching Amima would help us get Uncle and my father free?"

I stared, nearly tripping over my own feet. "I don't know. Maybe. Do you want to ask him?" I glanced up at the platform surrounding the stockade. He was up there with a few of his men. As if his attention had been hooked by our words, he was staring down at our shelter. "I'll go with you, if you do."

Samiqwas shook his head, a flush heating his cheeks. "Not you. I need Amima."

Leaving me standing with my mouth hanging open, Samiqwas crossed to the fire and spoke to Aunt Tuulah in a low voice. To my surprise, she agreed. They waited until they saw the black soldier approach the gate, then she whispered for Mother to watch the porridge and they headed in that direction.

I started to slink off after them, but Mother stopped me. "One boy running off is enough. Someone needs to amuse Seicu while I cook."

"But, Amima, I need to tell him what I saw, too."

She pointed to the hearth. "Sit. You can tell your story later, if he believes them and can help us."

I sat, sulking, trying to ignore Seicu playing with a grass doll.

When she grew bored and began to fuss, I pulled out my loop of string without thinking, and started making string figures to amuse her.

I made the figure called the Raven's Nest, and then Sled Dog Running and a few others I thought she might like. Then, without consciously being aware of what my hands were doing, I formed the pattern of The Seer's Pool. An image of Aunt Tuulah and Samiqwas talking to the black soldier formed in the centre diamond almost immediately.

In my mind I heard Samiqwas say, "But I saw them! I was just outside the shelter, on my belly, looking under the cover. There were three soldiers inside, Scar-Face, the one with the big belly, and the one with black woolly hair on his face and one tooth missing. They had waskyja and a cup with small painted rocks in it. When a Qwani'Ya man won with the rocks, they gave him waskyja from the jug they'd brought."

"My son doesn't lie, soldier man. Can't you do something to get my brother out of jail?" Aunt Tuulah said.

The soldier's full lips twitched into a ghost of a smile, but there was no mirth in his eyes. Aunt Tuulah folded her arms over her breasts and waited. He studied her for a long moment, then finally he asked "Your brother? And what of your husband? I hear he is also in the jail at the fort. What of him? Can we keep him?"

Tuulah flushed, then her mouth thinned into an impatient line, and she tossed her braids back over her shoulder. "I have no husband."

The soldier raised an eyebrow, and she added, "I took his things back to his mother. I repeat; I have no husband. Now are you going to help us or not?"

"So, it is as easy as that among your people? A woman just makes up her mind and returns a man to his mother." He smiled, his eyes travelling over her body in the way I'd seen men and women do when they wanted to couple with someone. Tuulah recognized his look, too. She raised her fist as if to strike him.

All teasing forgotten, he sobered and put up a hand to stop her. "Your people's ways are so different from my own; but I shouldn't tease you at such a time." He glanced down at Samiqwas, who looked angry enough to kill at that moment himself. "Be easy with me as well, young warrior. I believe your story. I don't trust those men. My Commander would never have men like that in his troop. They deserve a flogging or worse, but without proof, Commander

Magoss is unlikely to believe us."

Tuulah threw up her hands in frustration. "But surely there must be something we can do, soldier man, to convince the fort commander!"

"Ma'leubwey."

"What?"

"My name, pretty Qwani'Ya woman, is Ma'leubwey. I give you permission to call me Sergeant Ma'leubwey instead of 'Soldier Man'. What shall I call you in return?"

"Don't change the subject. Will you help us or not?"

He sighed and gave her his smile again. "I too won't lie to you and promise to do what I can't. But I will promise to speak to my Commander tonight. I know him well enough to say that he will do what he can. This is the best I can offer you. I am sorry it isn't more."

Tuulah's shoulders sagged in defeat. "I am sorry too. Thank you."

As they turned to go, my aunt looked over her shoulder at him one last time. "My name is Tuulah." She turned and walked quickly away.

It was only me who saw his smile—or so I thought.

"Soldier like Amima." Seicu said.

I choked and dropped my string, staring at my little cousin as icy chills ran down my backbone. I'd been so intent on my conjuring, I'd forgotten about Seicu, sitting in my lap. I'd grown too complacent—gotten careless—and Chumco was going to be furious with me. I trembled at the thought of Grandfather discovering my lessons and forbidding my apprenticeship.

How much had she seen or heard while looking into the pool with me? Feigning nonchalance, I asked, "What Soldier Man?"

She pointed to the sagging loop on my hands. "Man in picture, silly Rock Squirrel."

I felt my cheeks heat, but fear choked back my angry reply. I smiled instead and bounced her on my lap. She giggled. "Why do you think he likes her? Did you hear him say so?"

Seicu shook her head. "I just see. What him say?"

"I don't know either. I just saw the picture, too."

Well, that was a relief. It was disconcerting enough that she'd seen anything, but if she told people that she'd not only seen pictures in my patterns but heard them talk as well, that would be my doom. But everyone saw a picture in the string figures; that was how the patterns came by their names. If she talked about my pictures, people would believe I was playing a harmless game and think nothing of it.

"More, want see more now!"

"No, I am too tired." Her face puckered up as if she were going to cry. "And I won't ever make the pictures for you again if you cry, or tell anybody, understand?"

She sniffed, but nodded. To distract her, I took her hand and stood. "Come, let's go meet them, I think I see them coming back now."

Chapter Eleven

Dawn mist hung low over the stockade when I sensed Chumco's presence in my dreaming mind. "It's time, little warrior. If you still want to help me defeat our enemy, then rise from your blankets and meet me by the privy."

"I'll come."

"That's good. I'm pleased with you. Hurry, I'm waiting."

Still ensnared within my dream, I watched as my physical-self threw my blanket about my shoulders and headed for the privy.

All was quiet in the stockade, most people's awareness not yet surfacing from the Lake of Dreams. No one called a greeting as I wove my way between the shelters. For those who were awake, I was just someone roused from sleep with a too-full bladder.

Chumco met me by the privy's privacy wall as I finished relieving myself. As he brushed by, he pressed a small leather-wrapped object into my hand. "Take that to the priest's big tent. Conceal it somewhere inside, in a place where the bag won't be discovered. Put it among his things, if you possibly can."

He closed my hand around the charm. "Go now and don't be afraid. My Spirit will be with you and protect you from harm."

I asked no questions; I just walked away as he disappeared behind the wall. Moving like a wraith through the sleeping stockade, I was hardly aware of my bare feet touching the cold ground. On the walkway above, the sentries dozed at their posts. People snored and coughed. A baby cried somewhere up by the gate.

At the priest's tent the morning fire had already been lit. A few sleepy Converts sat nearby, waiting for a pot of tea to boil. My footsteps faltered. "What should I do now?"

"Continue walking," Chumco said. "When the people around the fire can no longer see you, turn toward the wall and approach the priest's tent from behind."

With my blanket over my head and partially covering my face, no one recognized me or paid me any attention. I continued until I could no longer see them, then stepped past a group of snoring men, and squeezed behind a lean-to near the wall.

Still keeping close to the logs, I crept through the next encampment. But in the one closest to the priest's, a young boy popped his head out from under his mother's blankets and stared right at me. The green eyes grew round in his pale yellow face. I froze, as still as a rabbit scented by the dogs.

He opened his mouth, and I thought he would give me away for certain, but in the next moment his mother pulled him back under her blankets without looking in my direction. I moved hurriedly away when I heard his loud suckling at her breast.

At the rear of the priest's tent, I threw off my blanket and got down on my belly to peek under the canvas wall. The gossip around the stockade claimed that the priest and his women slept together in there, even though they weren't married or related. His Converts defended Intercessor Raymonel by saying that the priest and the Qwani'Ya man studying with him, named Praiser Jon, slept behind one partition and the Mercy Women slept behind the other.

Looking into the dim interior of the tent, I saw no one sleeping in either straw-stuffed mattress on my side of the partition. The colourless dark robe protruding from a basket standing at the end of one of the beds gave me no clue, either.

"Go inside, before you are discovered."

Crawling to the nearest stake I wiggled it back and forth till I could pull it from the ground. I worked on another, glancing up at the lightening sky. I would have to hurry; many people would be awake soon. I pulled the stake free, then slithered inside and stood, looking around. Was I in the priest's sleeping chamber or that of his women? I couldn't tell.

My instructions were to hide the bundle in a place where it wouldn't be discovered—at least for a time. But where would be a safe place? Surely not in the lidded basket containing clothes, nor would hiding it in the chest of holy objects I discovered be safe. And not in the boxes of hard-cake stacked by the bed. All these places would be examined frequently during daily use. Where then?

I was considering searching the other sleeping chamber, when I heard someone come into the tent's outer room. Fear hovered at the edge of my consciousness, waiting to strike. But my Spirit was still safely ensnared within Chumco's trance. I ignored its warning, allowing it to flow away like water falling from a seal's oily fur.

I crouched behind the stacked pile of food boxes at the foot of one of the beds, hoping the person would leave soon. My eyes darted about the dim chamber, sensing the urgency of the one who guided me.

Then, I heard the voices of more people coming into the tent. To my dismay, it didn't sound like they were going back outside any time soon. Before long someone might return to this place to collect something needed.

"What should I do?"

Anger and maybe a hint of desperation coloured the mental voice when he urged, "Master yourself. Keep looking."

I took a deep breath and allowed my unfocused eyes to play across the items in the dim enclosure. I would find that special place; I would be brave....

Then, my attention happened to fall upon a small rip in the mattress by my shoulder. I pried my trembling fingers into the hole ripping it wider. I withdrew the talisman from my shirt and stuffed it deep into the moss and straw ticking. When it was done, I crept to the place where I'd pulled up the stakes and slipped out.

A wave of relief washed over me as I retrieved my blanket and threw it about my head and shoulders.

"You've done well, my young warrior. Your father will be proud. I will leave you now, but I'll reward you for this later. You would like that, hmm?"

A smile curved my lips at the thought. "Yes, I would." I had completed my task and pleased him—now I need only return to my bed and wait. Fearing the child and his mother might be awake and notice me if I retraced my steps through their camp, I decided to go in the opposite direction.

I was just easing behind the next shelter's wall when a rough hand grabbed my blanket from behind and jerked me backwards so I nearly fell. "I saw you sneaking around back there, boy. You nasty little Zaunk, what did you steal?" My head whipped backwards as the hard-faced older Mercy Woman spun me round to face her. She repeated her question, shaking me by the shoulders.

I saw her angry grey eyes widen as she recognized me. "You again? I should have known." She tightened her grip. "Confess, what did you steal?"

I tried to pull away without hurting her, but she held on like a wolverine. Her loud voice was drawing the attention of the people by the fire and onlookers from the surrounding campsites.

"I'm no thief!"

"No thief? Then why were you sneaking around here so early in the morning?"

Why was I here; what explanation would she believe? Without giving myself time to think, I blurted out the first thing that came into my mouth. "I wanted to find Intercessor Raymonel. I've something to show him before he leaves for the fort. That's why I'm here early."

"That's a lie and you know it. You're just trying to talk your way out of a beating like all you Zaunk brats."

I had been taught to respect people older than me, but this bitter woman was beyond my tolerance. Putting some force behind my blow I pulled free of her grasp. "If you don't like Zaunks and think we are all thieves and bad, then why are you here among us? Why don't you go back to where you came from?"

My smart mouth earned me a hard slap across the face, but before she could do more damage, the priest hurried over to us with some of his followers trailing in his wake.

"Celibress Vonica, what are you doing?"

She hadn't been aware of his approach until he spoke. Looking as fierce as a cornered mountain cat, she whirled round to face him. "I caught this lying boy sneaking round. There are some pulled up stakes over there," She pointed to the back of the tent. "He says he came to show you something before you go to the fort, but of course he is lying. He came here to steal."

The priest and the people with him turned their attention on me. I should have cringed at the anger and, yes, even hatred I saw in some of the Converts' eyes, but I was so indignant by that time, there was no room in my heart for fear. I reached into a pouch at my waist and drew out some of the papers I'd taken from the soldiers during the fight in Gagayii's shelter. I held them out to him.

"The scar-faced soldiers and the others say they weren't in the stockade until after the fight started, but that isn't true. They were there—many times. Grandmother was worried and so she sent my uncle to see what her daughter's husband was doing each day. My brother-cousin and I followed him. We snuck around the back of the shelter and saw what happened inside.

"The soldiers brought the waskyja with them and these pieces of paper with Chamuqwani writing on them. When a man won at the gambling the soldiers gave him waskyja. When a man lost, the soldiers made him put his mark on these pieces of paper. I picked these up during the fight. I came here to show them to you, because maybe they are important."

Intercessor Raymonel took them from my outstretched hand. As he looked them over, his face reddened, but I didn't think he was angry with me. The Mercy Woman asked him something in Chamuqwani and she wasn't happy with his answer, because she gave me a sour look.

"Are the papers important?" I asked him hesitantly when he continued to ignore me and stare at them.

Startled, he looked up and nodded. "Yes." He tapped them against his other hand and turned to an older man standing by his side. "Jon, this is all the evidence we need to get those poor men released." Returning his attention to me, he asked, "Son, why didn't you bring these to me sooner?"

I hung my head in shame, wanting to cry. So it was as Chumco had told me. I'd had the power to free my uncle all along, but I hadn't been paying attention. Feeling sick at heart, I stammered, "I forgot about them—I wasn't sure what they were—I didn't know they were so important."

I had just learned a hard lesson. I had known they were important in some way, if not exactly how. But I had allowed my Qwakaiva and my reason to be clouded by my emotions, and my Uncle Tli had suffered for my negligence.

Uncle and the others were released later that morning. Grandfather went to Shilshigua's camp to treat his wounds. He reported back to us that Tli was all right, though bitter and angry for the injustice done to him.

Ko must have gotten the news of his divorce, because he never came round, so Grandmother was denied the pleasure of turning him away.

As for Scar-Face and the other soldiers involved, they were flogged after the priest threatened to report the yellow-haired commander to the Father Emperor. But the soldiers were allowed to keep the pieces of paper they'd tricked the men into signing.

We had been cooped up in this terrible place for too long. It was getting colder. People were sick, and this further example of injustice only added fuel to the flames of our resentment.

Part Three

Chapter One

"You will be leaving in four days." Just inside the stockade gate Sergeant Ma'leubwey stood with the fort's interpreter on a cart, the people assembling around him. "In preparation for our journey, the women will be issued leather, wool cloth, and blankets, so they can make the necessary clothing and foot gear."

"Praise the Djoven the Mighty and the Chamuqwani commander for this generous gift," a Convert man shouted.

The sergeant cleared his throat, his eyes fixed on the treetops showing just above the stockade wall. "You misunderstand," he finally said, "the cost of these supplies will be subtracted from the treaty money owed you."

"As if we wanted their money; as if we wanted to leave our land!" Samiqwas grumbled in a low voice beside me.

"So, we are expected to pay for our own removal," Uncle Tli shouted angrily "How very kind of you, Chamuqwani."

The soldier's mouth hardened, staring straight ahead. "I have my orders. The supplies will be arriving soon. Each man must line up. You will be required to place your mark in the ledger book to receive your family's allotment."

Glaring at everyone, Tli folded his arms across his chest. "I'm not marking any Chamuqwani paper."

"Please," Shilshigua murmured. "Think of our baby instead of your pride for once."

Tli's eyes dropped to the baby tucked into a side sling on her mother's hip. She smiled and held out a tiny hand to him. For just a moment his expression softened, then his mouth thinned into its habitual bitter line. He sighed and gave Shilshigua a stiff nod.

"What about the sick ones among us?" a downriver man cried. "My old mother and my youngest son are too ill to walk these hard mountain trails. Please, let those of us with ailing relatives build winter shelters and stay here until spring."

Sergeant Ma'leubwey shook his head when the interpreter finished translating. "That won't be permitted. The sick will be carried on sleds or pony drags until we come to a place where there are paths wide enough for carts to carry them."

The sergeant also told us that Commander Mu'Dar and his soldiers had been chosen to take us through the mountains and down the big river canyon leading south to the Chamuqwani lands. "Better him and his soldiers than that fool at the fort," Grandmother muttered.

Sneaking a look to the walkway where the sergeant and his guards now stood, Aunt Tuulah grunted her agreement

On the fourth day the sun rose in a haze of chalky light. In the midst of a lot of cursing and shouting, we were formed into a column and marched from the stockade. Like a big disjointed snake-monster, the line twisted and curved over the rocky path, leading to the Copper Falls Portage. Along with the Qwani'Ya people and the soldiers who were going, there were also many pack beasts loaded high with supplies. Several pony drags carrying the worst of the sick moved slowly just ahead of the rear guard.

A cold wind blew in off the lake, knifing through our clothing as we turned our faces southward and began to climb. Willow and aspen flamed golden along the first portion of the trail. As we neared the higher elevations, the scrub was replaced by taller spruce and firs.

I was surprised when I learned that Intercessor Raymonel, his Mercy Women, and the big tent were also coming with us. He and his Converts walked in a tight column just behind the leading soldiers. The priest and his followers sang hymns of thanksgiving to their god for the new land. They made a great noise, but behind their show of enthusiasm, tears glistened in the eyes of many.

The rest of us straggled in disorganized groups in their wake. Walking by Mother's side with a blanket pack of our belongings on my shoulders, I breathed in the crisp morning air. We were leaving, never to see this beautiful land again. That terrible knowledge grieved my heart, but in spite of that I was also relieved at being free of the stockade. Adding to my turmoil, I was dimly aware of Chumco's black rage, churning in the depths of my consciousness. The intensity of his emotion frightened me. I suspected he wasn't aware of our link, and I didn't dare draw his attention to that fact, but it fuelled the disharmony of my Spirit.

My grandparents walked together, but Grandmother seemed

barely aware of her husband and his steadying arm. She moved with her eyes focused straight ahead, her mouth set into a hard line. From time to time, Grandfather glanced at her as if worried by the muddy fog swirling through her Spirit-Fire. She ignored him, refusing to answer any of his questions.

Aunt Tuulah followed them, carrying more of our belongings on her strong back. Samiqwas held his sister's hand and lifted her onto his shoulders from time to time when there was a rough patch in the trail.

Throughout the morning I heard many people sobbing, men and women alike. Often a person would stop to touch a tree or sing a song of farewell to a mossy boulder.

Grieving with the rest, I leaned my face against a tall birch, its pealing papery bark rough under my cheek. Small tremors vibrated through the trunk from the feet of the people and animals passing by. The tree's consciousness was sluggish with the cold. Winter and the long sleep filled its thoughts.

"Goodbye," I whispered, "I will miss you." A leaf detached and fell atop my head like a tear.

Then, a sharp blow on the back of my leg brought me to my knees. A soldier with a riding whip in one hand and his thunder-weapon in the other glared down at me. "Keep moving," he growled.

I cried out, looking up bewildered. "I only want say goodbye," I tried to explain. He raised his whip once more . I staggered to my feet and hurried to catch up with my family.

As I resumed my place, I noticed other soldiers riding along the column, shouting curses and threatening us.

"You must keep moving," Sergeant Ma'leubwey said when he passed us. Then, catching sight of my aunt among the waiting people, he offered a further explanation, "We have a long way to go today. It would be very hard on the children and the old people if we're forced to make a cold night camp on the portage itself."

All day we climbed with the booming of the falls ringing in our ears. The way was steep and slippery in places from wind-blown spray. We continued on until nearly dark and at last made a rough camp in a small hollow just off the main trail.

Wind gusted through the trees, spilling droplets of moisture on the soldiers watering the horses and mules. Men cut saplings and hammered them into the ground. Over them they tied large canvas tarpaulins to act as temporary shelters. The women and children cooked the evening meal and did camp chores, while our men were set to digging a shallow privy trench.

Most of the soldiers did no work and stood around with their weapons drawn, watching everyone. In spite of our pledge, they didn't trust our men; no Qwani'Ya man was allowed out of camp to hunt.

Women and children could forage for food, however. So, after seeing to the comfort of my grandparents within one of the shelters, I joined Samiqwas and the older boys in making simple rabbit snares from nettle cordage and willow wands. We slipped past the soldiers and laid our snares along the game trails up and down the creek, hoping for some fresh meat for the evening meal.

Drawn to the sound of rough water, I walked upstream past the others and found a tumbling little patch of rapids. In a sheltered pool several black trout were swimming. By lying flat upon a fallen log and crawling slowly out over the pool, I was able to reach my hand into the cool water and catch hold of several fine, big fish. I flipped them to the bank before the others caught on to my tricks and headed for the bottom out of my reach.

Returning to the bank I killed the fish to stop their suffering. I thanked them for the gift of their lives, then I strung them on some nettle cord and headed back to camp. Samiqwas, Matoqwa, and Cohasi met me with some rabbits flung over their shoulders. When he saw my fish, Matoqwa gave me a curious look. Remembering the Seal that was my father, I felt my face heat and dropped my eyes.

He laughed. "Trust a Siyatli to find fish where none should be."

"They were swimming in a pool by the rapids," I stammered and pointed back over my shoulder.

Cohasi cocked his head, giving me a quizzical look. "So. Why are you explaining? I like black trout. Want to trade two for a rabbit?"

I hesitated, then detached two from my string. "Sure." The transaction completed, Samiqwas called for a race.

Before returning to my own fire, I shared my catch with others among the People. Giving in to a perverse impulse, I offered a nice fat black trout to Sergeant Ma'leubwey, which surprised him. I wasn't sure how I felt about his obvious interest in my aunt, but he was a good man, and I reasoned that it didn't hurt to have a friend among these enemy soldiers.

When I proudly displayed the last of my catch to Mother, she smiled at me. Splitting both rabbit and fish open, she laced them between sticks and propped them by the fire to roast.

Heavy fog rolled in after sunset. Lit by the blurred yellow light from our fires, the silhouettes of our guards, looming unexpectedly out of the gloom, reminded me of disembodied demons. I shivered in my blanket and drew its folds closer around me.

But in spite of the fresh meat, our meal that night was a sombre affair. No one felt like talking. We were all exhausted. Someone, maybe Samiqwas, was coughing. Seicu was fretful, barely eating. Mother put an arm about my shoulder and drew me closer. She gave me an encouraging smile. Tiny droplets of moisture clung to her hair. I nestled up against her without shame, feeling her solid warmth, and drowsed.

That was the last night of comfort I had for a long time.

Chapter Two

The air when we woke two days later was cold, tasting of snow. The soldiers hurried us onto the trail as early as possible. No one complained over much; we all knew the signs of a big storm coming.

When the snowfall began around midday, it was gentle and sporadic. Large soft flakes fell silent as feathers for a time, then they would stop, leaving the trail clear ahead of us.

Pausing to catch his breath after a particularly steep climb, Grandfather looked up at the iron-grey clouds hovering just above the treetops. "I don't think we will be able to make it to a sheltered camping spot in time."

Grandmother lowered her blanket from her head and looked up. "We should turn back, make camp by the spring where we rested earlier."

The shrubs around us had been recently browsed by a herd of elk. Their musk hung heavy in the air. Grandfather shook his head, still studying the sky. "No, I don't think so. The spring is too high and exposed. It doesn't have enough firewood for so many people. Better for us to keep moving."

She barked a mirthless laugh. "Keep moving and die in the coming blizzard."

Giving me a thin-lipped smile, Grandfather sighed. Grandmother was already walking along the trail, her blanket once more covering her head. Picking up his bundle, he hurried to catch up with her.

The soldiers pushed us mercilessly as the day wore on. Now that we had crossed the portage around the great falls, we were descending through the mountains in a series of winding game trails that mostly paralleled the course of the Copper River.

As the day darkened into afternoon, the wind blew harder. Then, the clouds suddenly let go of their burden in a blinding shower of white.

As I trudged beside Mother and Samiqwas, my feet and hands grew more chilled at each step. Wind moaned through the branches of the trees, and frost-demons laughed and threw stinging icy flakes in my face. Seicu was coughing and wanting to be carried.

Samiqwas tried, but stumbled often, lagging behind. Over the wind I could hear her plaintive cries.

Finally Mother and Aunt Tuulah stopped beside the trail, waving other blanketed travelers to pass on by, while they waited for Samiqwas to catch up. "Go on; your Grandmother may need you," Mother said to me. "I'll stay and help my sister."

I glanced up the trail where the shadowed figures of the old people, Uncle Tli, and his family were disappearing into the gloom. Snowy sleet stung my face. I turned away. Samiqwas drew near, staggering through the drifts, Seicu clinging to his back under their shared blanket.

I wanted to hurry after the rest, but a tendril of warning stabbed at my heart, cautioning against it. "Uncle Tli is with them. I'll stay with you," I shouted over the wind.

She gave me a curious look, but wasted no energy on arguing. When Samiqwas reached us, Aunt Tuulah took her shivering daughter in her arms, while Mother divided up Auntie's pack between herself, Samiqwas, and me.

All that took some time, and when we resumed walking there was no one in sight. The light was fading; blowing snow quickly obscured the trail. Mother took the lead, her walking stick cutting deep furrows into the growing drifts. "We have to hurry," she called. "Stay close or we will lose one another."

Frost-demons mocked her words with their laughter. Tiny pale beings with asymmetrical faces and hard green eyes, they danced atop skeletal branches drooping under icy coatings of white. "Where are you going?" they called to me, as I passed.

"Come to us. Rest a while. We know you are tired. Feel our kisses upon your cheeks. Stay and soon you will be warm and safe with us. We will love you forever."

I raised my face into the wind and shook my fist. "Go away. Leave me alone! Your words are lies, Go away!"

They howled, throwing stinging ice crystals into my eyes, so I had to close them. I stumbled over a hidden tree root and nearly fell. They laughed louder and threw more missiles.

"Nasty little human, we will teach you to be respectful."

"Bad boy, we know your secrets. We know," one said.

"So arrogant—bad, bad, but you can't hide what you are and what you've done from us,"another cried.

"In your heart, you are no different than us. We know."

"No! I'm not like you—go away—leave me alone!"

The gloom deepened; my feet and hands were numb. I focused my eyes on the hunched form of Mother right in front of me. I concentrated on putting one foot in front of the other. Something deep in my Spirit trembled. I wanted to outrun their terrible words.

The storm closed in around us. The wind howled through the trees. I could see no one on the path ahead of us. Had we missed their sign and now were lost? I wanted to use my new skills and call upon Grandfather for help.

Back at the stockade, if he'd paid any attention to me at all, he would have seen with his Spirit-Sight what I could no longer hide. Engrossed in my secret studies with Chumco, I'd welcomed his indifference—thought it a blessing, in fact. I'd constantly worried that I might do something that would alert him to my apprenticeship with a man he had warned me against. And for that same reason, I feared calling upon him, even though I craved his comforting presence in my mind.

Well, if I was afraid of Grandfather discovering my secret, then I should contact my teacher. Chumco could be gentle and loving when I pleased him, but his mood had been so unpredictable of late that I hesitated. Ever since the morning I'd put his charm in the priest's tent, his interest in me had waned. On the few occasions when he did allow me to communicate with him, he was impatient to end the contact, promising me more time, later. But as the storm and the darkness closed in about us, I realized I had little choice. My relatives and I would die without guidance.

Chumco must have sensed the urgency in my summons, because he answered without hesitation. "Your mother has missed the path," he told me when I had explained our situation.

"The camp is to the south and west in the next sheltered hollow. Tell her you will lead and I will send a Fetch to guide you.'"

Forcing my numbed feet to go faster, I caught up to Mother and pulled on her arm. "Amima," I shouted. "We're going the wrong way. We'll miss where the People have camped if we continue this way."

She stared at me dully, snowflakes coating her hair and eyelashes. When she didn't answer I begged, "Please, the Unseen Ones have shown me the way."

Aunt Tuulah and Samiqwas had reached us by then. "What's wrong?" Tuulah said. "We have to keep moving. It will be dark soon."

"My son says we're going the wrong way," Mother explained.

Cold and swaying with fatigue herself, Tuulah seemed to take a long time understanding her words. Finally she motioned for me to take the lead.

Feeling the weight of the responsibility placed on my shoulders, I stepped away from the women and turned in a circle with my eyes closed, reaching out with my Qwakaiva to touch the pulse of the land about us. Chumco had said the camp was south and west. When I felt a tug on my awareness I stopped and opened my eyes.

The camp was in that direction; I could feel it now. And as if to confirm my judgment, I saw the glowing form of a Spirit-Lynx slipping through the trees ahead of me.

"This way," I called and took off through the forest after the Fetch.

Heading south once more, we climbed up a steep slope, staying in the trees as much as possible. Under the sheltering branches of the firs, the snow hadn't had time to collect into deep drifts. The travelling was easier. Before we reached the top, the Fetch turned us westward and began an angling descent downward onto a new trail.

My mentor lending me strength, I felt neither the cold nor my fatigue, but behind me I sensed the women's exhaustion increasing. Their strength was nearly finished. Ahead of us the Fetch was moving swiftly along this new path. I could barely make out its glowing form in the deepening gloom.

The snow was nearly to my knees in places along this new trail, and without snowshoes the going was difficult. "Wait," I called to it in desperation. "We can't go so fast over this deep snow."

The Lynx turned, its glowing yellow eyes surveying us with a cold indifference. "You have the Qwakaiva to float atop the snow. Leave them and come."

"No! I can't do that. They're my kin."

The Lynx turned its back on me and walked down the trail, disappearing into the gloom. "Please hurry," I shouted over the wind.

I don't know how long we struggled through the storm. I had lost the Fetch, but now knew where the camp lay, so I continued to plod in that direction with head lowered against the wind. Unthinking, more than half frozen, I focused on putting one foot in front of the other and kept moving.

Somewhere in that nightmare of wind, snow, and biting cold, a dark form loomed out of the storm in front of me. I raised my eyes and saw it was a man leading a mule, heading up the trail towards us. As he reached us, I recognized Sergeant Ma'leubwey.

I stopped, the others coming up beside me. I heard Seicu whimpering, complaining of the cold. Aunt Tuulah pulled the blanket over her face, trying to soothe her. Over my aunt's feeble protests, Ma'leubwey took the child from her arms and climbed onto the mule. Reaching down a hand, he pulled Tuulah up behind him.

"The camp isn't far," he told the rest of us. "Walk behind the mule and the going will be easier. Stay close and you won't get lost."

The sergeant left us beside the first roaring fire we came to, once we reached shelter. Someone pushed a hot cup of spruce-needle tea into my hand. I sipped it gratefully and stretched my feet towards the fire. Seicu cried as her feet thawed. I knew how she felt; my own limbs ached with such a burning pain that it left me gasping.

Now that my mind was awakening from its plodding stupor, I wondered how many more of my people would be lost in the storm. Surely we weren't the only ones gone astray. I couldn't see much in the darkness and blowing snow. But I heard the sounds of axes chopping down saplings to make shelters for people to get out of the storm. I shivered as melting snow from the fire's heat ran down my chest. Where was the rest of my family? Were my grandparents and Uncle Tli safe?

I must have dozed off, for the next thing I remembered was jerking awake when someone laid a hand on my shoulder. I looked up; Mother and a bearded soldier were standing above me. She held out her hand. "Come, we must get under shelter before the storm gets worse."

I rose slowly, glancing across the fire. Samiqwas and Aunt Tuulah were gone. An old man and woman I didn't know were squatting in their place. All covered in snow, these new arrivals were shivering and holding out their hands to the blaze.

Confused, I hesitated and looked up at Mother. "Where—"

The soldier made an impatient gesture, motioning us to hurry. "Come quickly now. They're all right," Mother reassured me.

The soldier brought us to a shelter of saplings and spruce boughs, piled shoulder high with snow for insulation. He pulled aside a blanket stiff with ice. I heard a stranger shout, "No room. Go away."

Another voice, a woman by the sound, called out a name I didn't recognize, then began crying when she realized we weren't the person she was looking for. The soldier yelled at the people to shut up and motioned us inside.

After we crawled through the low doorway, the blanket was closed quickly. People grumbled, shifting their positions to make room for us. Inside the air was dark and moist, clammy against the bare skin of my forehead. It was still cold, but warmer than being out in the storm. As I squeezed in between Mother and the sobbing stranger, I whispered, "Amima, where is our family?"

"Don't worry. They're well. There just wasn't enough room in one shelter for all of us. Try to sleep now. There's nothing more we can do till the storm is over."

Listening to the wind howl outside our little nest, I knew she was right. I tucked my feet up for warmth and leaned my head against her.

When we were settled, Mother called out a polite greeting to the unseen occupants of the shelter, giving our use-names and where we were from. In spite of the initial resentment to our arrival, the people answered her with courtesy. There were four others already in this shelter, two women who were not related, an old man who was related to one, and a small child who constantly coughed.

While the storm lasted I huddled next to Mother and tried to forget about my cramped and numbing limbs. The snow outside fell thick and heavy, as silent as a stalking lynx one moment, then slamming against the branches of the shelter with a stinging fury the next time the wind gusted. Frost-demons danced and gibbered around the shelter, taunting me. I was afraid and dared not allow myself to sleep as my mother suggested, for fear my Spirit would wander away and never return to my body.

Some time during that long night my teacher checked on me. He was glad I was safe, but he offered me little comfort. His touch was impersonal, nearly as cold as the storm outside. Power radiated from his Spirit-Fire, making me tremble with excitement. He had gathered the Qwakaiva of the storm about him to work some great enchantment. I begged him to let me help him, but he silenced my pleas with a stinging command that left me gasping.

"Then will you let me share my Qwakaiva with you, so I can at least help in some small way?"

"There's no need for me to draw upon your power at this time. The storm will lend me all I need. Later you can help, my brave Little Seal. You'll need all your strength to survive this night."

And with that he was gone, leaving me with the mocking laughter of the frost-demons ringing in my head. "Bad boy, bad boy. Come, lend us your Qwakaiva. We won't refuse you. Come, give us your Spirit's Power. Dance with us, we will love you forever."

The storm continued on into the next day. I ate flat, dry hard-cake from Mother's pack and melted handfuls of snow in my mouth when thirsty. Mostly I dozed between Mother and the woman separated from her family.

Though desperately afraid for her husband and little girl, she was also sensible enough to know that there was no point in looking for them until the storm abated. I tried hard to ignore her quiet sobbing, all the same.

Mother soothed her as best she could. "Your family might be safe. The soldiers are pushing people into any dwelling that has room regardless of kinship. So don't give up hope."

I learned later from Mother that thanks to Sergeant Ma'leubwey, we were some of the lucky ones who knew where all our family members sheltered. The sergeant had collected Aunt Tuulah and her children and put them in with my grandparents, and Tli and his family too were safe.

As the light began to fade the next afternoon, the storm finally died. The ache of my full bladder nearly bending me in half, I stumbled from the snowy mound of our refuge. When I returned to the encampment, I wandered over to a cook fire where I found Mother and Aunt cutting up dry-fish and tossing it into a large tin can with oatmeal and snowmelt. My stomach rumbled at the thought of something warm to eat.

Around me in the camp I heard the joyous cries of reunion and the frantic calls of lost family members searching by each fire for some of their own relatives. Pausing to brush the last of the clinging snow from my garments, I glanced up into the night sky. My heart felt swollen with gratitude for our good fortune. I offered up my prayer of thanksgiving to the Unseen Ones for their blessing. We had been lucky—this time. Above me the green serpentine Spirit-Lights writhed across an indigo sky already dotted with the shining eyes of stars.

While the women brewed spruce tea and cooked, the soldiers came around counting people. A low wind rattled through the branches of the firs, its breath against my face promised a cold night to come. I prayed there be no more lives lost tonight.

When I first saw Grandmother she was so stiff from the cold that she could hardly walk. She leaned heavily on Grandfather's arm as he led her to the fire. When she was settled, she sipped her tea and studied me with penetrating black eyes.

Waiting until I began to squirm, wondering what I'd done to displease her, she finally said, "My eldest daughter tells me that you saved her and her children from being lost in the storm. Did you call upon your father again?"

Grandfather's head turned sharply in my direction, awaiting my answer. I shook my head and dropped my eyes, suddenly finding much to interest me in the collection of spruce needles at the bottom of my cup. The wind gusted up just then, but the cold chill that ran down my back wasn't of the wind's making.

Grandfather's curiosity was aroused. And Grandmother's eyes were still boring into me, demanding more than a shake of the head in answer. She wasn't going to let the matter drop, so I took a deep breath and looked her in the eye.

"No, Ami, I didn't call upon my father. As I told you before, he can't help me now."

"Then who did help you, if not your father, hmm?"

I needed to be very careful how I answered. Grandfather could detect my dissembling, if he were of a mind. Chumco had told me, and I truly believed, that Grandfather's hatred for my father was so strong that he would do all in his power to prevent me from gaining any form of knowledge that wasn't his to control.

"There were wandering ghosts in the storm. I begged one of them to help me, and it did. To spite the frost demons, maybe, because they were tormenting me."

Grandmother seemed disappointed, but satisfied with my answer. Grandfather gave me a searching look, unconvinced. To my relief he let the matter drop. I took in a deep breath and let it out slowly. I hated keeping secrets from him.

After we ate, Samiqwas and I helped Ko set up a branch and blanket lean-to. A blazing fire in front would help heat the shelter's interior for the night. The weather was clear and cold. As the evening lengthened, the camp settled into an uneasy silence. I huddled with the rest of my family on a bed of spruce boughs and tried to sleep. We would have to be up before dawn. The soldiers wanted us to get an early start.

Chapter Three

Next morning the soldiers pressed us to hurry, allowing time only for a meal of their hard-cakes and tea, before urging us onto the trail. We had to leave these exposed lands behind. If real winter caught us in the high mountains, many more would die than the few lost in the blizzard.

During that day, and those that followed, I fell into a mind-numbing lethargy in which I had energy only to lift one foot after the other. Keeping my eyes closed to mere slits against the glare, I tried not to slip in the icy mud, praying I wouldn't fall down the bank into the growling river below us.

The weather grew warmer the further south we travelled, but there were still frequent autumn storms. The only difference was that instead of snow we had mud and bone-chilling rain to torment us. And the days were growing shorter, slowing our progress as well.

When it became clear to everyone that Aunt Tuulah had indeed divorced her husband, she began to receive the attentions of other unmarried men, including Sergeant Ma'leubwey. The sergeant rode alongside my aunt as often as he dared. When none of his superior officers were about, he would even take a turn at carrying Seicu to give my aunt a rest.

It was during such a time that I overheard him telling Tuulah how worried Commander Mu'Dar and his officers were. "With the growing number of sick ones among your people, plus the bad weather, all of this is slowing our progress much more than we expected."

Grandmother openly scowled her disapproval the moment the soldier joined us. Overhearing them, she complained, "It's a little late to worry now, isn't it? Your commander should have left us alone to winter in our homes—and protected us from those miners—instead of thinking only of the yellow rocks. Then none of this would be happening, would it?"

The sergeant had been carrying Seicu, Tuulah walking at his stirrup. Looking into my aunt's eyes he had ignored the rest of us after his initial greeting. I watched his mouth harden as he translated her words in his mind.

"My commander, like the rest of us, is one of the Father Emperor's soldiers. It isn't the duty of a soldier to question when he is given an order from a man carrying the Emperor's seal."

"So you obey without question or complaint, no matter how unjust the order, hmm?"

Aunt Tuulah shot her an exasperated look. "Mother, please."

"I speak only the truth, and this man knows it."

Tuulah stared at her mother's rigid back for a time, then sighed and held out her hands for her daughter. "Here, give her to me now. I'm rested. I can carry her. You had better go before someone comes looking for you."

"I only do what is my duty."

"I know. Mother is cold and hungry. Pay no attention to her."

Ma'leubwey leaned from the saddle to place the blanketed Seicu in her mother's arms. Seicu whimpered, calling out his name. Ma'leubwey said something soothing to her in his own language and brushed damp hair off her forehead. Tuulah fastened her daughter in the side-sling and balanced her upon a hip, then resumed walking. Ma'leubwey straightened. Without looking at any of us, he said, "I'll check back later. If the doctor has any medicine left, I'll bring some for her when I come back."

"That would be good. Thank you."

After he was out of hearing, Grandmother stopped on the trail and turned to Tuulah. "Must both my daughters show their wilfulness by choosing unsuitable mates for their beds? That soldier is an enemy. You had a good husband. Why do you bother with that Chamuqwani, Tuulah?"

Tuulah flushed, opening and closing her mouth several times before she could speak. When she finally found her voice, the words came out in an angry rush. "Wasn't it you who always told me I made a bad mistake in choosing Ko for the father of my children? And wasn't it you who recently told me that either Ko left, or I would be cast out, too?"

"Yes, I said those words, but that was before you began making such a fool of yourself in front of everyone. I would rather have a drunk for a son-in-law than that soldier. Have you no ears to hear what people are saying about you, about our family?"

"I don't care about what people say—"

"You should care—"

"Well, I don't. I'm not doing anything wrong."

"If you don't care for yourself, think about your children!"

Mother stepped between them. "Stop it!"

"Be quiet. I'm just stating the truth."

"I don't want to marry anybody," Tuulah cried. "So why are we arguing?"

"If you don't want Ko back under your blanket, there are plenty of good Qwani'Ya men in this column from whom to choose a new husband. You have no need to encourage that soldier."

My aunt didn't answer. Seicu began coughing, demanding her total attention. When the little girl dropped back into a fitful doze, Grandmother repeated her last remark. Tuulah said in a voice so filled with despair that I feared she too was becoming ill, "Leave me alone, Mother. I have no strength to argue with you. I'm not encouraging anyone. I've no time for suitors—of any kind. I only want to take care of my children."

"Mothers and sisters, husbands and wives, we all are saying cruel and bitter words to one another," Mother cried, wiping a hand across her eyes. "So many deaths—sickness—and what about our hurt and lonely children? Are all our Qwani'Ya people going insane?"

She might have said more, but Grandfather interjected his calming presence at that point, drawing Grandmother away.

We had been stopped for some time; people behind us had come up and stayed to listen. A sizeable gap was opening up between us and the rest of the column. As I began walking again, I glanced behind me. Samiqwas walked stiff-backed, facing straight ahead, acting as if he had heard nothing, but the colours of grief, fear, and yes, anger, writhed within his Spirit-Fire

Too exhausted to do more than eat, sleep, and walk, I hadn't felt much like talking and had accepted Samiqwas's long silences as a normal part of our harsh journey. Now I wasn't so sure he was right in his mind. Though Ko's family was never far from ours, Ko made no attempt to speak to us, or come to our fire of an evening to see his children.

Hearing Samiqwas coughing, I dropped back to walk beside him. "You sound like a seal out on the lake. I thought it was me who had a seal for a relative, not you," I said, hoping to make him smile.

He wiped his nose on his sleeve and stared, at first not comprehending my attempt at a joke. Finally his mouth curved into a faint smile. "But I do have a seal for a relative," he teased in return. "You."

We shared a laugh and I knew he felt a bit better.

Chapter Four

As the days passed while we made our slow progress down the Copper River canyon, I grew to hate the taste of the soldiers' rock-hard cakes. The cakes were filling when held in the mouth and softened by spit, but they were as tasteless as chalk, leaving the body craving something more substantial. But the soldiers kept us moving with few rest breaks during the day; there was no time to set snares or forage for more satisfying and nourishing food.

Commander Mu'Dar and his men ate no differently than the rest of us. I can't fault them for adding to our suffering on that account, and yet we weren't used to such fare and more sickened because of it.

Mother and I were fortunate in maintaining our health. We suffered only the constant hunger and fatigue plaguing Qwani'Ya and soldier alike. But Seicu's cough worsened, and that had everyone worried.

"Stupid soldiers! Don't they realize that people need better food to eat?" Aunt Tuulah complained as she hoisted her feverish daughter onto her hip.

"Father, isn't there anything you can do for her?" Mother begged as she settled her blanket pack onto her shoulders.

Grandfather looked up from scooping dirt over the fire we'd made to boil tea at our rest break. "I'll look for medicine herbs along the path as we travel this afternoon," he said.

Grandfather seemed helpless against a sickness that caused coughing so severe it brought upon bloody vomiting. If a person's Qwakaiva wasn't strong enough to defeat the disease on his own, the sickness progressed to a fever and diarrhea that left the person too weak to travel without help. Death usually occurred soon after that. And with Seicu and Samiqwas coughing, the fear of death in our family haunted all of our thoughts.

"What are you looking for? Maybe I can help." I said.

"To be honest, Grandson, I'm not sure." He brushed a hand across his haggard face and picked up his own pack. "This sickness is so powerful. The soldiers give me no time to search, and it's so late in the season, I don't know what plant I need to find. I just pray to all the Green Ones for their help. Hopefully one will speak to me if it has the Qwakaiva I need."

Most everyone had a touch of the coughing sickness, including many of the soldiers. But as Grandmother pointed out, "The soldiers may be getting sick, but none of them are dying like our Qwani'Ya people are."

Other relatives whispered that there was a darker reason for the sickness and misfortune stalking the column. "Fires that flare up without warning, burning anyone close, pack beasts going lame overnight, strange accidents, unexplained injuries, what else could it be but a Malicer's sorcery?" an old auntie confided to us one evening.

"No one's immune," Tuulah agreed, "The soldiers, too, are having their share of misfortune."

The auntie nodded solemnly. "Even if they say they don't believe in such things they can still be harmed."

Malicious sorcery. I tormented myself by day, worrying about my family's safety. At night, though, I was so exhausted from carrying my heavy pack I could hardly keep my eyes open long enough to finish my portion of the evening meal. I slept badly. My dreams were haunted by scenes of blood and killing.

I often woke to people coughing, tearful cries of mourning, the sounds of chanting and malice being conjured in the shadows. Nearly too afraid to breathe for fear the stalking evil spectres would notice me, I would lie shivering in my blanket, unable to sleep. Then, I'd sense Grandfather's Qwakaiva enveloping me. His whispered song in my mind would banish my terror and I would be lulled at last into sleep.

Like Grandfather, the priest was tireless in his efforts to aid the sick. He would care for both Traditional and Convert alike. I grew to admire him and believed he wasn't aware of the conjuring being done in the name of his god. That was one of the reasons his injury was so upsetting to me.

Grandfather and I were visiting the soldiers' camp when the tragedy occurred. We'd come to see if Supply Master would give us grease to make a salve for Grandmother's swollen joints. While Grandfather talked, I happened to look around and saw Intercessor Raymonel in conversation with Commander Mu'Dar and a few of his officers. Sergeant Ma'leubwey was also among them.

I was surprised and a little curious to see the priest without his usual entourage of Converts. I moved a little away from Grandfather, hoping to learn what had brought him alone to the soldiers. Their expressions were sombre, but I couldn't hear what the men were saying. Between us were several soldiers talking and joking while they groomed the horses and mules.

Further across the clearing, off-duty soldiers sat about small fires cooking their own measures of the evening's rations. They were talking to one another—sometimes loudly—thus adding to the distraction. It was growing dark, but still light enough to see quite clearly; nothing was out of the ordinary, and yet....

I was edging a little closer, when Grandfather called me. "Supply Master has no fat he'll give us. We'd better return to our fire."

We were nearly at the edge of the soldiers' clearing, when some unexplained premonition caused me to stop and turn. Intercessor Raymonel had just finished his conversation and had started walking back to his own tent. But instead of taking the long way round, as we had, he cut straight across the area where the soldiers were working.

Suddenly one of the mules broke away from the man grooming it and charged the priest. Lost in thought, the priest didn't notice his danger until someone shouted. By that time the crazed animal was nearly on top of him.

He flung up his arm to protect his face. The mule let out a loud bray as if terrified by something only it could see. Then, it reared. One hoof struck his upraised arm while the other slammed into his chest, knocking him to the ground. Shocked into immobility, no one stopped the beast as it disappeared into the brush.

In the next instant, pandemonium broke loose. Men shouted and other mules began kicking and braying wildly. Coming to my senses at last, I saw Grandfather running back across the clearing, heedless of his own safety. When I caught up to him, panting like a sled dog, he was kneeling beside the fallen man.

The young priest lay in a crumpled heap, groaning with pain. Removing the blanket from about his shoulders, Grandfather laid it on the ground and gently eased the man onto it, straightening his limbs.

The priest cried out as the old man touched his arm, jerking it away. Grandfather retrieved the arm and eased it down at the priest's side. With skilled movements the Otter's Qwakaihi next allowed his hands to travel over the priest's body checking for other injuries, all the while keeping up a low-voiced conversation with his patient.

The air about us tingled with power. I stared down at the priest wondering if he could sense how Grandfather was helping him. I decided after watching for a time that he probably couldn't. Maybe it was the pain that dulled his awareness or maybe it was as Grandmother claimed, and all Chamuqwani were too wilful and ignorant to see what was all about them.

There was mud on the priest's face and a growing stain of red on his blue robe. I noticed he had lost the amulet of his god's power. The silver thunderbolt was gone from around his neck. It was odd that it should have fallen off, I remember thinking. I knew the priest would want it, so I began searching the ground around him, hoping to find it for him.

I finally spied it half-buried in a pile of fresh dung, the chain broken, the pendant twisted nearly beyond recognition. I wiped it off on some dead leaves and tried to mould it back into its former shape.

To my surprise the metal wasn't soft and malleable as I had assumed. The pendant was made of hard silver and wouldn't yield to my efforts to bend it. I stared at the twisted remains. Could a mule stepping on this have distorted its shape so violently? Maybe, but I wasn't convinced of it. Some great power had done this, and it made me afraid just to think about it.

Unsure whether to return the pendant or drop it back in the mud, I walked over to Grandfather, still holding it in my hand. Though obviously in pain, the priest seemed lucid. With my Spirit-Sight I saw the flare of Grandfather's Qwakaiva as he helped his patient. I was very proud at that moment. Grandfather seemed so knowledgeable and self-assured. I hoped someday when I had completed my lessons with Chumco, I would be a great Qwakaihi just like Grandfather.

"How badly is he hurt?"

Sergeant Ma'leubwey, Commander Mu'Dar, and two other soldiers were standing over us. It had been the sergeant who had spoken to us in our language, acting as translator.

"He has two cracked ribs and some bad bruising on his abdomen, which may mean he bleeds inside," Grandfather said without looking up.

"I've made a mess of myself haven't I, Commander?" Intercessor Raymonel said, speaking in Chamuqwani directly to the officer.

"Stupid of me to be so careless around animals, wasn't it?" He tried to laugh, but the sound ended in a groan.

Grandfather laid a hand on his forehead, brushing back the priest's hair, checking for head injuries. "Lie still, Intercessor, while I finish my exam. You aren't to blame for what just happened. The mule—"

"Bespelled, possessed?" he grimaced, finishing the thought. "Don't look so startled; I've heard the talk. But I can't believe in such primitive foolishness. I was merely careless...."

"I don't believe in such nonsense, either, but you are not to blame for this accident, Intercessor," Commander Mu'Dar said. "The elder is right about that, at least. It's my soldier's fault, and he'll be whipped for his carelessness."

"No, please. There's no need—"

Cutting in on their conversation, Grandfather said, "This isn't important now. We need to bring him to a safe place where his injuries can be treated."

Commander Mu'Dar shouted an order and men were sent to bring a litter of canvas and poles to carry the priest away. In the distance I could hear many people shouting the news of the accident and I felt a knot of unease tangle in my gut. I glanced at Grandfather's face and caught his eye. He nodded slightly as if reading my mind. Yes, there was going to be more trouble over this; he feared it too.

The men had arrived by then with their litter of poles. He turned from me to caution the sergeant. "Tell them to be careful when they lift him. His arm is broken, too. He will need—"

"Don't touch him, you devil's spawn!" a woman shrieked. "Get away from the Holy Intercessor."

Racing towards us across the muddy ground came the older Mercy Woman. Wild-eyed and tangle-haired, the woman had lost her veil somewhere during her flight. Her face bleached white with anger, she shouted something else I didn't catch and held up the lightning-bolt pendant about her neck. The pack of grim-faced Converts trotting at her heels were furious as well. They glared at Grandfather and me as if this were our fault.

Breathing hard as she reached us, the Mercy Woman still had enough breath to spit out her bile. "Commander, keep that Malicer away."

Commander Mu'Dar's dark features moulded themselves into a stony mask. "Nonsense, Celibress. You're merely distraught. The

Intercessor was struck down by a runaway mule. The elder here was merely trying to help."

"Help, bah! He is an evil sorcerer. I tell you—"

"Celibress Vonica, please," the priest said in a weak voice, silencing the shouting combatants. "I'm all right. And you know as well as I do that there's no such thing as sorcery. Help me up."

"Have a care," Grandfather said. "Take the litter. Your injuries are serious. Your ribs, there may be bleeding...."

The commander motioned for his men to bring the litter and place the protesting man upon it. "Go rest, Intercessor. I'll send the regiment's doctor to set your arm and have a look at your injuries."

As we turned to go, I suddenly remembered the pendant I still held. In the confusion, I quickly handed it to the sergeant. He seemed puzzled at first by what I'd given him, then his eyes widened as he recognized what it was.

"I found it in the mud," I murmured, then raced after Grandfather.

The old man was silent as we walked back to our fire. Intercessor Raymonel's injuries were no accident. When I'd held the pendant, I'd felt such hatred behind the intent to cause harm, it made me shudder with fear for all of us. Unable to keep silent any longer, I quickened my pace and took his hand. "Ati, I'm frightened—you felt it, didn't you?"

He sighed and squeezed my hand. "Yes, I felt the conjuring, unfortunately not soon enough to deflect it."

"Does someone truly want to kill the priest?"

"It would seem so."

"But why, who would want to do such a thing?"

"I don't know, but I intend to find out."

I would have liked to ask him more, but by then we had reached our camp, and the women were bursting with their own questions.

Chapter Five

Next morning the priest's injuries were the talk of the entire column. Everyone had an opinion as to what had actually happened. The converts no longer sang as they marched. Tension grew among the various factions of the Qwani'Ya people. Accusations of sorcery were hurled back and forth by both Convert and Traditional alike. Everyone was afraid, never knowing who would be struck down next. Fights were a common occurrence each evening. The soldiers had their hands full keeping the peace.

In spite of his injuries, Intercessor Raymonel tried at first to go on with his usual routine of preaching and caring for the sick, but his wounds refused to heal. He developed a fever, which worsened as the days went on. Many begged him to rest and look after his own health, but he ignored them. Finally Commander Mu'Dar ordered him to be confined to a pony-drag litter for the march each day.

Within his blankets, he looked like a big baby in its cradleboard. I was sorry to see him so weak. Speaking low enough so no one else could hear, I asked Grandfather, "If his god is as 'mighty' as he and the Converts claim, how could something so bad have happened to him?"

"That's a good question, but one I can't answer."

"Is he going to die?"

Grandfather glanced at the loudly chanting Converts, and a frown creased his brow. "I have no way of telling that, Grandson. Only the Unseen Ones know a man's fate." He unfocused his eyes and I knew he was studying the priest with his Spirit-Sight. Turning away at last he seemed troubled by what he'd observed.

I focused my own Spirit-Sight on the sick man, but I was too inexperienced to detect what he'd discovered. "Can you help him?"

He shook his head. "I don't know, but there is such a wall of mistrust grown up between us that I doubt if the Converts, or the priest himself, would accept my help—even if I offered."

Grandfather rubbed a hand across his face and it suddenly occurred to me that he was an old man. This long journey and the needs of our Qwani'Ya people were taking their toll on his strength.

His powerful hunter's body was growing gaunt and bent with the burden of age and worry he carried.

Swallowing down my fear that he too might die, I placed my hand in his once more. He looked down at me, his smile forced. "Don't trouble yourself, my dear one, all will be well."

That night we camped in a sheltered hollow by a stand of aspens, their golden leaves aflame in the dying light. While the women made a fire and brought out rations for the evening meal, Samiqwas and I collected leather buckets from Supply Master and hurried to the creek for water. The evening was clear for once, the sky bright with stars and a silver crescent moon.

I raced Samiqwas to keep warm. Dead leaves crackled under my feet. Grey clouds of breath puffing away from my mouth, I pushed myself, hoping to leave the worries of my relatives behind. We filled our buckets quickly. But after several days of mist and rain, the night was so beautiful; I had no wish to return so soon to the encampment.

Lowering my head I placed my hands with fingers spread atop my head, snorted, then challenged my cousin to a mock battle. I was a deer, a young buck deer, with a rack of new-grown horns atop my head, kicking up my hooves, glad to be alive. Samiqwas sat down his own bucket and joined in my play,

An older girl shouted at us to stop fooling around. Others needed the buckets to bring water to their families. Still grinning and stomping, we picked up the buckets and headed back to our fire. It had been fun to play like we used to, even for such a short time.

When we came near the encampment, I saw Ko and several Qwani'Ya men I didn't know digging the privy trench. A bored soldier with his thunder-weapon held in the crook of one arm stood nearby supervising the work. Ko tossed a shovel of dirt out of the hole, then stopped to wipe sweat from his forehead. In the dim light I couldn't see his face, but his shrunken Spirit-Fire displayed his fatigue.

Samiqwas had seen his father, too, but he gave no sign of it. He would have walked on by without a second look, but I stopped him. "Those men look thirsty. Bring them a drink."

When he hesitated, I said, "I'll hurry on with my water so the women can begin the porridge. I'll tell them the soldier made you bring him and his men water if you are worried about Grandmother finding out that you were talking to your father."

Samiqwas blinked rapidly a few times then nodded and walked towards his father, who was still watching us.

When I got back to the fire Mother took the bucket and poured its contents into the big tin can we used as a pot and set it atop stones within the fire. Aunt Tuulah glanced up from rocking a fretful Seicu.

"Where is my son?"

I sat beside her and held out my hands for the little girl. "I can take her. Samiqwas will be along soon. He is doing an errand for the soldiers."

A couple elders were visiting; Grandmother was occupied and not paying attention to my news. Tuulah accepted my explanation without comment, handed Seicu to me, and rose.

With the women's low-voiced talk in the back of my mind, I focused my attention on my sick little cousin. She seemed to have lost more weight since last I'd held her. Nestled in my arms, Seicu felt as light as wild goose down, and as hot as a rock heated in the fire. Her breath was a phlegmy wheeze, and her eyes were glassy and unnaturally bright. When she coughed, her whole body shook, leaving her gasping and breathless.

The night about us was so filled with life: the waxing moon, the twisting fires of the Spirit-Lights, the distant howl of a wolf, the scent of rutting elk on the wind, so much life, so much beauty. My heart felt as if it would burst from my chest and shatter on the flinty ground. I wanted to suck up all the Qwakaiva of the night and pour it all into her tiny, feverish body.

"Hello, Little Bird, how is my baby feeling tonight?"

"I not baby."

"No, no, you're right. You aren't a baby. I'm the baby, right?"

"Little Rock Squirrel."

I forced myself to smile through my tears. "That's right; I'm your Little Rock Squirrel. Want to play with me?"

There was another bout of coughing, a long hesitation, then she whispered, "Yes."

"Shall we play hunter and sled doggie, or maybe fish in the net?"

She laughed weakly. "Silly Rock Squirrel. I too tired. Want see pictures."

"Pictures? I don't understand. Let's play another game."

"You know," she insisted. "Want magic pictures with the string."

"No, I can't make the pictures now. Maybe later."

"I want see pictures in string. Now." Seicu's last pronouncement had been quite loud and very clear. She'd promised not to tell, but she was so ill.

It took a moment for my refusal to penetrate her fevered brain, but when she understood, she screwed up her face as if she was going to cry. I glanced up to see if anyone was watching. When it appeared that no one was, I let out the breath I hadn't realized I'd been holding.

"All right, I'll make the pictures. Don't cry," I whispered.

"Yes. Show me."

Arranging the folds of my blanket as best I could to hide what I was doing, I drew out my string and held it out between us. Then I laced it through my fingers to form the diamond patterns of The Seer's Pool. "What picture do you want, hmm?"

"I want go home."

Home ...

My heart gave a lurch; that would be an easy request to fulfill. My own Spirit longed to return to those happy times as well. With little effort, my mind formed a picture of our village in the centre diamond. I saw once more the long green lake tucked among the ice-capped peaks of the Aseutl's Teeth Mountains. Seicu and I walked along the shore, eating long sticks of striped candy from the trading post and tossing flat stones into the water to watch them hop. She giggled at the antics of an otter sliding down a muddy patch of bank at Hot Springs Creek, and laughed when his mate stole his fish and they played a game of tag.

"What are you and Seicu laughing about, Tas?" Samiqwas asked as he sat down next to me. Startled, my hands jerked, the string figure falling slack and slipping off my fingers.

As I looked up, I gazed directly into Grandfather's face. Hastily I looked away. Oh, Ancestors protect me!

I swallowed hard and answered my cousin with a forced note of cheerfulness. "I was just amusing Seicu by making string figures while we waited for you to come play with us."

Now that the pictures had disappeared, Seicu wasn't happy. Her cough returning, she was ready to have a tantrum. Quickly drawing her attention to her brother, I bounced her up and down on my knee. "Look, Seicu, Brother is back and wants to play with us."

"Make pictures for brother, too, Little Rock Squirrel."

Hastily I bent over her and whispered, "Shh. You promised, remember?"

"Want—"

"No, I can't. Brother doesn't have the right kind of Qwakaiva to see them. The pictures are only for you and me. Now be still."

I was saved further explanations when Mother announced that the porridge was done, and Aunt Tuulah came to take Seicu.

I sat between Samiqwas and Grandfather, trying to act like nothing was wrong, but each mouthful of the gluey mass I swallowed lay like a rock in my protesting stomach. He said never a word to me, only sat calmly eating his porridge, but I felt his presence looming over me.

By the time I finished, my gut was twisted in knots. I excused myself and headed for the privy, feeling as if all that I had eaten would force its way up again. I had to get away from the fire, out of Grandfather's sight.

In the shadows, I leaned my brow against the smooth bark of an aspen and tried to compose myself. Chumco had warned me and I'd disobeyed him. But surely making pictures to cheer up my sick cousin wasn't a bad thing? Why was it so terrible if Grandfather learned of my apprenticeship? He wasn't a petty man. Surely he would be happy if I'd found another Qwakaihi with gifts similar to my own who could teach me.

I hated keeping secrets from him. But Chumco had sworn to stop teaching me if I told anyone, and I desperately wanted to learn all I could from him. He'd promised to show me how to communicate with my father.

All these disturbing thoughts were bumping around in my head, making it hurt. I was tired and it was getting cold standing out here without my blanket. I needed to sleep. Pushing myself off the tree, I headed back to my family's campfire.

Wrapped up in my own childish fears, I'd failed to sense the mounting tension in the encampment that night. Hearing the strident tones of Celibress Vonica's voice among the angry people coming my way, I hung back waiting for them to pass. To my horror, they seemed to be heading towards my family's hearth.

Chapter Six

Keeping to the shadows, I raced ahead to give my family a warning. Aunt Tuulah and her children were already in their blankets in the lean-to when I ran up. Only the old people and Mother still sat around the embers of the fire.

"Ati, the priest's mean woman is coming," I gasped, "and the people with her are angry."

Grandmother gave me a sharp look, her black eyes boring into my skull. "Angry? Why would they be coming here, foolish boy?"

My teeth chattering, I shook my head. "I don't know."

"Perhaps they want your help, Father," Mother suggested.

We could all hear them now, praying to their god to protect them, as they purged the camp of evil.

"No, my dear, " Grandfather said quietly. "I don't think so."

Handing me my bedding, Mother said, "Tasimu, go lie down in the lean-to. This doesn't concern you."

I needed no further urging. I slipped into the shelter and lay down, pulling the blankets over me. Once settled I peered out from under a fold of the covering. I was shivering.

"What's going on?" Samiqwas whispered from the darkness. Both he and Aunt Tuulah were awake now, lying stiff and silent in their blankets.

"I don't know. Some angry Converts are coming," I whispered.

Grandfather stood and added more sticks to the dying fire, as the group stopped just inside its light. Giving no indication that anything was amiss, he turned to face them. "Welcome, friends, will you be seated by our fire and have some tea? It will take but a moment to reheat."

Celibress Vonica held up Djoven's amulet like a shield. "Devil, evil sorcerer, I want none of your poisonous brew."

"Then, why are you here?" Grandmother said, rising to stand beside her husband. "It grows late and we need our rest."

"We have come to tell you, Malicer," said a mixed-blood, brandishing a heavy stick of firewood like a club, "that we know of your evil. If Intercessor Raymonel dies because of your foul conjuring, I swear, by Mighty Djoven, you'll die, too." The rest of the angry Converts chorused an agreement to back up his threat.

The noisy group had attracted the attention of others who weren't asleep. The crowd surrounding our fire was growing.

Aunt Tuulah tucked the blanket she'd been sharing with Seicu tightly around her daughter and stood. In a low voice that only Samiqwas and I heard, she said, "When no one is looking, one of you boys sneak out and go find the sergeant or some other soldier that can speak our language. Tell him to come before there is bad trouble."

"I'll go, Amima," Samiqwas said.

"Good. But don't let anyone see you." Then without a backward glance, she walked out to join her parents and sister.

"My father would never harm anyone!" As fierce as a mountain cat, Mother faced the Mercy Woman with eyes blazing. "Who has been looking after the priest and caring for his wounds—you? How dare you accuse my father of anything!"

Trembling with indignation, Mother pointed, and said, "Look at her hands; they are filthy. Does she ever wash them before she goes among the sick? Everyone knows that dirt can conceal a sickness. Did you people give up your good sense when you converted?"

"You foul-tongued liar, don't you dare talk about a holy Mercy Woman like that," a woman wearing a headscarf shouted. "One more word and I'll come over there and give you the sound beating you deserve."

"Beating, is it?" Grandmother said. "Since when does a Qwani'Ya person try to beat another into respect? That is the Chamuqwani way, and a foul practice at that. Have you no shame?"

Grandmother's words seemed to embarrass some of the people. Many dropped their eyes under the onslaught of my female relatives' ire.

Into the stunned silence that followed, Grandfather said, "As many among the People will tell you, I am a Man of Power, a Qwakaihi. I'll not deny it." His voice grew harsh as if barely controlling a deeply felt emotion. "But what I will also tell you, and swear it, by the blood of my ancestors—and Qwa'osi the Otter from whom I claim my power—I have never, and will never, use my Qwakaiva to harm anyone."

"So you say, Malicer," someone in the shadows cried, "but I saw you and that nasty boy by the Intercessor when he was attacked. I say it is you who sent the devil to harm him. And again this afternoon, I saw you staring at his fevered body, mumbling your wicked death chants. We saw. We know. You can't escape our punishment!"

"I repeat. I've done no conjuring to harm anyone."

"Then how do you explain this," Celibress Vonica said. Holding out her hand to the firelight, she unwrapped a piece of cloth and displayed a tiny leather object. "Praiser Jon found this tucked into a slit in the Intercessor's mattress. He explained the symbols' meaning to me."

She held it out towards Grandfather. "Come closer. Take a good look, then tell me it isn't a charm to work great evil."

"I've no need to examine it closer. I can sense its malice from here. You're correct about its purpose, but you're wrong about who made it. I neither made the charm nor placed it."

Until that moment, I'd nearly forgotten about the talisman. But I recognized the leather bag all too well. Chumco had given it to me and directed me to place it within the priest's tent while we were still back at the stockade. He'd never explained what was actually inside the charm. I knew only that by delivering it I was helping him, and also my father's struggle, against our common enemy.

No! It was impossible. The charm couldn't be what they claimed! My teacher was a great Qwakaihi, a warrior against evil! He would never.... Did I really know that? What if I had caused the priest's misfortune, and maybe others' sickness and injuries as well? What had I really done when I put that charm in the priest's tent? And now, these crazy people had come here to hurt Grandfather—blaming him—but it was me they really wanted.

Me!

I trembled like an aspen leaf in the wind. I wasn't a bad boy; I wasn't evil. They were lying about the charm; they had to be! Chumco could explain everything. But no matter the truth about the bag, I couldn't let my Grandfather be blamed for something that I had done. I had to confess, before someone was hurt. Teeth chattering from fear, not the cold, I put aside my blankets and crawled from the lean-to.

"L-leave Grandfather alone. He d-didn't do anything bad. I—"

"Celibress Vonica, what is the meaning of this?"

The voice of the unknown speaker from the shadows hadn't been loud, but something in its timbre captured everyone's attention.

The Mercy Woman gasped and turned to face the man dressed

in a dirty blue robe who staggered into the firelight, supporting himself with a sturdy walking stick.

"Intercessor Raymonel! You should be resting."

The priest swayed, leaning heavily on his stick. When one of his followers offered to help him, he waved the man away with the arm tucked into its sling. The gesture made him grimace, but he gritted his teeth against the pain, refusing to cry out.

"Maybe I should be abed." He glanced around, taking in Grandfather's calm expression, the defiant postures of the women standing shoulder to shoulder with the old man, and the Converts' angry faces. "But so should all you good people. We have a long day's march ahead of us tomorrow. We all need our rest. Go back to your shelters now and get some sleep."

"But Intercessor, we've found the evil one who has cursed you and so many others," someone shouted. "We're here to make him pay for his crimes, so he won't cause any more sickness among us."

There was murmured agreement to that statement. The priest held up his hand for silence. "Curses and evil sorcery?" Intercessor Raymonel shook his head as if he was very disappointed with them. "That's superstitious nonsense. I've told you many times before, Djoven the Mighty One will protect us. You must set aside your primitive ways and have faith in His justice."

"Show him the charm found in his mattress, Mercy," someone cried.

"Charm? Let me see this so-called evil charm then," the priest said, holding out his good hand for it. Reluctantly, Celibress Vonica showed him the leather pouch she was holding. To gasps of horror he picked it up and examined it. After taking a long look he turned to Grandfather, and asked, "This pouch, should I assume that it was designed to make the ignorant believe it has power to do harm?"

"To do harm is its purpose, yes."

"But my father didn't make such a thing," Mother said angrily. "He would never use his Qwakaiva in such a terrible way."

"I agree, daughter," the priest said and tossed the bag into the flames.

Mother stiffened, then her eyes opened wide, as the bag burst into blue flame. She stared like the rest of us at the incinerating charm.

"Now, let there be an end to this foolishness," the priest said into the awed silence. "Go back to your beds and leave these good people alone."

"But, you were injured, and now you're ill. Someone among these devil worshipers, has caused—"

Raising his voice to drown out the rest of the Mercy Woman's words, he said, "Whether I am ill or in good health is up to Djoven. Celibress, I am very disappointed in you—all of you. I have given myself and my life into His keeping. I am His devoted servant and no idiotic jabbering of spells and witchery will harm me; I truly believe that." He fixed his followers with an angry stare. "Where is your faith, your acceptance of His will? All the time I've been among you haven't you learned anything? Celibress, how could you encourage this violence?"

Seicu coughed several times, then began to cry for her mother.

Her voice catching on a sob, Tuulah said, "If my father had the power over this sickness that you people claim, do you think he would harm those in his own family?" She headed for the lean-to. "My daughter is very ill. Go away. Your noise has awakened her."

"I'm sorry for that. I will pray for her."

Suddenly drained of energy, the priest stumbled and would have fallen if a burly Convert hadn't steadied him.

"You heard the Intercessor," a stern voice said. Commander Mu'Dar stepped into the light, a cluster of armed men fanning out around him. "Go to your fires and your beds. Any more disturbances like this one, and you will be punished severely."

"There will be no more trouble, Commander," Intercessor Raymonel assured him. "Isn't that right, Celibress? Praiser Jon?"

"Yes, Intercessor."

Chapter Seven

Within the realm of Dreams, Chumco's Spirit-Body had as much substance as did his physical one. I smelled the scents of smoky leather, tree resin, and lynx musk that always clung to him. Laying my face against the smooth skin of his chest, I allowed his ghostly arms to enfold me and hug me close. His lips were a feathery caress upon my hair as he spoke, "Tell me what has happened."

I knew without asking what he meant. And so I told him about the Converts, the Mercy Woman's accusations, and how Intercessor Raymonel had stopped them from doing us harm.

"The Converts found the bag you gave me to put in the priest's tent. They said it was meant to do evil. Grandfather agreed with them. Is that true? Am I bad for putting it there?"

Chumco sighed and stroked my hair to calm me. "Sometimes, my Little Seal, I despair of you learning anything. Good, evil, haven't I told you countless times, that such concepts vary with a difference of perception? What may appear good and noble when seen from within the backwater pool in which we swim today, may turn out to be something entirely different when viewed from an eddy further down the river of time. There are no absolutes in the universe, only ambiguities."

An echo of the frost-demons' mocking laughter tormenting me, I pressed, "Did you know what the charm would do before I placed it among his things?"

"Not exactly. I knew only that the power placed in the bag by our Spirit's Companion Kunai would teach a lesson. How the lesson was taught was unimportant to me."

"But what type of lesson was so significant that people must die to learn it?"

His voice hardening, he spat, "The lesson is to teach you, and those deluded Qwani'Ya converts who have forsaken their ancestors, that Chamuqwani power isn't as great as the priest and those other chattering gulls, the Father Emperor's men, would have you believe. We have power, too. If you remember nothing else of what I teach you in the years to come, remember that. The

Chamuqwani aren't omnipotent or invincible. You can fight against them and win."

"But—"

"No more talk. I've allowed you to question my actions enough for one night. Can't you hear the Spirit-Lights singing to you? Let us dance with them, and renew our strength." Giving me no time to protest, Chumco pulled my Spirit from my sleeping body and we were away.

Shape-shifting into the Spirit form that gave me power, I soared high on leathery wings, my tail whipping out like a banner behind me. Gliding on the Spirit-Lights' fiery currents, I swooped and dove, my mentor laughing at my antics. Opening my mouth wide, I drank in their Qwakaiva, my belly growing round and tight with my gluttony.

I danced and sang to them of my joy, until, passing by a luminous cloud, a shadowy being darted out of concealment and flung a net of glowing fibres over me. I shrieked and clawed frantically at the net, but the strands only tightened about me.

I heard a voice exhorting me to stop, but my terror made the voice unrecognizable. "Free me," I roared. "I will burn you with Qwakaiva if you don't!"

Matching my words with action, I opened my mouth to spew out the fire already rising from my belly, but I never got the chance. My captor had anticipated my plan. As soon as my mouth was open, he stuffed rotting lake weed down my throat until I choked.

"Calm yourself, Grandson. I don't want to hurt you. Resume your true shape, so you can listen to me in a human fashion."

Keeping a tight hold on the mouth of his net, Grandfather's winged body hovered above me in a ball of golden light.

When I lay naked and gagging in human form at the bottom of his net, he said, "I should've guessed the truth before now, but like a fool, I allowed my bitterness towards your father to blind me to what's been happening right under my nose. But that's not important now. Your apprenticeship is over, and I'm taking you back with me."

"No! I don't want to go—"

"I'm giving you no choice. You're still a child in my care. You have no idea of the dangers Chumco placed in your path when he tricked you into helping him."

"Not true; he didn't trick me, and he wouldn't harm me. I won't go with you, and I'm not a child. Teacher, help!" I clawed and kicked at my luminous prison, but to no avail.

"You speak of blindness," a cool voice said, "but perhaps you've been blinded in other ways than your opinion of his father. Your grandson isn't the child you perceive him to be. He is a young warrior, and he can make his own decisions in matters of power."

My heart swelling with pride and relief, I ceased my struggles and looked up. Chumco, in the radiant body of a winged Aseutl, floated lazily in the sky above us. He grinned, displaying his fangs and flexing his claws, threatening.

"You'd better release my student now and return to your sleeping body, before someone gets hurt."

"It's my grandson who is being hurt, Chumco. And I won't let him be tutored in your corrupted ways."

Chumco flew a little closer, his tail lashing the air like a mountain cat before it strikes. Still showing his fangs in a draconian smile, he said, "Don't be too sure of that. I won't give him up easily. He's mine."

Grandfather ignored his threats and my struggles, continuing to keep a tight hold on the mouth of the net."Yours? You have no right to use my grandson in your schemes."

"Are you such a fool that you haven't realized that we are at war with these foreigners? They have come to claim our bodies, minds, and spirits, and they will stop at nothing, including corrupting life itself, to achieve their ends. Maybe you haven't seen the future, as I have. I tell you our end is coming. Do you want our people, our way of life, to be destroyed?"

"Whatever the future may bring to us, if you use an innocent child in your schemes, then you are no different than those you claim to fight."

"Innocent child?" Chumco shook his head in mock reproof, the blue scales of his long neck glittering. "I think this innocent child, as you call him, understands better than you—man of power though you claim to be. Tasimu is a warrior, as is his father, and as am I."

His voice hardening with emotion, Grandfather said, "I understand well enough. You would use him, placing him in danger, or drain him to death if it suited your plans."

"Not willingly. He is a very talented student. But if the need arose, yes. He is a warrior and knows the risks. In any combat there are bound to be casualties."

"Casualties." Grandfather focused his attention on me, making me squirm. "Hear what he's saying? Can't you see his evil now? Are you willing to sacrifice not only a portion of your Qwakaiva, but perhaps your very life for this man?"

In truth, Chumco had spoken to me little of risk and sacrifice. Like the father I longed for, he'd given me instruction, and what I thought was love. But even more binding than pleasure and affection, was our mutual affinity for Kunai's power.

Grandfather loved me, thought he knew what was best for me, but he could never teach me as Chumco could. The Great Aseutl, companion of my Spirit, swam in dark currents, where those bonded to Qwa'osi the Otter could never survive. I was my father the Seal Man's son, and as Chumco repeatedly told me, Kunai, Master of Enigma, was the wellspring of my Qwakaiva.

"I see no evil in him, Grandfather. My teacher is right. I am a warrior. I would willingly give my life to help my people, if that is required of me someday."

"You see? Are those the words of a child? He has no need of your protection any longer. Release him and be gone."

Ignoring Chumco, Grandfather gave me a pitying look. "Ah but, Grandson, does Chumco truly see our future? I know his Spirit's Companion is named Master of Enigma, but what does that truly mean? Think, my dear one, Enigma. Like any greedy dragon, Kunai hoards his secrets. Can he be trusted to reveal all that is his to know, even to one who has his favour? Are Chumco's schemes worth your life if he's wrong?"

"I'm not wrong. Have you looked into the future? Have you seen the destruction that will befall our people if the pattern is allowed to continue as it is now unfolding? Blackened forests, dead and starving animals, the waters and air of our home fouled and stinking? Do you want this to happen? The Chamuqwani will make it so, if we don't stop them. The lives of our entire People may depend on what we do. What does the life of any one of us matter when we are playing for such high stakes."

"I repeat; we can't afford to win if it means becoming like the enemies we fight."

"And we can't afford to lose by being timid as you suggest. Enough talk. Let the young warrior choose for himself. It is his life and Qwakaiva after all. Now that he has been awakened to his Gift, he has that right."

Did I have that right? My Spirit trembled with the prospect of making such an important decision. This whole argument was so confusing. When I had agreed to become Chumco's student and help him, I'd wanted only to learn, so I could speak to my father and get to know him. I hadn't wanted to cause harm to anyone. But if we were at war as Chumco claimed—and Grandfather didn't disagree—then it was my duty to....

Oh, I wished they both would go away and just leave me alone; how I wished my father was beside me to help me know what to do!

"Grandson, there is one more thing you must know before you make your decision."

Startled, I looked up. "What?"

"If you choose to continue your apprenticeship with this man, you will have to leave the family and go to live with him."

Leave Mother, Samiqwas, Grandmother, and everybody? A tightness coming into my throat, I felt my vision blur. "But why?"

"That is how these things are usually done, if you didn't know. And in this case I would insist on it. His ways are too different from mine."

Chumco must have seen my horrified expression. "That won't be such a bad thing, my Little Seal. You would have to leave your family in a few years when you marry. And by coming to my household you will get the training you desire that much sooner— think on that."

Turning to Grandfather, he added. "This is a very good idea. And to satisfy wagging tongues, I can even offer a marriage to explain his move. I have a niece with a daughter of a suitable age. Tasimu's Qwakaiva need be the only groom-portion exchanged. I will see to it."

"Is this what you truly want to do, Grandson? If so, I will tell your mother and grandmother to make the necessary arrangements."

Marriage? A few moments before, I was happy, dancing with the Spirit-Lights, determined to continue my studies. Now, however, I wasn't sure what I wanted. Everything was happening so fast.

Suddenly a vision of Seicu's feverish eyes and stick-thin body, cradled in her mother's ragged blankets, flashed before my inner eye. Then my Qwakaiva gave me the vision of her coming death. Choking on a sob, I buried my face in my hands.

"What's wrong, Grandson?"

Snarling, Chumco blew out a breath of flame Grandfather barely dodged. "See what you have done with your threats of leaving? There is no need for him to come to my family's hearth until he is older. It is only your stubborn pride that would have it so."

With another breath of flame Chumco banished the net from around me. I was free now to go where I wished, but I ran to neither man. Instead I backed away, wishing only to run, but forcing myself to stand and face them.

I felt suddenly like a rabbit trapped between two hungry sled dogs. They both loved me, thought they knew what was best for me, but beneath their concern for my welfare I suspected there lurked a darker purpose. Each seemed willing to tear me apart if it meant getting what he wanted.

"Come to me, my Little Seal. Tell me what's wrong."

Chumco's voice had been filled with worry and tenderness, which made my question all the harder to ask. "Tell me one thing before I decide. Did the charmed bag I helped put in the priest's tent also make my cousin ill? Am I the cause of her suffering?"

"It's impossible to know that, young warrior. The seeds of my conjuring drifted like cattails down on the wind. The spell was meant to harm the priest and cause disorder among the Converts, but it had no particular focus other than that. We're making a hard journey, and your sister-cousin is young. Her ailment may have no greater cause than that."

"Grandfather?"

Grandfather had no further words of wisdom to offer. He shook his head. "I honestly don't know. I've done all in my power to protect my family. It may be as Chumco claims. She is young, and the ghosts of our ancestors have always called to her. Perhaps her Spirit feels it's her time to go to them. But whatever the cause of her illness, you aren't to blame. Don't trouble yourself on that account."

I laughed, hearing the rising note of hysteria in my voice. "So much power, so much wisdom, and neither of you can give me a straight answer. Am I to blame or not?"

"Kunai's Gift of foretelling is stronger than those of my own Spirit's Companion. Have you had a vision?"

"Yes. And I'm to blame for her death."

"The Chamuqwani are to blame," Chumco said angrily. "They have forced us from our homes. Haven't I told you that often enough?"

"Yes, you have."

Losing Chumco as my teacher filled my heart with fear, my untrained Gift snarling like a wolf caught in a trap at the thought. And yet I couldn't abandon my family and go with him, not for the love of my father or what Chumco might reveal to me.

Throughout the years of my childhood, Grandfather's wisdom and quiet strength had always been there like a guiding beacon to show me the way. Suddenly I realized I was more the child of his lineage than I had ever imagined. I could fight no combat where the innocent might be harmed by my actions.

My vision blurring with a bottomless sadness, I turned to Chumco. "I love you ... but my choice is to give back your token. I'm sorry."

Chumco laughed bitterly. "I'm sorry, too. I have misjudged you. Of all whom I have taught, you are the one I had hoped would inherit my power." His voice was taunting when he continued. "Such a gentle little ptarmigan, how noble, you don't want to hurt anyone. And the priest is such a good man—as are the rest of those carrion birds. They are all good people, hmm?" He laughed again at my expression.

"Ah, my Little Seal, someday when the priests take you to their special prison for children, you'll look back and regret your cowardice this night. Then you'll remember my offer and weep. You will wish you could swim against the currents of time to change your mind. But by then you will be alone and powerless, with no one to blame but yourself. Remember that. You have been warned."

"Stop, you're only trying to frighten him," Grandfather shouted.

"I'm not trying to frighten him or to sway him to what I desire, as you've done. I am merely predicting his fate."

"Don't listen; he can't truly know your future."

"I hope he remembers that when your treachery nearly destroys him." Chumco spat.

"My treachery? You're talking nonsense."

"We shall see."

"He has made his choice, Chumco, leave us."

Chumco glanced at me for confirmation. I stared unblinking, unable to verify or deny Grandfather's claim. "So be it." Then with an anguished roar, Chumco pumped his leathery wings and vanished into the swirling patterns of the Spirit-Lights.

Resisting Grandfather's attempts to comfort me, I fled into the void of dreamless sleep.

Chapter Eight

The clear sky next morning gave me no pleasure. I awoke fatigued, my body aching, my heart heavy with grief. When I remained curled in my blanket long after the rest of the family was up, Mother came over and anxiously felt my forehead.

Too bad for me. I wasn't physically sick.

At her insistence I rose, made up my travelling pack, then went to squat by the cook fire. I sipped at my spruce-needle tea and poked at the porridge Aunt Tuulah handed me. I stared into the flames, wishing I was going to die—like maybe Seicu. My Qwakaiva writhed within me. Half-taught, half-alive, how could I face the empty years to come? I was nothing, a dried husk. Maybe the frost-demons were right; I was bad. Maybe I should join them.

Startled out of my reverie by a sharp jab in the ribs, I looked up. Samiqwas grinned at me. "Hurry up and finish. I'm hungry."

I handed over my nearly full bowl to him. I'd forgotten that with only three bowls and four birch-bark cups between us, we needed to take turns.

"Here, you finish it. I'm not hungry."

Samiqwas stared at me as if I had just grown antlers on top of my head. "Not hungry?" He coughed and took a quick swallow of the cooling tea I had also given him. "Tas, are you getting sick, too?"

I laughed. I wanted to feel sick. I wanted to feel something—anything but the emptiness engulfing me. "No I'm not. I'm just not hungry. Leave me alone."

From her place across the fire Grandmother handed her cup to Tuulah. With a voice unusually gentle, she asked, "What's wrong, my dear one?"

The last thing I wanted at that moment was Grandmother focusing her attention on me, no matter how kindly intended. I didn't want anyone wondering why I was in such a foul mood. Swallowing my irritation, I took a deep breath, and answered meekly, "I'm just tired, Ami, nothing more."

Neither Grandmother nor Mother seemed convinced, but I was saved the need for a further explanation. Grandfather had returned.

When I recognized who was coming, I dropped my eyes to the

stones encircling the fire. I felt the tug of his power in my mind, but I refused to meet his eye. After what had happened between us, I was determined to deny him the satisfaction of seeing my pain.

When at last I gave in and looked up, he stood in front of me, holding the loop of string Chumco had made from my hair in one hand. Without saying a word, he held out his other hand. I knew, without his asking, what he wanted. I reached into the pouch at my waist and handed him the loop Chumco had given me.

Grandfather took both loops and tossed them onto the dying cook fire. I watched the flames devour my last link with the man and the knowledge that I craved. I heard the women's whispered questions, but I was beyond caring what he said to them. Tears were blurring my vision, running silently down my cheeks, and I was powerless to wipe them away or stop them.

Sometime later Grandfather sat down beside me. I sensed his nearness, but he made no attempt to touch me. He sat watching me cry, waiting for me to acknowledge him. When the flood of my grief had slowed to a trickle, he at last spoke.

"I know this has been hard for you. You are hurting now, but you did the right thing, Tasimu."

When I made no answer, he sighed. "It's true that I've no love for the Seal Man who sired you, but what I know of him I have to respect, —however much I hate to admit it. Kunai's kin—be they related to Co'yeh the Seal or other changeable creatures—some are more human in their perceptions of the world than others. Your father's Qwakaiva was nothing like that of your former teacher, I am sure of that. I don't think he would have wanted you to study with a man whose Qwakaiva is so ... dark. Not all who share your affinity are like Chumco. When you are older and can better judge these things, you will find another mentor. One who is more suitable."

"Suitable to whom, you?" I laughed, my voice catching on a sob. "You know, Grandfather, you and Kunai's Qwakaihi are more alike than you would care to admit."

He seemed annoyed by the comparison, making me smile. "How so?"

I choked down bubbles of hysterical laughter. "How so? Both you and Chumco tell me I will please my father when I do what you want."

"You're hurting and can't see the sense of my words now, but

I promise you this pain won't last. You'll find a better teacher someday." A ghost of a smile curved his lips. "That's my prediction for your future."

Thinking of the pain I'd endured to master Kunai's crystal gift, I barked a laugh. "That easy, hmm?" I shook my head sadly and rose to get my pack. It was time to go. The soldiers were shouting for the People to line up for the day's march.

Chumco and many of his family members vanished from the column some time during the march that day. I doubt if Commander Mu'Dar and his men even noticed their leaving, but my Spirit knew, adding to my misery.

As well as I knew my own name, I knew they were returning north. With Chumco's power to aid them, they would survive in spite of the Chamuqwani. I could have been going home, too, if I had chosen otherwise. Had my teacher only stayed with the column as long as he had because of me? I would never know for certain.

Chapter Nine

I remember very little of the country through which we walked for several days after Chumco left. I put one foot in front of another, trudging through the mud, willing myself not to think, not to dwell upon my loss. Cold winter winds at my back, I ignored the drizzling rain falling from the iron-grey clouds overhead. The bleakness of most days was in its way comforting, matching my mood.

Samiqwas traveled beside me whenever the trail widened enough to permit it. But after several refusals of conversation, he remained silent and just walked. I was unable to tell him how much I needed his company, but I think he knew.

Perhaps respecting my wish not to be near him, Grandfather chose to walk with other relatives, taking Grandmother along with him. Seicu's blanketed form straddled her mother's hip, tucked into a sling strapped across Aunt's back, head lolling on Tuulah's shoulder. Mother walked beside Tuulah, the two sisters speaking softly, so as to not disturb the little girl.

From time to time Seicu's harsh coughing jarred me out of my misery. My fault. No matter what Chumco or Grandfather said. Seicu and many others were paying a high price for my knowledge. Ignorance of Chumco's purpose—if it had been ignorance—was no excuse.

And though I cursed myself for my wickedness, my hunger to learn was still so intense that I could barely hold back my tears. Conflicting emotions were tearing me apart. I hated myself for helping spread the illness, and yet I wasn't sorry for my decision to accept tutelage from Kunai's Qwakaihi, not sorry at all.

After a late morning rest break on one of those endless days, I saw Ko waiting beside the trail up ahead. Samiqwas must have seen his father about the same time, because a wide smile suddenly illuminated his face, and he quickened his pace. Not wanting to be left alone I hastened to keep up with him.

Wiping a drool of saliva from her daughter's cheek, Tuulah's head jerked up as Samiqwas hailed his father. Ko waved to his son and stepped out of the firs to walk beside his former wife.

Tuulah's expression soured as she recognized him. "What do you think you're doing?"

"Walking." He grinned hesitantly, "Same as you. I thought maybe—"

Tuulah quickened her pace. "I don't need any help."

"Tuulah, please, let me—"

"Go back to your mother, and your bottle. Leave us alone."

Ko swore a Chamuqwani curse as he hurried to catch up with her. "Woman, what bottle? I've drunk nothing but water for a long time now."

"So you say, but do I believe it?"

"You should.—"

"Why? When there is opportunity again, you will drink; we both know it."

Samiqwas's strangled cry of protest made her look down at his stricken face. "What's wrong with you?"

"Amima, please."

Ko cursed again and put a heavy hand on her shoulder, forcing her to stop and look at him. His big-nosed face was flushed with emotion. "Stop, you're hurting our children with this talk. There's enough anger and sadness among the Qwani'Ya people. Don't make the disharmony of the world worse."

Tuulah seemed startled by his reminder of such a basic Qwani'Ya teaching. She glanced down at Samiqwas's pleading expression, and her expression softened. Ko saw the look and he continued in a rush. "I don't care if you want that Chamuqwani soldier under your blankets—that's your right—I won't stop you. Make a fool of yourself over the man if you want."

"Fool? You're the fool, drinking and letting Chamuqwani trick you, then fighting with my brother and landing in jail." Tuulah's voice rose with indignation. "After all that, you have the nerve to call me a fool?"

Ko held up a hand as if to ward off a blow. "I'm sorry—a bad choice of words. But don't change the subject. This isn't about you and me alone. Whatever is between us, don't think for a moment that I've forgotten about my son and daughter, just because you gave my things back to my mother.

"Tuulah, I love them. I miss them, and they me. I want to see them, and help you care for them. Can't you find it in your heart to let me do that? Will that soldier be there to hunt for you and the old people in this new place? I don't think so. He'll follow his leader somewhere else as soon as we arrive there. He'll forget about you, and all of us."

Hearing her father's voice, Seicu roused from her fevered doze, and began coughing and crying. "Appi carry. Want Appi!" Raising her thin arms she held them out to him.

"Hello, my sweet baby." Ko's face suddenly contorted as if he were trying very hard to hold back tears. He glanced at Tuulah, eyes pleading. She hesitated, then lifted Seicu from the sling and handed her over.

Ko took his daughter carefully and cradled her in his arms. He brushed a hand across the little girl's forehead to push back her damp hair and spoke in a soothing voice till her coughing subsided, and she settled once more into a fitful sleep.

They walked along in silence for a time. At last, he said, "Why didn't you come tell me how sick she was?"

Tuulah snorted. "Why didn't you come ask, if you were so interested in your children's welfare?"

His voice low and gentle, Ko said, "Tuulah, my heart, please don't be angry. I wanted to come, but I,I wasn't sure if you or your mother would allow it."

The rock-strewn trail narrowed just ahead, tall spruce crowding the slope on either side of the path. Ko hung back to allow her to precede him. When the trail widened so they could once again walk abreast, he said, "I wanted to, but yes I will admit it, I was afraid to come."

She stared at him, incredulous. "You afraid? Why?"

He laughed softly and smiled. "You are a formidable woman— like your mother. Hasn't anyone ever told you that? Yes, I was afraid...."

I heard no more after that. Mother placed a hand on my shoulder, forcing me to drop back. " Let them have their privacy," she murmured. I looked from my cousin's beaming face, to his parents talking in low voices as they walked together, and I nodded.

Then I heard the clop, clop of a horse's hooves and turned to see Sergeant Ma'leubwey riding down the column toward us. I watched his welcoming smile fade, as he saw Ko and Aunt Tuulah talking. His expression blank, he rode on past us without stopping. Mother turned her head to watch him pass, and sighed. "Poor man.

I believe he truly cares for my sister."

"Does Ko walking with Auntie today mean that he will be coming back to live with us, Amima? Samiqwas will be happy if he does."

"I don't know. It's too soon to tell. Right now Seicu's illness has brought them to an understanding. For that to become permanent, many things would have to change."

"You mean Ko would have to stop drinking waskyja."

She made a face but nodded. "There are other considerations as well. No one person is at fault when a marriage sours."

"You mean Grandmother would have to let him return. But she said she wanted Ko to come back."

Mother laughed softly and reached across to tousle my hair. "Your grandmother's approval would certainly help matters, but most important of all, Tuulah has to want him back—and she may not."

Then I understood. "Sergeant Ma'leubwey? But surely Auntie would choose a Qwani'Ya man, father of her children, over a foreigner?"

"The Sergeant's ways are strange to us, but he's a good man, too, don't forget."

She laughed as if at a private joke. Then, her eyes unfocussed, as if remembering another time, another man, her voice softened. "There's no way of telling what will sway a woman's heart when all is said and done, now, is there?"

Recalling how I'd abused my Gift to probe her dreams, I saw again a man with violet eyes and long brindle hair tangled in a passionate embrace with her, and flushed. "No. I guess not."

The sound of my voice seemed to pull her out of her reverie. She turned to me and smiled. "Enough talk; we should hurry ahead and find the old people. We'll be stopping for the night soon."

Chapter Ten

That evening when the column halted for the night, Ko, still carrying Seicu, followed us to our campsite. Grandmother was startled to see him, but greeted him politely, and then she offered him a place at our hearth. Ko seemed flustered by her welcome, but after a quick glance at Aunt Tuulah to see if she would take offence, he accepted the old woman's invitation. Excusing himself, he went to his mother's fire to explain his absence.

I followed Samiqwas to the creek for water. I returned to our fire without stopping to trade good-natured insults with Matoqwa and some of our friends. Seeing me, Grandmother asked me to bring firewood, so I rose without a protest and went back to the creek.

After collecting an armload of branches from under the firs, I squatted on my heels by the fire to wait for the porridge to finish cooking. I had no wish to talk to anyone or go off with Samiqwas and Matoqwa to set rabbit snares, even though they'd come back specially to get me.

"Maybe tomorrow," I said. "I'm too tired tonight."

Samiqwas made a rude noise, then trotted off with the others. I thought Grandmother was going to order me to go with him, but instead she pointed with her lips to my sister-cousin. Seicu was fussing, wanting her father, but Ko hadn't returned from his mother's encampment. Aunt Tuulah was hard-pressed to calm her, while still trying to help with the evening's chores.

The little girl felt as warm as cakes fresh off the griddle stone when I took her from her mother's arms. I smoothed the damp hair from her forehead and plastered a cheerful smile onto my face. "Hello, baby-girl, how are you tonight?"

Seicu's eyes brightened with indignation, her breath a phlegmy rumble in her chest. "I not baby."

I could feel the corners of my mouth wanting to smile. I had to work hard to control myself. "I'm sorry. I forgot." I straightened her blanket and fitted it securely about her head and shoulders to keep the cool evening air from chilling her. Seicu coughed and I held a rag to her mouth. It came away spotted with blood.

An owl hooted in the surrounding forest. It wouldn't be long. I could sense the ghosts hovering in the shadows to carry her Spirit back over the mountains to our true home by the Big Ice Lake. I planted a kiss on her cheek and hugged her, knowing I was going to miss her.

At that moment I would have willingly renounced my Gift. I had no desire to possess a power that tormented me with such terrible knowledge of the future. "What would you like to play with me while your mother fixes your meal, hmm?"

"No want porridge—icky. Want Appi hold me."

"I know; he'll be back soon, but for now let's you and me play."

"Yes, you show me pictures."

Show her pictures—pictures in the patterns of a string loop empowered with Qwakaiva. I took in a deep shuddering breath, wanting to cry, forcing myself to put aside self-pity and think only of the sick little girl.

Reaching up I untied the leather thong that bound back my hair and retied it into a large loop that I draped across my hands. "I'll try to make the pictures for you, my Little Bird, but I've lost my special string and I may not be able to do the magic with my hair-tie, but I'll try, very hard, —just for you."

"Grandfather is watching you," Seicu said.

Startled, I looked up. She was right. His blanket about his shoulders, he squatted across the fire from us, sipping a cup of hot tea. I shuddered and took a deep breath. "So he is. It'll be all right; he knows our secret now. I'll make the pictures if I can."

Ah, but could I? Fear knotted itself in my gut. The string looped over my hands quivered with the intensity of my emotions. Could I summon the Qwakaiva now that my link with Chumco had been severed? I had been afraid to attempt even such a simple conjuring as the string pictures. What if I discovered for certain that my power was ended, gone—forever. I wasn't sure I could survive such a blow.

Better not to try—not to know.

I looked into Seicu's feverish eyes and took another deep breath. For her sake, I would do my best. For her sake, I would master my fear and make the attempt. Giving Grandfather what I hoped was a defiant look, I stilled my trembling hands. Seeming to have a will of their own, my fingers pulled upon the cord until they had formed the pattern of the Seer's Pool.

As the power of the conjuring built, my Qwakaiva responded in kind. The knot of fear untangled itself inside me. My Qwakaiva wasn't lost to me! This small bit of the power was still mine to claim.

"Where shall we travel within the pool, Little One?"

"Want go home."

Home. Yes, I should have expected that. We all wanted to go home. And so, I took her. Flying north on the wings of my conjuring, away from the sickness and heartache of this brutal march south into a future that I refused to know. Back to the Big Ice Lake we went, and a past where there was joy and love. In truth I needed the distraction as much as Seicu. Reluctantly I dissolved the pattern when Aunt Tuulah came to feed her daughter and put her to bed.

As soon as I had eaten and done my chores, I collected my blankets and crawled into the lean-to. I lay like a caterpillar in its cocoon, listening to the sounds of people settling for the night. I tried to sleep, but the knowledge of Death's messenger hovering nearby kept me wakeful. In truth, no one in our family slept much. Seicu's fever rose as the night progressed. Ko held her wrapped in blankets by the fire while Aunt Tuulah brewed cup after cup of a tea made from willow bark and pine gum that Grandfather had collected the afternoon before.

His palm slapping rhythmically against his thigh, taking the place of the drum he no longer owned, Grandfather, in a low-voiced chant, begged Qwa'osi for the power to heal her. I wished him well with his effort. I added my own prayers to his, but with little hope of success. The cold chill of certainty formed like ice around my heart.

There was no way back for Seicu now.

The ghosts had always been jealous of her leaving them for the living world. We all knew that—had known it from her earliest babyhood. And now they had followed the little girl through the cold mountains to take her home.

Throwing my blanket over my shoulders against the chill, I gave up any pretence of sleep and rose to gather more wood for the fire. When I returned, I saw that the rest of the family had arisen to join the death watch.

Aunt Tuulah had given up offering Seicu tea. She sat cradling her daughter, singing a lullaby. Ko sat beside them, his blanketed arm thrown over one of Tuulah's shoulders, holding both of them. Samiqwas huddled next to his father, his face a rigid mask, trying to hold back tears.

I stacked the dry branches near the fire and went to crouch next to Mother. Grandmother looked up, nodding her thanks for the wood. No one spoke much. I drank tea when it was offered me, but mostly I leaned against Mother and stared numbly into the shifting patterns in the flames.

I wished there was something more I could do besides wait. I wished there was something I could say to change things. But there wasn't.

Towards dawn, Seicu's breathing grew laboured. One by one we each came forward to take her hand and say our farewells. As I crouched in front of my aunt and took Seicu's thin hand in mine, she opened her eyes.

"Little Rock Squirrel."

"Yes, I am your Little Rock Squirrel," I whispered and kissed her hand. "Safe journey, my Little Bird."

She looked at something over my shoulder and smiled. I turned my head and saw the impatient spectre, its dark wings unfurled. "Farewell, Little Bird." I squeezed her hand and rose so that Samiqwas could take my place. There wasn't much time.

Grandfather had stopped chanting and sat holding Grandmother's hand. His expression remained calm, but I was sure he had seen the skull-headed Owl, too. Grandmother cradled a forgotten cup of tea in her lap, her posture rigid. Her eyes dry, she stared at nothing.

As I took my place once more beside Mother, the death rattle began deep in Seicu's throat, and then she breathed no more.

Tuulah moaned, the sound welling up from the depths of her being. She hugged her daughter tight, sobbing and rocking. Ko cried out, throwing his arms about them both, whispering words of comfort, but she angrily pushed him away. He made no complaint, but I saw the bleakness in his eyes.

Mastering his emotions, he leaned over to touch his son on the shoulder. Samiqwas was curled in a ball upon the cold ground, his head and face covered by his blanket. I could hear his uncontrollable sobbing coming from within its woollen folds. At his father's touch, he pulled down the blanket's corner. Ko's voice was low but firm.

"Get up, my son. I need your help. It grows light. There's much to do before the day's march. Let us see if one of the soldiers will give us a pick and shovel. They won't want us to stay behind, and they won't wait for us to bury your sister."

Grandmother and Aunt Tuulah were keening, joined now by other relatives from nearby campsites. My vision blurred and I turned away. I could feel the tears running down my cheeks and made no effort to stop them. It was right to mourn for a lost loved one, so the old people always said, but why did it have to hurt so much?

Mother touched my arm and spoke my name. "Tasimu, we'll need water to wash the body. Take the big tin can there by the fire and go to the creek." When I returned, Mother placed it over the flames to heat.

Tuulah made a strangled protest and clutched her daughter tighter. Grandmother crouched before her, holding out her arms. "You must give her to me now, my girl, it's time."

Tuulah shook her head, but Grandmother was persistent. Both Grandfather and Mother added their encouragement and at last, she gave her daughter's body into the old woman's care. With Mother's help, Grandmother laid the little girl on a blanket and together the two women began singing their prayers for the dead, as they washed and prepared the body for burial.

Relieved of her daughter, Aunt Tuulah sobbed hysterically, collapsing into Grandfather's arms. Murmuring soft endearments to her as if she was once more a child, he sat rocking her.

With the light, soldiers roused the camp to get ready for the march. It didn't take long for the news to spread that there had been another death during the night. Auntie Qwatsitsa came over with cooked food for those who could eat. Other relatives kept showing up to pay their respects and offer a hand with whatever needed doing.

When I saw I was no longer needed, I whispered to Mother that I was going to find Samiqwas. She nodded for me to go ahead. I found him with several of our men in a stand of young birches near the creek. He was helping his father dig the grave. To my surprise Sergeant Ma'leubwey and a few of his soldiers were also there, helping some of our relatives gather stones to place upon the mound as a marker.

Seicu was a little girl and even with such flinty winter ground, it didn't take long to make the hole. When all was ready, Ko leaned on the shovel looking exhausted. Uncle Tli tapped me on the shoulder and sent me back to our fire to tell the women.

When I returned, Seicu's body had been cleaned and shrouded in the ragged blanket in which she'd been carried throughout her illness. A few feathers, pretty stones, and other special charms had been laid beside the shroud as final gifts from friends and relatives.

When Grandmother saw me she rose to her feet. Still holding Tuulah's hand, Grandfather rose and stepped to the shroud. "Would you like me to carry her?"

Tuulah shook her head and picked up her daughter. With the old people on either side, she led the procession to the gravesite. I fell in beside Mother as Auntie Qwatsitsa raised her voice in a high-pitched keen.

The People stopped by the grave, forming a circle around Aunt Tuulah's family and my grandparents. I stared at that dark hole dug into this land that wasn't our home, my heart numb with grief. I didn't want my last sight of her to be a blanketed bundle lowered into that cold lonely ground. Instead I focused on pleasant memories. Seicu coming home with Esusi from picking raspberries, her mouth and chin stained with juice. Then I saw her atop her brother's shoulders as we walked to the trading post for candy. I recalled Samiqwas and me on his bed, tickling Seicu until she screamed with laughter. They were all images to treasure in my heart.

The gathering fell silent as Grandfather raised his arms to the sky and sang the prayers to aid a Spirit upon its journey. I closed my eyes, feeling the tingle of power in the world about us, summoned by his Qwakaiva. The Unseen Ones dwelling in that land stroked my face with a feathery touch cold as ice. Among the birches a raven cawed, then took to the air, heading north. "Good bye, sweet baby, I will miss you," I whispered as I followed the raven's flight.

"I not baby," a faint voice said, and the wind ruffled my hair.

In spite of my tears, I felt my lips curve into a smile. "I know. I forgot again."

When it was over, Grandmother put an arm about her daughter's shoulders and led her back to our fire to collect our belongings. It was full day by that time. The soldiers were shouting for the People to get on the march.

As we were leaving the gravesite, I happened to look back and saw the Qwani'Ya man studying to be a priest, called Praiser Jon, and a few of the Converts, standing among the mourners. I touched Grandfather's arm to draw his attention to them.

"Yes, I saw them earlier."

Recalling the hateful words spoken by those people not long before, I couldn't keep the bitterness from my voice when I asked, "What are they doing here? What do they want now?"

Grandfather shook his head, giving me a reproachful look. Then he headed in their direction. Not thinking he would mind, I trailed along in his wake. Stopping in front of Praiser Jon, Grandfather spoke a greeting, then waited to see what he wanted.

Jon cleared his throat a couple times before he could bring the words out. "We came this morning to offer our condolences on behalf of both Intercessor Raymonel and ourselves. It's hard to lose such a young child."

Grandfather nodded, his expression solemn. "It's difficult. Your sympathy and your prayers are welcomed. How is the Intercessor?"

Jon rubbed a hand across his tired face. "Not so good."

"I'm sorry to hear that. I will pray for him."

Jon made a face at that, but voiced no objection. Unspoken words fluttered between the staring men like ptarmigans disturbed by a lynx, but neither seemed able to voice them. At last a soldier shouting for them to hurry up broke the silence.

As Jon turned to go, he said, "I'm sorry for what happened the other night. I've been told there was another Qwakaihi among us, one whose reputation is ... well, it is of no importance now, because he has left us. I believe he was the one. You won't be bothered again."

Chapter Eleven

Not long after we buried my cousin, the land through which we walked began to change. Gone were the snow-capped peaks and fast water of the high country. The river slowed and widened, its green depths an enigma. The mountains shrank in size, becoming thickly wooded hills. Spruce and fir gave way to aspen, willow, and other kinds of leafless giants unknown to me.

As broken in Spirit as the rest of my relatives by Seicu's death, I trudged the endless trails in silence. But, unlike them, guilt lay like a heavy blanket about my head and shoulders, smothering my Spirit with its weight. I was growing skeletal and listless, barely able to force down the food that was offered me. I'd developed a nagging cough, and I knew my relatives were worried about me, fearing that I might fall victim to the sickness still following our march like a scavenging dog.

Finally one day as we walked alone in a seemingly endless silence, Mother decided she had had enough of my moping and stopped on the trail to confront me. "Tasimu, you can't go on like this. Please tell me what's still weighing down your heart."

Her question was like a cup of icy water thrown into my face, it was so unexpected. "Wrong? Nothing's wrong; I'm just tired, that's all."

She folded her arms across her chest and continued to glare at me. "I'm your mother, remember? The birth cord has been cut, but we still share a bond. Please tell me."

I thought about not answering her, or making up some frivolous tale to explain what she had witnessed when Grandfather threw both loops into the fire and severed my link with Chumco.

Now that she'd confronted me, I realized I didn't want to keep my feelings all stuffed inside any longer. It hurt too much, and if anyone could understand my longing for the Qwakaiva, and the Seal Man who had gifted it to me, it would be her.

So I told her—all of it.

After I finished we walked along in silence. The roar of a nearby creek tumbling down from the crags above would have made talk impossible, anyway. The rain had stopped, and a watery autumn sun came out from behind the clouds. It painted the yellow aspens and dark spruce with a golden hue that reflected off each glistening raindrop. The air was damp, smelling of tree resin and rotting leaves. In a nearby tree a raven cawed and took to the air at our approach. I felt strangely at peace.

When we rounded a bend and left the noisy creek behind, Mother finally spoke. "Father's right, you know, Tas. You aren't to blame for what happened to Seicu or anyone of the People. Perhaps you are too young to understand, but Father, and yes, I too, must take some of the blame for what has befallen us."

I gaped, tripping over a root in the trail. "You? Grandfather? How can you say such a thing? Grandfather warned me to stay away from Chumco, and you had nothing to do with any of this."

"Ah, but I did in a way. You were growing up and you needed to know about your father. I knew that in my heart, but still I kept silent. I wanted to keep you forever young, never old enough to ask painful questions, never old enough to leave me—alone. With my selfishness, I fear I've done you a great wrong."

"No, Amima, that isn't true—and I will never leave you—I promise."

She laughed and tousled my hair again. "Of course you will some day, when you marry, and I would have it no other way." She laughed again at my expression, and added to reassure me. "But your marriage day isn't for a few years yet, so we'll enjoy our time together while we can."

We walked in companionable silence for a long time before she spoke again. "I sense that you're still troubled in your mind. What else is bothering you? Does it concern your Qwakaiva?"

I nodded. She knew my heart better than I'd guessed.

"I can't give you the teaching you crave, no matter how much I wish it were so, but I can share with you what little I can about your father. I will answer any questions you wish to ask me about him, and I'll give you this."

Mother paused on the trail and removed a braided cord from her neck and handed it to me. The cord was threaded with a stone having a natural hole through its centre. I'd seen this talisman since my earliest babyhood; she'd never removed it before that moment.

Like the string Chumco had given me when he taught me to make the magical patterns, this cord was made from plant fibre and two colours of hair. My heart pounding, I glanced up and met her eyes. She nodded, affirming my unvoiced question.

"He found that special rock for me and I wove the cord to carry it, from my own hair, and some of his, left in my comb. This is all I have of him. Now, I give it to you."

"But—"

She put the cord over my head and patted my arm to reassure me. "It's all right. It's time I left the past behind. In this foreign land I'll make a new life for myself. I would have burned this or thrown it into the Socanna River to find its way back to him, but something held me back. Now I know why. I was to give it to you."

I opened my mouth several times to reply, but I couldn't push the words past the lump swelling in my throat. I heard the sound of people talking. They were coming up behind us; we had lingered too long in one spot. Mother touched my shoulder and I moved with her.

I blinked tears from my eyes and kept walking. What a great sacrifice it must be for her to let this last token of their love go. I was grateful, yet....

"Tas, you still look sad. Don't you want it?"

I wanted to be angry, blame her, but she hadn't known about my studies. Unable to keep the tremor from my voice, I blurted, "Yes, I just wish you'd given it to me sooner. With Chumco's teaching to guide me, and with such a powerful talisman to aid me, I could have reached out to my father, told him of our plight, asked for his help, told him how I needed...." Furious with myself I swiped at my brimming eyes. " ... loved him."

She heard me out, then said, "I'm sorry I didn't give the talisman to you earlier when you confronted me that day before the soldiers came to our village. And later ... I thought you had forgotten about him again. But, you speak as if there is no hope of you ever getting to know him or learn more, and that, my dear one, isn't necessarily true."

I stared as if she had sprouted flowers from her fingertips. "How can that be? Grandfather isn't about to let me study with another bonded to Kunai."

"Father has taken away what he felt was an unsuitable tutor, but he can't take from you the knowledge that has already been gifted to you."

If that were indeed true, then the cord made with my parents' hair was powerful Qwakaiva. But would it be enough? "Father said he would wait by the Big Ice Lake for us to come home; he said he would teach me. But we aren't going back. We have no home. And, when I am a man, in this new place, we'll be too far away for his power to reach me."

She laughed softly, waving to Aunt Tuulah who had stopped in the trail ahead to wait for us. "I'm no Qwakaihi, but I do understand a little of how the Spirit-Power works. And remember this as well, my dear one. Water is all about us no matter where we go. Even in the driest land, there is water under the ground. And Kunai and his kindred can always swim the black rivers under the earth. Wherever you are, Kunai's power can help you and your father travel the hidden rivers to find one another."

Her words were an unexpected revelation. Could I someday find the strength to contact the Seal Man on my own? The idea made me tremble with hope. But I also feared she might be wrong. Maybe I wasn't worthy—maybe my Qwakaiva wasn't strong enough to withstand the trials I knew must come to challenge me. But like Samiqwas, I would be brave. In the uncertain future that awaited us, the People would need my gift—and me.

❋ ❋ ❋

No matter how much hardship my people and I endured during that time, or what we continue to suffer, I am still Qwani'Ya Sa'adi. Whether they are living or dead, my kindred surround me with their love and wisdom. I never walk alone. My daughter's mentor says he wants to understand our past and help us. I wonder if he has the courage needed to set aside the lies he's been taught and fearlessly embrace the truth.

We shall see.

The events I've recalled in this narrative grieve my heart. I have to stop, renew my Qwakaiva, before going on. I'm an old man now and I must tell my story in my own way. But no matter my personal wish to bury the past, I can't allow myself to forget, nor let my people forget. I'm the only one left alive to speak the truth of that time.

I will continue—later. And if my daughter and her mentor wish to discard some of this record as not important for their work—so be it.

Celu Amberstone

Of mixed Cherokee and Scots-Irish ancestry Celu Amberstone was one of the only young people in her family to take an interest in learning Traditional Native crafts and medicine ways. This made several of the older members of her family very happy while annoying others. Legally blind since birth, she has defied her limitations and spent much of her life avoiding cities. Moving to Canada after falling in love with a Métis-Cree man from Manitoba, she has lived in the rain forests of the west coast, a tepee in the desert and a small village in Canada's artic. Along the way she managed to also acquire a BA in cultural anthropology and an MA in health education. For the past 10 years she has been a frequent contributor to the SF Canada professional writers website. Celu loves telling stories and reading. She lives in Victoria British Columbia near her grown children and five grandchildren.